SECRET NEED

SATIN RUSSELL

Secret Need

Copyright © July 2017 by Satin Russell.
Visit Satin at www.satinrussell.com
Or Email: satinrussell@hotmail.com

Edited by Debbie Robbins
Cover and formatting: www.damonza.com

To my husband, first and always.

To Lynne, everyone should be so lucky to have a Lynne in their life.

CHAPTER ONE

PETER GRIPPED THE steering wheel to still his trembling hands. He wished he had a hit to take the edge off, but his boss insisted he make the drive sober. After all, the shipment of heroin was worth more than his life.

The job was almost done. Once he'd completed it, he'd have enough money to stay high for at least a week. He just had to make it through the day and not do anything stupid.

He flipped the radio on and scanned through the stations until he found one playing the Beastie Boys. Perfect. The familiar green trusses of the Piscataqua River Bridge rose before him and he breathed a sigh of relief.

Peter swung to the right and passed the car in front of him. Just as he pulled ahead, his stomach dropped at the sight of the police cruiser crouched on the side of the road. Dread clenched his throat and his heart pounded in his chest. With his breath suspended, he kept one eye glued to the rearview mirror. If he could just crest the hill and make it out of sight…

Lights flashed to life. In an instant, all his fearful fantasies became reality. "Shit. Shit. Shit. Shit." Each curse was punctuated by slamming his hand into the steering wheel. The last thin thread of hope – that the cop was going after someone else – was crushed when the cruiser rushed up behind him and began honking his horn.

For one brief moment, Peter played with the idea of making a run for it. But who was he kidding? He was too chicken-shit to get involved in a police chase. He was just going to have to play the situation out and hope nothing more happened.

Fear and stress wracked his body in a fit of quivers. He wiped the sweat off his forehead as the officer approached his window.

"Sir. Roll down your window, please."

Pressing the button, he offered a weak smile. "Hello, officer."

The man looked him over carefully, then let his eyes wander over the passenger seat before returning his gaze. "Do you know why I pulled you over?"

"Um…" Peter glanced around the cab of his car. "I'm not sure."

"You were going seventy in a fifty-five, you changed lanes without using your indicator, and you passed someone on the right."

"Oh." Damn. He was such an idiot! He had been given one job. One simple job. "I'm sorry…"

"I need to see your license and registration, please."

The request had Peter wiping his brow again. "Is that necessary? Wh-what if I promise not to do it again."

He watched as the officer's demeanor hardened. He leaned closer to the window, letting his shadow fall across Peter. "License and registration, please."

"Well, uh…" Peter went to reach for his wallet, sensing the tension emanating from the other man at his movement. "See, the thing is, this is my friend's car, but here's my license."

He watched as the officer looked at the license he handed to him. His brow furrowed and Peter's heart sank further. "Sir, I need you stay here for a moment. I'll be right back."

Peter watched as the officer went back to his vehicle to run his license. What was the possibility he drove away from this with just a warning?

He doubted his luck was that good. Sure enough, the cop was back a short moment later. "Sir, I need you to step out of the vehicle."

"What? Why?"

"Sir, step out of the vehicle now, please. Move slowly and keep your hands where I can see them."

This situation was sliding from bad to worse. How could he possibly get out of it? "Wait, can't we just talk about this?"

"You have until the count of three. One…"

"Okay! Okay." Peter took a deep breath, trying to steady his nerves. "I'm coming out. Just, just, don't shoot me or anything, okay?"

Before he could come up with a plan, he was facing the car with his hands spread on the hood, his legs apart, while the cop frisked him. Cars roared by, buffeting them with their passing. A small part of him was tempted to jump out in front of one of them. It was probably a better alternative than what was in store for him. He stared into the cab of the Ford Explorer, hoping against hope he'd wake up from this nightmare.

The cold bite of metal around his wrists brought him back to the moment. "Wait, what are you doing?"

"This vehicle isn't registered to you and there's a warrant out for you. It's not the first time you've been caught speeding, is it? You have the right to remain silent. Anything you say can and will be used against you in a court of law."

"You're arresting me?!"

"You have a right to an attorney. If you cannot afford an attorney, one will be appointed to you."

"This can't be happening! All this because I passed some old lady on the right?"

"Watch your head, please."

Any further protest Peter may have made died on his lips as the door slammed in his face. He looked at the SUV parked in front of them on the side of the road. The cop climbed into the front seat.

"What's going to happen to my car?"

"It's not your car."

"You know what I mean, man. What's going to happen to it?"

"It'll be impounded while we try to track down the owner. If that doesn't work, then worst case scenario is that we'll put it up for auction."

Peter would have dropped his head in his hands if they hadn't been handcuffed behind him. His boss was going to kill him. Hell, he might as well have jumped in front of one of those cars. "Auction?! Well, how long do I have before that happens?"

The cop turned in his seat to look at him, keen curiosity in his eyes. "About ninety days, give or take. Why?"

Three months. Shit, he was *so* dead. Peter squirmed under the other man's scrutiny. The last thing he wanted to do was give this guy any more reason to look at the vehicle too closely. He knew better than most that the compartment the drugs were hidden in was hard to find, even if you knew it was there. But, given the way his luck was running, he'd rather not tempt fate any more than necessary. "No reason. Just wondering for my friend."

After another beat, the cop turned to face forward. "I think you should be worrying a little more about yourself, don't you?"

The cop had no idea how true his words were.

CHAPTER TWO

STEEL-TOED BOOTS TAPPED in time to the driving beat. A rock song blasted from speakers strategically hung on the walls of the garage. The familiar smells of grease, sweat, and exhaust filled the air as Liz quietly cursed the hulking metal looming above her head. Giving a final yank with her wrench, she pulled herself up out of the bay.

The transmission on the old car had been a pain in her neck, but at least she was satisfied the car would keep running. As long as the owner did the proper maintenance, Liz knew she would would be able to get at least a few more years out of it.

Once again, she found herself grateful to her dad for teaching her a useful skill. It might make for long days, but no matter what the economy was like, a good mechanic was always in demand. Living in a somewhat financially depressed region made buying a new car unlikely for most people in the area.

Overall, it was fulfilling work. It provided her with a sense of security and purpose. That had been a comfort in the months after her parent's death.

Now, it was not only a means of earning a living, but also a way to give back to the community that had supported her and her sisters during that terrible time. Just as her father had done before her, she'd offered a payment plan to the single mom who had come into the shop needing her car fixed, even going so far as to give her a break on the labor costs.

"Hey! What are you still doing here, Lizzie-girl? Did you forget about your sister's dinner thing tonight?"

A small smile passed her lips at hearing Paul call her by the nickname he'd been using since she was a girl. "Nope. Actually, I just finished this car. I'll be taking off soon. You're going to be there – right, old man?"

He shot her a scowl at the old man remark, but she knew it was all bluster. "Yeah. I figured Jimmy and I could use a decent meal at least once this week. One of us is going to need to give in and learn how to cook. I'm telling you right now, it's not going to be me."

She laughed. "Yeah. Good luck with that." Rolling her shoulders, she began to lower the car on the lift. "Why don't you go ahead and take off? I'll close things up here."

"Alright. See you later."

Glancing at the clock by the door, Liz wiped her hands with a rag that had seen better days. Good, still on schedule. There was just enough time to take a quick shower before heading over to her sister's house.

Liz hurried to turn off the bright fluorescent lights and the radio, letting silence and shadows take over for the night. Instead of going through the front office, she gave the hood of the old Toyota Camry an affectionate pat and headed out the back door.

Wood creaked beneath her boots as she trudged up the steps to her place on the second floor and let herself in. The apartment couldn't be mistaken for luxurious, but Liz had never felt the need for anything fancy. As long as it was serviceable and clean, she could handle the sparseness of plain white walls. The living room was filled with a mix of second-hand furniture and some pieces she'd picked up at Ikea.

She headed into the kitchen and downed a glass of water. The most-used appliances in the room were the refrigerator, coffee pot, and microwave, which reflected her preference for reheating her sister's leftovers. There was a stack of takeout menus in the drawer by the fridge for those nights when she didn't have Olivia's cooking to fall back on.

Hydrated, Liz grabbed a clean towel and hopped into the shower. Five minutes later, she ran the towel through her short, pixie-cut hair and slapped a bit of gel in before getting dressed.

Her bedroom was her sanctuary, the place she'd taken care to decorate and personalize. The walls were painted a warm toffee color, which soothed her after a day surrounded by dark grays. A luxurious king-sized bed sat prominently in the room, covered in a sage green comforter and accented with a mound of turquoise throw pillows.

As much as she loved her job, being surrounded with metal, loud noise, and the smell of burnt rubber could get overwhelming. Here she could connect to the lighter, more feminine side of herself. The décor and earthy colors brought her back to nature and served as a much-needed counterpoint to her working environment.

She gave the mystery she was reading a rueful look and wished she could slide into a comfy pair of yoga pants and relax. Unfortunately, it wasn't going to happen tonight. She knew she'd have a good time at Olivia's dinner party; it was basically going to be everybody she cared about under one roof. However, attending still meant sacrificing a quiet night.

Liz slid into a clean pair of jeans and t-shirt, grabbed a light jacket and keys, and was out the door. A blanket of heat swamped her as she stepped out. The whole summer had been unusually warm. It was great for the tourists who flocked to Maine every year, but she was looking forward to the cooler weather.

She just hoped this next cold season wouldn't be as traumatic as the last one. The previous winter had been long and especially difficult. Not only because of the harsh weather, but because of her sister's ordeal with a stalker.

Luckily, everything had ended well – better than well, considering how happy Olivia and Mason were. The last few months had helped to relegate those events to the past. Once the new restaurant was open, they'd all be free to move forward.

She pulled her Jeep into the driveway, unsurprised to discover she was the first to arrive. Her youngest sister, Fiona, was perpetually running late. Liz knocked on the front door and was immediately greeted by Mason.

"Liz! Nice to see you." Mason gave her a quick hug and a cold beer. "Thought you could use one of these."

"Hey, Mason, thanks." She smiled and took a quick swig from the bottle. "Small-town life looks like it's agreeing with you."

Mason had been a Boston police detective until he moved to Bath to be closer to Olivia. Luckily, there had been an opening in the local department when the head of the Detective Division retired at the end of last year. Now, instead of working missing persons and stalker cases in the Boston Metro area, he was the new Detective Sergeant for a three-man division.

"Maybe too agreeable. I need to be careful with Olivia's cooking." Mason patted his stomach.

Liz laughed. "How's work going for you?"

"Not too bad, actually. There was one guy who resented me taking over the department, but everybody else has been fairly positive about it. It's a bit slower than Boston, but there's still plenty to keep me busy. Overall, I'm liking the change of pace."

Liz was happy to hear it. Olivia wasn't the only one who had a tough year. Especially after Mason's partner was shot and killed by the same man who was stalking Olivia. She suspected he still blamed himself for leading danger to Olivia's front door. As far as Liz was concerned, if any couple deserved their happily-ever-after, it was them.

"There's no question you have the right experience for the position. I'm glad to hear it's working out for you."

"I appreciate that. Why don't you head back to the kitchen and catch up with your sister? She's sending me to the store to pick up more ice."

Liz followed the spicy scent of comfort food, and caught her sister with a spoon in her mouth, tasting a batch of something that smelled like heaven. It was a cozy scene, one she'd seen a thousand times growing up. However, the black polka-dotted apron Olivia was wearing was completely out of character. "Where'd you get the fancy smock, Livvy?"

Olivia blushed. "Mason got it for me." She fingered the ruffles. "I know it's over the top, but I kind of love it. What do you think?"

Although it was a big departure from Olivia's usual plain garb, Liz liked the smile it put on her face. "It's perfect."

Turning towards the sink, Olivia asked, "Hey, can you do me a favor?"

"Sure, what's up?"

"The dishwasher is acting up a bit, and I was wondering if you could take a quick look at it."

"Okay." Liz set her beer down and went to turn the dishwasher on. "What's it doing, exactly?"

"I'm having difficulty locking it closed, so the whole machine won't turn on."

"Huh. Sounds like it may be the latch." Liz bent down to look at the dishwasher door. "Do you have a screwdriver handy?"

"You know where the toolbox is in the basement. Help yourself."

Liz headed down the stairs and was immediately transported back to her childhood. She'd spent a lot of time down there with their dad, watching him work on parts and handing him various tools. Those memories always caused a pang in her heart.

Not wanting to linger in the past, she quickly located the Phillips screwdriver she needed and headed up the stairs.

Her mouth watered as she entered the kitchen. "It smells amazing, Livvy. What are we having tonight?"

"Shrimp gumbo. Here, have a taste."

Liz took a sip from the spoon Olivia held out to her and was pleased to find it had some kick.

Olivia watched her face closely for a reaction. "I was feeling like something with a little personality tonight. Do you think it will be too hot for Abby?"

Abby was the daughter of Olivia's best friend, Jackie. She was only six, but Liz knew from past experience the kid would eat anything from sushi to Indian curry. "No, I think it's just right. In fact, if I remember correctly, Tom's chili is hotter than this, and I've seen her devour bowls of it."

Olivia laughed, "I admire the way Jackie has introduced Abby to a variety of foods so young. It probably doesn't hurt that Tom and his cooking have moved in with them."

Liz agreed. "Am I going to be in the way if I work on this while you're cooking in here?"

"I think it'll be okay. Everything is nearly finished and just has to simmer for a bit longer. Thanks for taking a look at it."

Liz nodded and began the task of unscrewing the panel on the dishwasher door. Even though this was a newer model than the one she'd learned on as a kid, she was sure the general concepts were the same. "Let's just hope the issue isn't anything electrical. If it is, I'll have to grab my VOM from the shop."

"Oh." Olivia looked confused. "Vom?"

"Volt-ohm meter." At her sister's blank expression, Liz explained, "It measures volts, currents, and stuff. Let's me know if something is getting enough juice."

"And it's called a volt-o-meter? Sounds like something out of a science fiction book."

Liz laughed. "Volt- Ohm- Meter, not Volt-o-meter." Ever since she could remember, she had liked taking all manner of machines apart and seeing how they worked. It used to drive her mom a little crazy whenever Liz would accidentally break something, but eventually she grew to appreciate having someone who could fix things around the house. Things had also gotten a lot better once her dad started bringing home small used appliances for her to dissect instead of household items.

Olivia poured herself a glass of wine and sat down at the kitchen island, watching her sister tinker. Liz glanced over at her. "So, who all is coming tonight, anyway?"

"Let's see. Paul, Tom, Jackie, and Abby..."

"Oh right. Paul mentioned giving you a call to see if he could bring Jimmy tonight."

"Yeah, I told him of course he should bring him."

"That's what I said. It'll be good to see Tom and Jackie again. I haven't had a chance to talk to them much since the grand re-opening of the café. How are they doing?"

"Very well! Business has been good. Everybody seems to be happy to have their favorite breakfast place available again."

"Good. I'll have to make a point to stop in and grab lunch from them this week."

Her sister nodded. "I'm sure they'd appreciate that. I also invited Mason's sister, Melody, and Brad said he might come by after he gets off shift. You know, I think he has a thing for her."

Liz glanced up from her task. "I was wondering about that. I thought I noticed a strange vibe between those two during Thanksgiving last year."

"Yeah. So far, she hasn't seemed overly eager to follow up with him, but I think they'd make a cute couple."

Liz gave it some thought as she removed the latch from the door and re-aligned it. "I could see it. But Melody seems as independent as me, if not more so. I'm guessing it won't be easy for him to convince her to take a chance."

"We'll see." Olivia wore a knowing smile. "Funny how things have a way of working out."

Liz grunted. She understood that Olivia and Mason had found their happily-ever-after, but not everybody was lucky enough to get that. Or even want it. She sure wasn't looking to settle down anytime soon.

"Well, including Fiona and me, it sounds like you'll have a packed house."

"Yeah, should be fun. Oh, and I also invited my subcontractor, Alex."

Liz got a little flutter when Olivia mentioned that last name, but she quickly squashed it. Funny how years later, the thought of him could still elicit the same response.

It was annoying.

Liz shouldn't have been surprised he was coming. She knew he'd been working on her sister's new restaurant for the last few months. Of course Olivia would have befriended him and invited him over. In fact, it was more surprising that Liz hadn't run into him before now.

Oh man, Alex Weston, she thought. Morse High's quintessential golden boy. Football player, straight 'A' student, and the most popular kid in school – loved by his fellow students and teachers alike. He was the kind of guy they made high school movies about.

In essence, the exact opposite of who Liz had been.

The group of friends he used to hang out with liked to make Liz's life a living hell. And while he didn't usually participate in the bullying himself, he never stepped in to stop it, either. That hadn't stopped her from mooning over him like every other lovesick high school girl.

Trying not to sound too interested, Liz turned to her sister.

"Huh. I haven't seen Alex since he moved back here. How has it been working with him on the restaurant?"

"It's going very well. He's been receptive to my ideas and gets what I'm trying to communicate, even if I'm having a hard time describing it. Yesterday he informed me that we should be able to open in a few weeks."

"Oh, Olivia, that's great news! I can't believe it's almost finished." Liz took a moment to closely regard her sister, and realized Olivia was looking happier than she'd ever seen her. Apparently pursuing your dreams and finding love was good for a person.

Well, hell. If Alex helped contribute to her sister's good mood, then maybe she could keep an open mind. At the very least, she could be civil.

CHAPTER THREE

"I REALIZE THAT, Dad. Just because you've hired a property manager doesn't mean you shouldn't check on them once in a while." Alex gripped the phone a little tighter.

"You already have so much going on, son. Let the girl do her job. She's been nothing but helpful to me."

Alex turned into a quiet neighborhood. "You know, we wouldn't even be having this conversation if you would just consider selling some of these properties. What do you need with this much real estate, anyway?"

"I will sell when I'm good and ready. Neither you, or anybody else, is going to force me to do it a moment sooner!" Alex winced. Even in anger, he could hear the weakness in his father's voice.

The last thing he needed was for his dad's blood pressure to spike. "Fine. We can talk about this later, but I have to go for now. I'll be by the house tomorrow." Alex hung up and let out a deep breath.

It was late afternoon by the time he pulled up to the modest white ranch house. Shadows were just beginning to stretch across the street. The afternoon held a kind of contented silence, filled by the sound of crickets and birds. Off in the distance a dog barked, and Alex could hear cars passing a few blocks over.

As a contractor, his mornings typically started early, and it had already been a long day. He knew coming back to Bath to care for his ailing father was the right move. He just hadn't realized how hard it would be to juggle that and a full-time job, let alone check in on the various properties his dad owned.

On the other hand, this was the main reason he'd moved back to the small town. His father's health left him unable to move around and it was up to Alex to look after his assets. He hoped to convince his dad to downsize his holdings, but Alex was finding it difficult to broach the subject. Until then, there was nothing to be done but make sure the properties stayed in good repair so the houses could be rented out easily.

As if in defiance, the path leading to the front door was over-shadowed by weeds. The yard was starting to look ragged. The drought affecting the region was making itself known. As he let himself in, he made a mental note to stop by that weekend and mow the grass. It was just one more thing to add to his grow-ing list.

The stench of urine and feces confronting him was so over-whelming that Alex stepped back in revulsion. He gaped at the room in disgust and dismay. Littering the front room were fast food wrappers, beer cans, chip bags, juice bottles, tiny plastic pill bags, and used syringes.

He made his way down the hallway, poking his head into the various rooms as he went. There was a pile of dingy blankets and an old sleeping bag in the back room. The offending toilet in one of the bathrooms was clogged. There was a half-melted candle and scorch marks in another room. They were lucky the whole place hadn't burned to the ground.

Irate, he pulled his phone from his pocket and called the police. After discussing his findings, they agreed to have an officer meet him to take a report. He watched the cruiser pull up to the curb ten minutes later. "Well, hey, Alex! How have you been?"

"Josh? Josh Carver? I didn't know you'd become a cop."

"Yup. Can you believe it? I was such a delinquent back then, it's kind of surprising even for me." He let out a self-deprecating laugh. "I'd heard you were back in town. Sorry I haven't tried to get ahold of you."

Alex shrugged, looking at his old high school buddy. Well, maybe buddy was stretching it. Josh had been a damn good defensive linebacker, but Alex had never liked the way his former teammate used his status as an excuse to bully other students. On the other hand, since he'd never been the target, he hadn't exactly intervened, either.

Maybe he wasn't being very fair. After all, Alex had changed quite a bit over the years, and besides, Josh was a cop now. "No problem. I've been so busy since getting back, I haven't been able to hang out much, anyway." He ran a hand through his hair, then gestured towards the house. "And now it looks like I'm going to have to deal with this, too."

Taking his cue, Josh pulled out a pad and pen before getting down to business. "You told dispatch someone was trespassing?"

"It's more than just trespassing. The place has been completely trashed. Let me show you." Alex led the way up the steps and gave him a tour of the damage he'd discovered. As the two men walked through the house, Josh noted any obvious damage and took photos with his phone.

Alex had to admit, he was impressed and a little relieved at the professional way he was handling the situation. "So, law enforcement, huh? When did that happen?"

Josh took another shot of the bathroom then took a step back, his nose wrinkling in disgust. "I got out of the academy a few years ago."

"That's great, man. How do you like it?"

"Oh, you know…" he waved his hand towards the ruined bathroom, "it's so glamorous." He shot Alex a grin. "Actually, it's not bad. Eventually I'd like to make detective, but it hasn't happened yet. Maybe in the next year or so."

"Sounds good. My client's boyfriend is a detective. In fact, he just moved here from Boston. You probably know him — Mason Clark?"

A dark shadow passed over Josh's eyes, but it was gone so quickly that Alex wasn't sure whether he'd seen it or not. "Oh yeah, I know him."

He wondered if Josh resented Mason coming in and taking over the department, or if there was some other bad blood between them. Either way, he wasn't going to pursue the topic. Josh's terse answer reminded him of the cold ruthlessness that he'd displayed back in high school and he wasn't someone Alex wanted to rekindle a friendship with.

It took another thirty minutes for the two of them to walk through the house. Afterwards, Josh assured him he had everything he needed to file the report and would keep him informed of any progress.

As the other man pulled away, Alex contemplated the dark and neglected house in the twilight that had stolen across the sky. It sat like the last wallflower that hadn't been asked to dance. It was sadly different from the homes surrounding it with their warm, glowing windows. They were filled with young families eating their evening meals or older couples sitting in the blue light of their televisions. Realizing he'd done everything he could for the time being, Alex decided to lock up and go home.

Once again, he made his way through the house towards the back door. He debated cancelling his plan to attend Olivia's dinner party. If it had been anyone else, he probably would have. But he'd enjoyed getting to know her and Mason the past few months and was looking forward to becoming better friends with them. It would be nice to spend an evening in good company, away from all the responsibilities that had taken over his life.

He'd just flipped the deadbolt on the backdoor when someone came through the front entrance. The soft pad of footsteps was barely audible on the carpet. Alex froze as a rustling sound came from the living room. Acting purely on instinct, he stormed across the kitchen with more speed than caution.

He burst out the front door, just catching sight of the fleeing figure of a man dashing across the front yard. He cursed his lack of stealth for giving the unwelcome visitor a head start.

At 6'2" Alex easily had a few inches on the guy and was still physically fit from his years spent as a football player. Working in construction, he had managed to retain an athletic physique. Unfortunately, it wasn't enough to compensate for the other guy's fear driven speed. Rounding the corner of the house, he watched as the man drove off in a beat-up sedan.

"Dammit!"

He took a good look at the car. Knowing Bath wasn't that big, if the intruder was from around this area, there was a good chance he'd see it again or was known by the cops. With a growl of frustration, he glanced at his watch and knew he had to get going if he didn't want to be rude. Not wanting to waste any more time, he decided he'd call Josh about the car on the way home.

Alex locked up the house and headed back towards his truck. A terrible grinding sound filled the air before the truck reluctantly started. He clenched his fists on the steering wheel, barely restraining himself from pounding on it.

Why couldn't he catch a break lately? He'd known the starter was on its way out for the last week. Couldn't it have lasted just a little bit longer? Was that too much to ask? Now he'd have to find the time to take it in and get it looked at. By the sound of it, he wasn't going to be able to put it off much longer. The last thing he wanted was to get stranded somewhere because his damn truck wouldn't start.

Before Alex pulled away from the curb he called Josh and left a message about the car and intruder. He was going to go back to the house, take a quick shower, and set everything else aside for the night. As he drove, he realized part of the reason he was so stressed was he hadn't been able to relax since moving back to Bath.

Sure, his childhood home was full of good memories, but ever since he'd arrived, he couldn't help feeling his life was moving backwards. Working on Olivia's restaurant was a worthy way to pass the time while he took care of his ailing father, but he knew his dad wasn't going to recover. The realization that this was a temporary living arrangement made it hard to fully commit to living in the small town.

His uncomfortable thoughts were interrupted as he approached the other side of the town's limits. There, sitting in the back alley behind a mechanic's garage, was the car he'd seen the intruder flee in. He probably wouldn't have even noticed it if he wasn't familiar with the business owner.

What on earth could Eliza Harper have in common with a man who broke into vacant houses and left drug paraphernalia lying around? This complicated matters. Josh Carver may be a police officer now, but he remembered the level of animosity Josh had shown towards Liz back when they were in school together.

Alex wondered if she was still the outcast he remembered from high school. She'd been an enigma back then, so unlike the other girls who threw themselves at him. He'd been intrigued and a little intimidated by the fact that she hadn't simpered or giggled the way the other girls had. Maybe that's why he'd never gotten the courage to show his interest.

He put off calling the police with an update on where the car was located. Instead, he'd go to the dinner party tonight and see if there was a good way to broach the subject with Liz. There had to be some other reason why that car was behind her shop. He hoped she wasn't associated with that sleazebag from earlier. As he pulled the truck into his driveway, Alex resolved to find out what the connection could be.

*

Nearly an hour later, Alex checked to make sure he was at the correct address, then parked the car across the street. He grabbed the bottle of wine sitting on the seat beside him. The sound of laughter drifted out into the air to greet him and he couldn't help but smile as he pushed the doorbell.

Mason let him in and gave him a friendly slap on the back. "Alex, glad you could join us." It was a much different response than the one Alex had received the first time he'd met the man.

Of course, Mason had mistakenly thought Alex was Olivia's new love interest at the time. Funny how much can change in the span of a few months. It had been a pleasant surprise to find himself becoming friends with the couple.

"I appreciate the invitation. I have to admit, I haven't had a home-cooked meal in forever."

"Well, you're in for a treat. Olivia's made shrimp gumbo tonight, with some fancy cornbread she calls johnnycakes."

"Johnnycakes, huh? What's the difference?"

Mason cast him a grin. "Your guess is as good as mine, but I have a feeling we're going to find out."

The two men walked into the kitchen, and Alex immediately fell in love with the room. It was obvious that whoever had designed it had been a cook because the floorplan was logically arranged for the greatest efficiency and flow. However, beyond the utilitarian aspects, it was readily apparent it was also created to be the heart of the home.

He glanced around the room and noted how all the finishes were sophisticated without being stuffy. While there were accents of chrome in the pendant lights and brushed cabinet handles, there was also the warmth of the wooden floors. Since he'd been working with Olivia on the design and feel of the restaurant, he recognized her sense of style and approved. It made him even more excited to finish the project.

Most everybody had arrived and they were standing around the kitchen island chatting. Smiling at them, he set his bottle of wine down on the counter. "Wow, it smells great in here." He gave his hostess a hug. "Hello, Olivia. Sorry I'm a bit late."

He nodded to Mason's sister, Melody. "Mel. Long time, no see."

She gave him a smile. "Nice to see you, Alex."

"Alex! I'm so glad you could make it," Olivia gave him a warm squeeze before turning to make introductions. "I don't know if you remember Jackie from high school? She was in my class, a couple of grades ahead of you. This is her boyfriend Tom and her daughter Abby."

Alex shook both of their hands, and winked at the little girl shyly looking up at him as Olivia spoke. "Paul is the co-owner of the shop with Liz, and his nephew Jimmy just started working there this week."

"Yeah, I'm doing all the paperwork and stuff that Liz and my uncle can't stand." Jimmy smiled. "I'm not complaining. At least now I get paid for the work I do, which is more than I can say for high school."

"Better you than me," the older man said gruffly before shaking Alex's hand. "Nice to meet you. Olivia has been telling us how well the remodel is going."

"I think we've been making good progress. It's a fun project to be working on."

Olivia gestured towards a woman setting the table, "My youngest sister, Fiona...and of course, Liz. You two were in the same class together."

Alex was hardly surprised when he saw that Liz had taken the dishwasher apart. There were a handful of screws and parts piled on the counter beside her. What did startle him was the way his pulse jumped when she turned to look at him.

The long brown hair that she'd always worn in a practical ponytail had been chopped into a sharp, edgy pixie cut that was sexy as hell. It perfectly accented her big, pale-green eyes. Even just standing there, he imagined running his fingers through it and mussing it up. Feeling like an idiot for staring at her, Alex struggled to find his voice. "Eliza, you're looking good."

He loved watching the way her eyes fired up at the use of her full name. "It's Liz. Not even my own mother called me Eliza."

He knew using her full name would rile her, but he couldn't resist the urge. Alex had always secretly liked how feminine her name was. Especially when compared to her badass attitude.

An attitude he was receiving a full dose of at the moment.

"Well, it's nice to see you," he said. She stared at him for a moment, then turned back to what she was doing. Maybe it hadn't been such a good idea to tease her right off the bat. He wondered why he always became tongue-tied around her. It felt like he was fifteen all over again.

Alex could feel everybody holding their breath as they watched his exchange with Liz. Conversation lulled in the room for half a beat longer than was comfortable before Jackie carefully stepped into the quiet. "So, Alex…Olivia tells me you've been living in Seattle for a few years. How did you like it?"

Grateful, he turned towards Jackie. "I loved it. Seattle, actually the whole Pacific Northwest, is a beautiful place."

"I've heard it always rains there. Is that true?" Jimmy asked.

Alex laughed. "Sort of. It's cloudy most of the year and even when it isn't downpouring, there's usually a drizzle." He shrugged. "Believe it or not, you get used to it. Besides, the summers are amazing and the winters aren't nearly as harsh as they are here.

"Plus, Seattle is booming right now. Amazon and Microsoft

have been expanding in the region, so the real estate bubble never popped like it did for the rest of the country."

Fiona handed him a beer. "It sounds like you'll be happy to return."

"Thanks." He took a swig before continuing, "I miss it, that's for sure. The company I work for is one of the largest in the region, so there was a lot of work. I'm just hoping I still have a job when I get back."

"It shouldn't be too long, right?" Paul asked. "Olivia says the restaurant is coming together well. Do you honestly think it could be finished in a few weeks?"

He nodded. "Yes, I think we're on track to open the last week of August."

"It must be quite a challenge," Fiona said.

"Actually, it's not so bad. It's sitting on a beautiful piece of land and the underlying structure still has good bones." He looked at Melody, who owned the old barn they were converting into the restaurant. The restaurant would be right next door to her bed and breakfast. "Plus, you can't get large beams like those anymore."

"I admit, that's my favorite part," Melody agreed.

"Mine, too," said Olivia. "Although I have a feeling my opinion may change once the wall of windows goes in and we get to take advantage of the view." She began ladling gumbo into bowls and passing them off to Fiona to place on the table. "Dinner is ready. Why don't you all grab a seat?"

Everybody came to the table. In the jostle for chairs Alex tried to find a seat next to Liz, but was disappointed when she maneuvered her way into a spot at the other end of the table. Although it wasn't obvious, he got the impression she was doing her best to avoid him. Was he a sucker for punishment because he secretly hoped he'd have another opportunity to talk to her?

The start of the meal passed quietly as everybody savored their first few bites, murmuring their approval. Gradually, conversation resumed. With Mason on one side and Melody on the other, Alex was content to discuss the progress of the restaurant with them. Periodically, he would look up to find Liz glancing in his direction, but she never jumped into the discussion.

For his part, he noticed the way she interacted with her family and the people she considered friends. It struck him how relaxed and in her element she appeared to be. It was a far cry from the quiet and socially inept girl he'd known back in school.

Alex suspected Liz would be a great person to have as a friend. She was the kind of person who would do just about anything for the people she cared about, like breaking down a dishwasher in the middle of a dinner party. What would it be like to be a part of her inner circle?

The evening progressed and, to his dismay, the opportunity to interact with her was quickly slipping away. He'd be waiting there forever if he relied on her to initiate a conversation. "So, Liz, I drove by the shop earlier. The place looks like it's doing well."

As he suspected, she was too polite to ignore a comment made specifically to her. "It is, thanks." Then, after a brief pause, "What brought you by?"

Alex hesitated to talk about discovering the intruder's car outside her garage. The ugly topic of drugs didn't fit into polite dinner talk. Besides, until he could better assess how Liz might be involved, it would be best to be discreet and give her the benefit of the doubt. He'd already bungled one conversation tonight, and he didn't want to alienate her again so quickly. "The starter on my truck is grinding and I thought I'd see if you could fix it."

"Oh, that's an easy fix." Paul chimed in. "Liz here has been doing that since she was fifteen."

Liz's cheeks blushed at the words of confidence. She nodded at Alex. "Sure, come by tomorrow. I'll take a look at it."

"Thanks, I appreciate it. I remember how much you used to like working on cars. It's nice to see you're still doing it."

She gave him a wry look. "Yup, I'm still a good ol' grease monkey. Never used to hear the end of it back then. Now I service most of their cars in my shop, and laugh all the way to the bank."

Alex cringed at the memory. "Most of us have managed to grow up since then and can appreciate good work."

The look of surprise that crossed Liz's face had Alex wishing he could go back and kick his younger self's ass.

A couple of hours later, Alex left with a grin on his face. The rest of the evening had gone well. Discussions spanned the gamut from music and travel destinations to architecture and food. While his direct interactions with Liz were limited, he was tuned in to her conversations. He learned she liked jigsaw puzzles and spicy food, and noticed she preferred beer over wine.

Overall, spending the evening surrounded by good conversation and friends was exactly what he needed. Plus, it didn't hurt that he'd been in the company of an intelligent, beautiful woman. He couldn't remember the last time he'd been on a date. Maybe it was time to do something about that.

Liz called to him from the front steps. "I thought you said you drove a truck."

Alex turned just in time to see her saunter towards the end of the driveway. This was definitely not the Eliza Harper he remembered from high school. No, this version was much more confident...and *hot*. He watched as she propped a hip up against the back of the Jeep sitting in the driveway before answering. "My truck is for work. This is for pleasure."

"A 2014 Audi R8 is kind of impractical for Maine winters." When he didn't immediately respond, she added, "Although I like that you chose the royal blue as opposed to the typical red."

"Glad you like it," Alex couldn't prevent the dry tone that entered his voice.

"Well, it's a little newer than I like my cars, but not bad."

Alex barked with laughter. "Not bad, huh?"

She crossed her arms and shot him a cocky grin. "430 horse-power, 0-60 in 4 seconds…"

"And a top speed of 168 miles per hour," he said, finishing her list of statistics. Leaning up against his car, he mirrored her stance from across the street. Who knew it could be so sexy to hear some-one rattle off car specs? Impulsively, he asked, "You wanna go for a ride?"

A shadow of doubt crossed her face before she straightened and made her way to her car door. "Nah, I've gotta get going. Early day tomorrow."

"Oh. Okay, then. Well, I'll stop by in the afternoon."

"What?" She turned to him. "Right, your starter. Yeah, sounds good." She opened her door.

With that, he watched her get in. His eyes followed her tail-lights all the way down the road until they turned at the intersec-tion. Well, she didn't bite his head off or ignore him, at least there was that.

CHAPTER FOUR

THE MAN LEANED back on the wall, deeper into the shadows, and waited for the other end to pick up. He didn't bother identifying himself when it did. "The house has been compromised."

There was a sharp intake of breath from the person on the other end. "Well, shit. This location didn't last long. It's getting harder to come up with places. What the hell happened?"

"The golden boy came by to check on his dad's property."

A heavy sigh came over the phone before the voice grew colder. "That's the least of our problems. We need to find the shipment, or we're all fucking dead. Have you located it yet?"

The man hesitated. He didn't want to be the bearer of more bad news, but there was no way around it. "Not yet, but we have everyone looking. It'll turn up."

"It better. I am not going down for this alone. Don't forget who's running this operation."

The man swallowed against the rage building in the back of his throat. There wouldn't be an operation if he wasn't doing the dirty work and covering their tracks. Instead of voicing his thoughts, he just grunted. "I'll let you know if anything happens. I had them clear what was left from the house. There's a new location already lined up, but I'll need to confirm its status."

"Well, put a rush on it." The voice on the other end was little more than a growl.

He heard the click and shook his head. Getting saddled with all the work was starting to get tedious. It might be time to start thinking about branching out.

First, they had to find that damn shipment and get themselves squared away with their supplier. Then maybe it would be time to consider his options. In fact, if he played the situation right, this mistake could be an opportunity to take over the entire operation.

CHAPTER FIVE

LIZ SANK FARTHER down in her seat and held her breath. She didn't want to have to deal with the group of kids who had just entered the coffee shop. She watched as they teased and pushed each other, cavorting and making enough noise for her to hear everything they were saying from across the room.

From the outside, she scowled and cast them a look of distaste, but inside, she secretly envied their camaraderie. Almost against her will, her eyes were drawn to the center of their group where Alex stood. How was life fair that the rich kid was also blonde and handsome and so damn perfect? Even light seemed to get a little brighter where he walked.

Her stomach fluttered at the same time she rolled her eyes at herself. As if someone like Alex Weston would ever be interested in a rangy grease monkey like her. Surreptitiously, she cast a look down at her stubbornly flat chest. It was a good thing she was a tomboy by nature. She certainly had the look right.

Maybe they won't see me…

Just as the thought crossed her mind, Alex's teammate Josh looked up and caught her eyes darting away. From her peripheral view, she watched him lumber towards her.

*"Hey, look, Alex…they actually let the monkey out of her cage."
He looked down at her, every line of his face full of derision. Liz*

thought his beady eyes and square face made him look more like a bullfrog than a boy.

"Shut up, Josh," Liz responded. She stuck her chin out and stared at him defiantly. No way would she ever let these jerks know how much they got to her.

"Why, what are you going to do about it?" He reached for her biceps, but she yanked her arm away, "You look like a ten-year-old boy."

Cynthia, the high school's freshman darling, flounced up and began to giggle. "Yeah she does! She's not a monkey, Josh, she's a plank!"

Josh bent over and let out a loud guffaw. Anybody who didn't know him better would think it was the funniest thing he'd ever heard. His eyes took on a crueler glint.

Liz furtively looked around to see if any of the adults were close enough to notice what was happening, but they all looked too preoccupied with their newspapers and Blackberries to pay any attention to the little group in the corner.

She should have just stayed at the garage with her dad, instead of letting him convince her to take a break. In a small town like this it was virtually impossible to avoid the toxic popular kids during Spring Break.

Cynthia turned to her best friend and sidekick. "Awww, poor little plank, both dumb and mute!"

Ashleigh let out a high-pitched giggle. "Yeah!"

Liz wasn't sure which was worse. The fact that someone as pretty as Cynthia could be so ugly on the inside, or that Ashleigh followed her around like a puppy dog and didn't seem to have an independent thought in her head. She supposed it didn't matter. They were both terrible.

She looked up at Alex from her seat at the table. Up to that point, he'd just watched. Liz was curious to see what he would do. Something in his gaze flickered, but it was impossible to tell what he was thinking. Finally, he said, "Come on, guys. I think our drinks are ready, and my dad said he'd come pick us up. Let's go back to my place and hang out at the pool."

With a final look of disdain from Cynthia and Josh, the little group left Liz sitting alone at her table, as easily forgotten as a piece of toilet paper stuck to the bottom of their shoe. Distasteful, but hardly worth noticing once flicked away...

Liz woke with high school taunts echoing in her mind. Seeing Alex last night had dredged up those terrible years of being subjected to mockery by the mean girls.

She hugged her pillow and smiled. That wasn't how things had gone a few hours ago though, was it? In fact, all night it felt like she and Alex had been circling each other. She'd caught him looking at her more than once. Each time, a little frisson of electricity would shoot through her. Liz wasn't the only one who noticed, either. Even Fiona had pulled her aside and asked what was going on between them.

Plus, what was that invitation to give her a ride? At the time, part of her couldn't believe it. The other part of her had felt victorious, as if the younger, high-school version of her was vindicated by his interest.

She frowned. And didn't *that* thought piss her off? The last thing she needed was Alex Weston's approval or interest. Liz reminded herself that she was a strong, sexually confident, successful business woman who had gotten over those old insecurities a long time ago. She'd been getting along perfectly well without the likes of him for years now.

Even if he had looked good leaning up against his car. Liz wrinkled her nose and silently chastised herself. "The last thing you need is to get involved with a guy like Alex Weston," she muttered to herself.

He was the kind of guy who stood silently by while his friends bullied her. A nice guy to your face, but not the guy who would defend you when you were down. He was not to be trusted. The dream was her subconscious reminding her of that.

Liz climbed out of her bed and pulled a ratty t-shirt out of the basket of clean clothes she'd neglected to put away. Picking up her favorite pair of jeans, she gave them a sniff test before shrugging and climbing into them. There was no point in being picky. They were already oil-stained and would be getting just as dirty again today.

Feeling good, she decided to walk the few blocks to the café. If she hurried, she'd have just enough time to grab some breakfast with her cup of coffee.

The air was thick with humidity and lay heavy on the back of her neck. In minutes, she had started to sweat. Crossing the street to walk in the shade, she waved to Frank, standing behind the counter of the hardware store. Despite what had happened to her sister a few months ago, she'd never known a more welcoming and safe town. There wasn't any place else she'd rather live.

Blessedly cool air washed over her as she stepped into the café. Jackie and Tom had taken it over from Olivia after the fire last winter. It still felt weird to see the sign saying "Abby's" as opposed to "The Three Sisters Cafe," but she couldn't help but approve of the changes they'd made.

Not that there were many, she thought, stepping into the front door. They'd kept the same cheery colors and sunflower motif, as well as the bank of coffee selections along one wall. In fact, they'd done a remarkable job of restoring the place to exactly the same as it had been before the fire. It was hard to believe the whole area she was standing in had been charred ashes just a few months ago.

"Liz! How are you doing this morning?" Jackie asked as she spotted her.

Liz gave her a quick hug. "Good! It's going to be busy today so I decided to get an early start."

"Do you know what you want?"

"Um, I'll have my usual – blueberry pancakes, bacon, and a cup of coffee. Oh, and can I get three Italian subs to go, please? May as well pick up lunch while I'm here."

"Great. Why don't you take a seat at the counter while you wait? I'll grab you that cup of coffee."

Jackie moved to get her order in as Liz took a stool at the breakfast counter. Overall, she had to admit, things had worked out to everybody's satisfaction after the fiasco last winter. She nodded a greeting to Tom in the pass-through window, then turned to her phone.

A while later, as Liz was happily digging into her pancakes, she heard Cynthia's distinctive voice and felt her good mood deflate. Liz looked over and wondered what she was searching for. As she watched, Cynthia headed directly back to the corner of the dining room where Alex was sitting. Her stomach dropped. She hadn't even noticed him sitting there.

Liz watched the two of them greet each other. Were they dating again? She supposed it was natural they would reconnect. After all, they had dated until he'd been sent to boarding school. And, Liz happened to know, through the local rumor mill, that Cynthia had recently finalized her divorce and was already on the prowl for a new husband.

What Liz hadn't counted on was how seeing them together gave her that old familiar sting.

Was it wrong to harbor a resentment towards the woman who'd made her teen years a living hell? People changed and grew up all the time. Liz knew she wasn't still the shy, self-conscious girl she'd been back then. In fact, she had worked hard to overcome being the sad, gangly girl who bore the brunt of so much bullying.

Bullying that Cynthia Monroe, as head cheerleader and most popular girl, had been all too willing to dole out.

Maybe it had been her imagination that he'd been flirting with her last night. Did it matter? She'd already decided she was going to keep her distance from him.

Liz hunched down in her seat, frustrated with her train of thought. After taking another long pull of her coffee, she casually tried to peek over her shoulder at the exchange behind her. Her heart lightened a bit when she noticed the way Alex seemed to pull back from Cynthia's arm.

He looked up in that moment and caught her eye.

That same spark of heat from last night shot between them. Lis feigned interest in her phone. Secretly, she began to hope he'd come over or acknowledge her presence. That would certainly give Cynthia a surprise, wouldn't it? Instead, she watched as he stood up, gave her a slight nod, then walked towards the door.

Shuttering her disappointment, Liz stared sightlessly at the kitchen. She was good enough to talk to when no one else was around, but it was the same old thing when there were witnesses. Apparently, some things never change.

Liz struggled to dismiss the hollow feeling settling into her chest. What was she thinking? Just because he had gone to her sister's house for dinner didn't mean anything. So, they'd managed to have a decent conversation afterwards and had what she thought was a moment. It was silly for her to read too much into it.

"Here you are." Startled from her thoughts, Liz looked up to see Tom standing in front of her with subs and three bags of chips tucked into a to-go sack.

"Thanks, Tom." She slapped a bill down on the counter. "This should cover it. I need to head back. It's Jimmy's first week at the shop and I want to make sure I'm there, just in case."

"That's right. He mentioned it last night. You going to be teaching him to work on cars?"

"Nah. He's not exactly the mechanical type. He's been helping out with the customers, answering phones, and doing the never-ending paperwork and filing. You know, all the stuff I hate."

Tom laughed as she gave him a wink. "Well, good luck to him. Tell them both I said hello."

Liz stalked back to the garage, grumpy about what she'd seen at the café. She didn't know if she was more irritated at Alex for flirting with her last night, or herself for hoping things had changed since they were kids.

Paul and Jimmy turned to greet her as she walked into the garage, but she wasn't in the mood. Instead, she just nodded to them both and headed directly to the office/ break room, stashing the sandwiches in the mini-fridge she kept back there.

"You okay?" Paul asked as she made her way to the first car scheduled for the day.

"Yeah. Just have a lot to do today and not enough time to do it."

Liz was glad she didn't have to plaster a smile on her face and sugarcoat her feelings with him. Having watched her grow up throughout the years, it certainly wasn't the first time he'd seen Liz in a funk.

All she wanted to do was get her hands on a car and lose herself in the work for a few hours. She liked those mornings when she could get in a groove and shut the rest of the world out.

Cars were infinitely easier to deal with than people. They were like puzzles. If something wasn't working, it was because a piece was worn or broken. Fix that and you could get the vehicle to run again. Simple.

People, on the other hand, were another thing entirely. Who could say what made a person tick? And what worked for one wouldn't necessarily work for another. People were constantly different, never consistent.

Right then and there Liz decided to put Alex out of her mind for good. She didn't need to experience the hurt of being a high school loser again. She was now a full-grown adult woman who was accomplished in her own right. There was no sense in rehashing the past.

The familiar opening strains of Proud Mary began to blare from the speakers, instantly transporting her to childhood weekends and afternoons spent in the garage after school. Now that her father was gone, Paul was all she had as a father figure. He always knew how to cheer her up.

Taking a deep breath, she felt the tension that had been building in her shoulders begin to release. This was where she belonged and always knew what to do. Liz couldn't help shooting a little smile toward the older man before disappearing under the car. Gradually, her mood began to improve and her steel-toed shoes once again kept time with the music as she worked.

CHAPTER SIX

ALEX WAS HAPPY to see Liz enter the café, and took a moment to admire her. It was amazing to him how much she'd changed since high school. Back then she'd been all skin and bone and scowls.

He knew he and his friends were part of the reason why she'd walked around with such a large chip on her shoulder. Thankfully, judging by the events of last night, she didn't seem to be holding it against him. With that thought in mind, he was just about to get up and go talk to her when he heard his name called from the door.

"Alex? Oh my God, Alex!" The high pitch of the woman's voice carrying over the rest of the dining room instantly grated on his nerves. It was all Alex could do to paste a smile on his face and turn towards the woman making her way over to him. "I heard you were back in town. Look at you!"

Something about her looked vaguely familiar, but he couldn't quite put his finger on it. It wasn't until she was standing directly in front him that he recognized his old girlfriend.

He tried to hide his shock at seeing the changes in her, but wasn't sure if he succeeded. Gone was the chipper cheerleader with the bouncy ponytail. Even from this distance, he could tell she must regularly see the inside of a tanning booth to have skin that color, especially in Maine and this early in the season. Her hair was a shade of blonde that only came from a bottle and was perfectly coiffed into a sleek, chin-length bob. Had she always had such a plastic smile? How had he ever found her attractive?

He shifted uncomfortably in his seat as she made no attempt to hide her admiration of him, from head to boots. "Well, you've certainly grown up well," she said after her initial inspection.

Alex wasn't sure how to respond to that. "Cynthia...what a surprise. How have you been?"

"Oh, you know." She waved her hand carelessly. "Still stuck in this place, but otherwise I've been well."

The tables around him had become hushed and it felt like everybody in the dining room had an ear cocked toward their conversation. He'd forgotten the way gossip could spread in a small town. Alex self-consciously glanced towards the breakfast counter, wondering if Liz was aware of the scene unfolding behind her.

Green eyes filled his vision. She looked back down at her phone. He wished he could sink through the floor. Belatedly, Alex realized Cynthia had been chattering, but he'd missed the first part of what she'd said. She must have asked him a question, though, because she was standing there looking at him as if waiting for a response.

"I'm sorry, what?"

"I asked how you liked being back in town? When I spoke to your dad last, he mentioned you're a contractor now."

That caught his attention. Oh right. His father mentioned he'd hired her to manage his real estate. At the time, Alex felt like his dad was trying to set them up and resisted meeting with her. The last thing he wanted was his dad to be coordinating his love life. But now he was reminded that assuming she had things under control had been a mistake. It was partly her fault that the home had been vandalized and left in the state which he'd found it.

Seeing his hesitation, she turned and rooted around in her designer handbag, handing him a card. Alex clenched his jaw as he looked down at the professional photo on her business card. After what he'd found at the house last night, he couldn't say he was impressed. In fact, he was downright furious. He wondered how many other properties had been neglected under her watch.

Not sensing the turn of his thoughts, Cynthia stepped closer and laid a hand on his arm. "It's been a long time, Alex. We should get together and catch up."

He pulled his arm from her grasp and stepped out from where she'd hemmed him in. His cool voice had her smile dimming. "Actually, I've been meaning to set up a meeting to discuss a disturbing incident that happened on one of Dad's properties last night. I'll need to check my schedule, but why don't I call you and make an appointment?"

Alex could see disappointment flicker in her eyes at the business-like turn of the conversation, but watched her quickly recover. "Absolutely. We can plan to grab a few drinks afterwards, if you'd like."

He doubted she'd want to be social after his discussion with her. Without answering, Alex turned to leave. He cast a glance towards Liz, but she still had her back towards him. He wished he had a moment to go over and greet her, but now he really was running late to his meeting. After paying his bill with Jackie, he quickly strode out the door.

*

Hours later, after a successful meeting with the building inspector, Alex decided to take off early. He needed to stop by Liz's shop to get the starter fixed on his truck, and she'd been in his thoughts since that morning. He wanted to see her.

Pulling his truck into one of the last spots available in the lot, he walked up to the shop. His pulse thumped to the driving bass line of Royal Blood being blasted from one of the garage bays.

The space behind the counter was empty. Alex glanced around

the front office before peering down the hall towards the bays. There, through the glass door separating the office area from the garage, his gaze snagged on the hottest, tightest, jeans-clad ass he'd seen in a long time...hell, probably his whole life. His eyes roved along the curve, noting the way a wrench and handkerchief were tucked into the back pocket. It was obvious the jeans were a favorite pair, judging by the way they seemed to have faded to a soft white around the edges.

The way those jeans loved her, she could be a Levi's advertisement.

The sound of a throat clearing in front of him broke Alex from his reverie. Jimmy stood looking at him from the other side of the counter, one eyebrow raised. He'd just been caught ogling and it was obvious by the expression on the other man's face that there was no sense in denying it.

Deciding it was better to cut his losses before the situation got any more embarrassing, Alex focused on the business at hand. "Hey, Jimmy, nice to see you again. Thought I'd stop by and see about getting that starter fixed on my truck."

Jimmy let him off the hook with a knowing grin and turned towards the computer. "Right. Let me check the schedule." After a brief moment spent tapping keys, he shook his head. "Looks like we don't have any appointments available until Thursday."

It wasn't surprising. Judging by the number of cars outside, Alex felt lucky she could fit him in this week. "That'll work. Sign me up." After giving him the pertinent information, he headed over to the door leading to the garage. "I'm just going to take a second to say hi."

The other man didn't even look up as he plugged the information for the appointment into the computer. "She doesn't like customers going into the shop," he warned. "If you get hurt, she'll have my head."

Alex gave him a nod to show he understood, but was

undeterred. As he drew nearer, he noticed Liz had started tapping her foot to the music and bobbing her head under the hood.

He was impressed with the wave of sound that poured over him when he opened the door. What he'd heard in the office had been a fraction of the volume currently hijacking his senses. How on earth could the little unit sitting on the workbench produce so much volume?

Strangely, Paul, working in the next bay over, didn't seem to mind. Alex yelled, trying to get Liz's attention. On his third attempt, the song abruptly ended, leaving his voice to hang in the air like a roar.

Liz shot up and promptly smacked her head hard on the hood. "What the hell?" She snapped, before turning and noticing Alex standing behind her. "Oh, Alex."

Alex felt like an idiot. Why had he thought it was a good idea to stop in and say hello? "Shit. Sorry. I didn't mean to startle you."

Another song started to fill the air and Liz rushed over to pause the track. "Kind of hard to hear with the music sometimes." She was still rubbing her head, but didn't apologize for the volume.

"Yeah, I noticed. It's almost five, are you getting off soon?"

Liz stayed a few paces away from him and gestured towards the car. "Probably not. I still have quite a few cars to look at." She looked down at her scuffed boots. "You bringing your truck in to get the starter fixed?"

Alex shifted the weight on his feet. Something was wrong. She hadn't looked directly at him once since she'd noticed he was there, and she seemed more fascinated with the rag in her hand than with him. He wondered at the change.

Glancing back at the office, he said, "Yeah, I got off a bit early. Your next available appointment for the truck isn't until next Thursday. Plus, I wanted to see if you'd like to have dinner with me."

Liz's head popped up and he finally got a good look at her.

There was a light smear of grease across her left cheek. "Thursday?" She scowled. "Jimmy's still new. Let's go check the schedule. I might be able to get you in earlier."

Surprised by her reaction, Alex trailed behind her back to the office. She hadn't even acknowledged the dinner invitation. Damn, he'd thought there might have been a spark.

"Hey, Jimmy!" A thread of tension and irritation laced her voice.

The other man swallowed and glanced over towards Alex. "Yeah?"

"Did you just say we can't get to Alex's starter until Thursday?"

He gestured at the computer. "Your schedule is packed, Liz. Besides, don't forget Uncle Paul is taking a half day on Wednesday and will be gone the rest of the week."

Alex watched with interest as Liz bit her bottom lip. "Damn, I did forget that."

Paul walked in from the garage, catching the tail-end of the conversation. "I'd offer to stay, but those fish aren't going to catch themselves."

Alex looked at Liz. "It's not a big problem. I can deal with a finicky starter for a few days."

Right as the words left his mouth, the bell hanging above the door chimed and another man walked in. He hesitated by the threshold when he saw how crowded the small office was. "Uh…"

Liz turned and greeted the other man with a warm smile. "Hi there. What brings you in today?" Alex felt a slight pang of jealousy. The woman who had been so cool and distant a moment before transformed instantly. Was he the only one she was keeping at arm's length?

He watched as the other man immediately responded to her smile with one of his own. "Oh, uh, well…I just bought a vehicle from a police auction a few weeks ago and the damn air conditioner doesn't work. Pardon my language." He rubbed the back of his neck. "I should have known better than to buy a car "as-is", but with my limited funds, it was the only choice at the time. Now it looks like it's going to cost me more money, anyway."

Liz made a sound of commiseration. "That sucks, but we do offer payment plans to help cover the cost of repair. What kind of car is it?"

"2007 Ford Explorer."

Paul started choking and broke into a coughing fit.

"You okay?" Liz turned and pounded him on the back.

After another moment to catch his breath, Paul nodded, "Yeah, yeah, sorry about that. Why don't I go outside and take a look at his vehicle? I can get him sorted out."

"Sure, although I probably won't be able to take a look at it tonight."

Paul waved his hand in dismissal. "We'll make it work." He turned back to the customer. "If you leave it overnight, we could probably take a look at it first thing, before tackling the other cars. Depending on how much work is needed, we'll be able to make an appointment from there." The client had already begun to nod as the two men walked out to the lot.

Alex was just about to reissue his invitation to dinner when the bell jingled over the door once again.

"Alex!" The bright tinkle of laughter that followed had him cringing. He reluctantly turned to find Cynthia standing in the doorway. She laid a hand on his arm. "What a pleasant surprise to run into you again so soon."

Unsure of what to say, Alex stammered. "Ah, yes... Hi, Cynthia."

He couldn't help but slide a glance toward Liz to gauge her reaction. Her whole demeanor had once again changed from warm and welcoming to cool and distant. The way she was holding her shoulders and shifting her weight made him think of a fighter balancing on her toes, preparing for an attack.

Despite the stance, he found himself feeling very protective. "Well, I have it on good authority that Liz is the best mechanic in town." He was rewarded with a look of surprise and a subtle softening at the corners of her mouth.

The effect was instantly erased a moment later with Cynthia's response. "Well, I suppose it figures. We all know how long she's been working on cars."

Alex noted the way she talked about the other woman as if she wasn't in the same room with her. If he hadn't been watching Liz's reaction so closely, he would have missed seeing the sharp flare of anger in her eyes before it was quickly doused.

Before Alex could respond, Cynthia continued. "We never did set up that time to get together this morning. Why don't I give you a call later?"

Alex knew he had to discuss finding drug paraphernalia at the house, but making plans in front of Liz made him feel distinctly uncomfortable. "I'll get back to you after I discuss it with my father."

At that point, Liz seemed to reach the limit of her patience. "Jimmy would be happy to make an appointment for you, Cynthia. I need to get back to work." Her voice, while tinged with a wry edge, was unfailingly professional. Her face was a carefully cultivated blank mask.

As Jimmy took over the conversation with Cynthia, Alex turned to find Liz looking back at him, almost as if she were surprised he was still there. "Right. Well, I guess I should get going, then. I'll be back on Thursday."

Liz looked like she wanted to say something, but instead she shoved her hands in her pockets and turned down the hallway towards the garage. "Sure. See you then."

Alex watched her walk away, confused. He wasn't sure whether he'd read the whole situation wrong, or if things had just gone off track, but one thing was for certain – this visit had not gone the way he'd expected. He'd hoped to maybe catch her at the end of the day, ask her out to dinner, and get a chance to see if the sparks he'd felt last night had been mutual.

Not that they had made their presence known today.

The funny thing was, he kept getting glimpses of the warm, caring individual he knew her to be. The way she interacted with her family and friends, or even her customers, all spoke to an open, loyal, hard-working woman. The kind of woman he'd like to be better acquainted with.

So why was it so hard for him to connect with her? Sure, it had been awhile since he'd actively dated anybody, but he didn't think he could be off his game that much. Could he?

Deciding he'd better beat a hasty retreat before Cynthia managed to corner him again, he made his way to his truck. He shook his head as he pulled out of the parking lot. One thing was for certain. Eliza Harper was still an enigma, one he was becoming determined to figure out.

CHAPTER SEVEN

"WE FOUND IT."

"You're kidding. How?"

"You won't believe it, but it drove right into the garage."

"Is it intact?"

"As far as I can tell. Our contact said a customer brought it in."

"We have to get it out of there."

"No shit. The vehicle was left overnight, we can take a look at it tonight. This might be the only shot we have to get it back."

"Arrange for a couple of guys to stop by. I want you to be there to oversee things. We can't afford any more mistakes."

The man clenched his fists. As if he didn't already know what to do. "Got it. Oh, one more thing."

He could hear the impatience coming over the line. "Yes?"

"Our contact wants to make sure this goes towards paying off the debt."

"It can't hurt, but that all depends on what we find."

"Right. That's what I said."

"Just get in there and get it. We'll worry about the rest later."

Click.

CHAPTER EIGHT

LIZ POPPED THE final spark plug into place and stood to stretch the kinks out of her back and neck. She was surprised to find it was only a little after nine at night and was happy this was the last car of the day. A hot shower and a cold beer were calling her name.

As she went around and flipped the lights off in the shop, she stopped to take another look at the vehicle that had been dropped off earlier. Knowing she'd want to check it out first thing in the morning, Paul had parked it in the empty bay before leaving for the day. As she looked at it, she realized the dash would need to be completely dismantled in order to figure out what the problem was.

A problem for tomorrow, Liz reminded herself as she turned the music off. Even though Jimmy had locked up when he left for the day, she double-checked the front door before slipping out the back and heading up the stairs to her apartment.

Half an hour later, she stepped out of the bathroom, happy to be in her pajama pants and a tank top. She'd been listening to her stomach rumble for the last hour and knew she needed to find something to eat before indulging in the beer she pulled from the fridge. Deciding to let the food come to her, Liz went to order pizza when she realized she'd left her phone down in the garage.

Irritated, she stuffed her feet into slippers and pulled a cardigan around her shoulders before heading back downstairs. It might be summer, but the nights could still get chilly up in Maine.

She was halfway across the garage when she heard muffled voices approaching the door. What the hell? Did Paul come back to get started on that car? The old man worked harder than she did. She turned and was just about to call out when she spotted two strange men carrying a car jack and a large, red toolbox.

BOOM!

Liz's heart jumped into her throat as she instantly dropped to the ground behind a car. Anger and panic warred in her chest. Had they seen her? Part of her wanted to flee; the other part wanted to confront whoever was in her garage. Before she could decide on a course of action, her attention tuned into what was being said.

"Peck! What did I tell you?! Did I not just say she lives upstairs? You gotta be fucking quiet!"

"Geez, Jonesy. You just get back into town and you're already on my case? The toolbox is heavy. Next time you carry it."

"Man up, will you? Damn crybaby. He's going to be here any moment. If you wake her up and we're discovered, both our heads are going to be on spikes."

Liz froze in the shadows, unsure of what to do. She couldn't call the cops until she got her phone, which was clear across the bay on the workbench. Deciding it would be better to get help some other way, she kept to the perimeter of the garage and began to circle back towards the door. She almost reached the exit when steely fingers grabbed the back of her neck.

Some deep, primal switch flipped in Liz. She clawed up at him, trying to wrench out of his grasp, but the man was too strong. Instead, he dragged her in towards the center of the room, out of the shadows and into the light.

"You idiots were *supposed* to be quiet." At that last word, he tossed Liz to the ground in a heap. Instantly, she was back on her feet and vaulting towards the backdoor. Her slippers threatened to slide out from under her but she willed herself to go faster. The men shouted, their heavy boots pounding the concrete behind her.

Almost there! Her palm slammed against the door. Cool night air greeted her just before a pair of strong arms grabbed her shoulders and hauled her back into the shop. "NO!"

Liz struggled with everything she had. Desperate and trying to twist out of the man's grasp, she screamed. Her assailant was too strong. He lifted her up and slammed her back down to the floor, knocking the breath out of her.

Shock ran through her as she came face-to-face with the man straddling her. Not even the polish and brass of his police uniform could hide the cruelty in the depths of his sneer.

His face filled with dark glee the moment he saw that she recognized him. Josh laughed. "Surprise! Bet you weren't expecting to see me." He let out a loud, mocking sigh. "Lizzy, Lizzy, Lizzy... what are we going to do with you?" Glancing up, he noticed the other two men, watching the scenario unfold before them. "What the hell are you two waiting for? Get back to work!"

Liz craned her neck to the side to see one of the men jump. "Wh-what are you going to do with her, boss?" he asked. Stringy hair hung down into his eyes. His pale, thin arms hung limply by his side. She could see a trail of track marks running up the length of them; some looked more recent than others. No wonder he'd dropped the heavy toolbox. There was something vaguely familiar about him, but she couldn't quite place where she'd seen him before.

It was apparent there would be no help from that corner. Even if they both weren't completely cowed by Josh, it was obvious they were shackled to a drug that would quell any real rebellion against their dealer.

She took a deep breath, refusing to let the anger, fear, and confusion muddle her thinking. Liz clenched her hands into fists as

Josh flipped her over and pulled her arms behind her. Her chin scraped against the concrete floor as he slapped her wrists into cool metal cuffs that dug into her skin. Holding her breath, she hoped he didn't notice the way she tensed her arms so they'd stay slightly loose.

She thought she had gotten away with it until he double checked to make sure they were secure. With a grunt, he clicked each of the shackles tighter, gauging her reaction as he did so.

It hurt like a bitch. She could already feel her fingertips prick in pain from the lack of circulation, but Liz stubbornly refused to make a sound. She knew from past experience that he was the kind of guy who got off knowing he'd hurt you. He fed off the pain he caused.

Liz's heart beat faster as she recognized the small victory for what it was. How was she going to get out of this mess?

Suddenly, Josh gave a cry as his weight lifted from her back. Freed from his heft, her lungs filled with invigorating oxygen. It took her a second to register the sounds of an intense struggle happening behind her. Flipping herself onto her back, she wiggled her way back into a seated position, shocked by the scene before her.

Was that Alex on the ground grappling with his old high school buddy? What was he doing here?

Both men grunted with the impact of each other's fists. Liz flinched as Josh landed an especially brutal hit to Alex's ribs. Alex had kept himself in better physical shape, but it was obvious that Josh had more training in hand-to-hand combat. There was also a glint of viciousness in Josh's eyes that Alex lacked.

After a few minutes, Josh had begun to breathe heavily. He was obviously struggling with the unexpected exertion and Liz began to think she and Alex might have a chance to escape. Relief turned into horror as one of the other men stepped up behind Alex. They'd seemed so weak and inconsequential before that she'd forgotten about them.

"Behind you!" Liz cried.

It was too late.

She winced as the wrench cracked against the back of Alex's head and watched as he silently slumped to the floor in a heap. Josh panted as he bent down to check his pulse.

He stood upright and took a moment to straighten his hair before turning to the other man. "I was wondering how long you were going to just stand there and watch me fight," he said, glowering at him. He adjusted his uniform before adding, "I want the dash out of that car in the next hour or you will regret it."

One of the men, the one called Peck, jumped like a scared rabbit and hurried back to the car to do his bidding. The other, Josh's rescuer, stared insolently at him before pivoting on his heel and heading back to the project. Moments later, Liz could hear them ripping out what was left of the dashboard.

Satisfied that he'd sufficiently motivated the help, Josh once again glanced down at Alex, lying unconscious at his feet. Anger infused his face when he spotted the little device on the concrete beside him. Snatching it from the floor, his face turned an even darker shade of red when he saw the screen. "You sneaky son of a bitch! Thought you could record me for evidence, did you?"

Liz flinched as he slammed the phone to the ground. Little bits of glass and plastic went spinning away as it shattered against the concrete. "This – is what – you – can do – with your – evidence!" Josh punctuated each word with a slam of his heel against the little device until there was nothing left but unrecognizable debris.

Liz cringed as he began kicking Alex in the ribs for good measure. "Not quite the golden boy any more, are you? Bet you're glad you came back to town now, aren't you?"

"Stop it! Just stop it!" The last thing Liz wanted to do was draw attention to herself, but she couldn't sit and watch Alex be tortured while he was unable to defend himself. Where was all this anger coming from? Hadn't they been best friends back in high school?

Josh turned to Liz. "Why the hell is he here?"

"I- I- don't know." Dammit. Being subjected to such unexpected violence, especially from her high school tormentor, had Liz stuttering. Being at Josh's mercy had never been a good position to be in, but this had gone way beyond the everyday level of bullying she'd experienced from him before. The fact that he wasn't bothering to hide who he was or his position could only mean worse things were in store for her.

It was the sharp ring coming from Josh's pocket that cut short anything else he may have done. Glancing at the display on his phone, he secured Alex in the same manner as Liz and forced her to sit on the cold concrete floor beside him. Satisfied they weren't going anywhere, he turned and answered the phone. "Hey, we've got a shitstorm here."

He gave her a warning look before turning away from her. "No, it's nothing I can't handle, but it is going to take a bit longer than originally planned."

"I understand that," he ground out. "They're taking the dash off now, one second." He yelled at the other two men working on the car. "Well? Is it there?"

The muffled response came from the second guy, his head all the way under the dash. "Yeah, boss, it's still here."

A dark, satisfied gleam entered Josh's eyes and Liz wondered what, exactly, they were looking for.

"Good. Get it out of there! Clock's ticking." He turned back to the phone conversation. "Yeah, it looks like it's there and still intact. Nothing has been touched as far as we can tell. They're pulling it out now."

Liz watched as Josh moved closer to the car and further from where she sat on the floor. She paused for another moment to make sure he wasn't going to come back right away, then leaned forward and inspected the locking mechanism on Alex's cuffs. She was relieved to find they were standard issue, the same kind Mason left lying around the house.

If she could find some kind of shim, there might be a way to jimmy it open. Liz began searching the floor around her for something that might work. Alex wheezed and groaned as he slowly came to. The sharp intake of pain had Liz wincing in commiseration as he struggled to breathe while lying on his side. She could tell his ribs were killing him where Josh had kicked them. She wondered if they were fractured.

"Shhh, take it easy and try to catch your breath. Can you sit up? It might help," she whispered.

Gritting his teeth, Alex began to move. He shifted closer to Liz and leveraged his back against her leg. Sweat dampened his forehead from the exertion and pain, but with her help, he managed to get himself sitting upright with a low groan. "Damn. Guess I need to work on my rescuing skills." His fingers searched around him. "Have you seen my phone?" Liz nodded her chin towards the fragments scattered across the floor. Focusing on the path her eyes took, Alex noticed the sad pile of broken plastic shards and grimaced. "There goes that idea."

They both sat slumped and leaning against each other. Alex took stock of his injuries and the situation, while Liz kept scanning the area, looking for anything that might help free them. Finally, she had to ask. "Why are you here, anyway? How did you even know I needed rescuing?"

"I didn't, it was a coincidence. I don't know why Josh is here, or who those two other guys are," he gestured with his chin, "but I recognized the car they arrived in as the one I chased off from one of my dad's properties yesterday. I found evidence of squatting and drug use at one of his houses. Hard-core drugs – the kind that requires needles."

"Yikes."

"Exactly. I called the police about the vandalism and Josh was the officer who came to file the initial report. He'd already left by the time the intruder arrived, so I left him a message and gave him an update."

"And you followed the car?"

"I tried, but my starter wouldn't work. However, on my way home, I spotted the same car parked in the alley behind your garage."

"You mean, before the dinner party?"

"Yeah. But I remembered that you and Josh never got along back in the day, so I was hesitant to say anything until I knew more. I came back tonight hoping I'd be able to grab a license plate number or something else tangible to add to the report. When I got here, I saw the car from yesterday, but I also watched two guys going through the back door.

"When the police cruiser pulled up, I assumed someone must have seen the same thing and called it in. When Josh got out of the car, I assumed he was following up on a lead. Only something about how he entered the building seemed off."

"What do you mean?"

"I don't know. He just seemed a little too relaxed. He didn't have either his gun or his flashlight out. And trust me, its dark back there.

"I couldn't help myself. I stuck around for a moment out of curiosity. Just when I was about to leave, I saw you try to run out the door and get yanked back in. That's when I knew something was really wrong and started recording. I had no idea it was going to be this bad, or that Josh would be involved." Alex winced. "I can't believe he kicked me like that."

As Alex talked, Liz was casting around for anything she could find that might be useful in getting out of the cuffs. Now she scoffed, "What? Like you didn't know he was a dick?"

Alex winced. "Actually, when I was talking to him last night,

54

he struck me as different, like he'd grown up a bit. Especially since he'd become a cop. I knew he could be an asshole, but I never would have guessed he'd do something like this."

Liz decided it wouldn't do any good trying to convince him that Josh had always had it in him to do this. In fact, if her instincts were right, he was capable of doing much, much worse. She grimaced. Not exactly a good scenario for either one of them at this point.

"Why didn't you say anything about all of this last night at the dinner party?"

Alex shrugged, but didn't look up. Her eyes rounded. "You suspected I might be involved somehow, didn't you?"

She stopped to regard him more closely. Well, at least he had the grace to look embarrassed. A small object on the floor behind him caught her eye, "Hey, can you lean to your left a little bit? I need to try and grab something."

"What are you doing?"

"Shh. Just keep an eye out and let me know if anyone heads over here."

Liz fell to her side and wiggled her way slightly behind him. She grabbed the pen cap from the floor then levered herself back into a seated position. Alex was so close, she could smell the subtle scent of his cologne and the shampoo he used. It was tempting to take a moment and lean against him.

"He's coming back."

They could just catch the tail end of Josh's conversation as he made his way over to them. "Hey, I know. It's all of our heads if we lose this shipment. I'll give you a call in the morning." His voice turned frosty as he pinned them under his stare. "No, I got this."

Liz didn't know who was on the phone with Josh, but it was obvious he wasn't the one in charge, and that Josh didn't like having to answer to somebody else. He listened to whatever instructions he was being given then promptly hung up.

Josh gave Alex a smug look. "Welcome back, sleeping beauty."

"Asshole."

Josh grinned, grabbed Liz roughly under the arm, and hauled her to her feet. Her hands were trapped behind her and for a brief moment he held her tight against his body.

Liz dug the pen cap into her palm, reminding herself not to struggle. She knew it would be giving him exactly what he wanted. Instead, she kept her gaze steady on his, refusing to flinch in embarrassment.

"Not quite the plank you used to be, are you?" he leered. "I don't usually go for grease monkeys, but for you I might have to make an exception."

He reached down and grabbed her ass, grinding his pelvis against hers in a lewd gesture. Liz narrowed her eyes and tasted blood from biting her lip so hard. She would be damned before letting him see the fear that sat quivering in her stomach.

"Come on, man!" Alex protested from the floor. "Don't do this."

"Shut. UP!" The force of his anger left Liz trembling, but she was thankful he had been distracted. There had been something dark and lascivious in the way he'd looked at her that made her want to take a shower and scrub her skin. With mock regret, he said, "Too bad I don't have time to go slumming."

Josh spared a glance at his former buddy. "We knew Liz was a workaholic and there was some chance we'd have to dispose of her, but your presence is unexpected. What are you doing here? Cynthia not putting out for you anymore?"

Alex gave him a look of disgust. "What happened to you, man?"

"What happened to you, man?" Josh parroted back at him in falsetto. He sneered. "I'm not the one with my hands bound, sitting on a filthy floor, am I?" He gripped Liz tighter in his anger. "Damn sanctimonious piece of shit. You always did have to be the best at everything, didn't you? First in your class. Most popular. Dating the head cheerleader. Well, you know what? Screw you, you fucking asshole. You leaving town was the best thing that ever happened to me."

Alex gaped at him, taken aback by the ferocity of his words. Liz felt the anger and tension in Josh's body as he caught his breath from the outburst. "You know, if you'd stayed where you were supposed to, you would've had a much more pleasant role in all of this. As it is, you're going to the trash heap with your little friend here."

Trash heap. There was an unpleasant image, Liz thought. Wait a minute. What did he mean by Alex having a better role? Was he in on this? Was she being played? She considered him, his battered and bruised body prone on the floor.

Alex being knocked unconscious was a mark in his favor, but she hated the fact that she still couldn't fully trust him. She gripped the item she'd obtained and prayed she could make it work.

With a rough shove meant to keep her off balance, Josh pushed her towards the back door. Fear locked her knees and threatened to paralyze her.

Holy shit, was he going to kill her right now? Here? She couldn't let him do it, not without a fight. With one swift jerk, Liz managed to catch Josh off guard and twist out of his grasp.

She whirled and ran towards the door. Before she could take more than two steps, Josh shoved her hard in the back, using her momentum against her. She tripped over her toes and fell face first towards the floor. Liz barely managed to twist in the air and land on her shoulder instead of her chin, but it was enough to have her crying out in pain before she could stop herself.

The sound had both of the junkies whipping their heads around to see what the commotion was about. The timid one was biting his lip and had a look of regret on his face. *Peter.* Memories surfaced with his name before the reality of her situation came crashing back.

She could hear Alex yelling from his spot on the floor as she desperately scrabbled for the pen cap she'd dropped in the fall. She felt its reassuring presence in the palm of her hand before Josh hauled her back to her feet. "Bet you feel stupid now."

"Where are you taking me?" She'd meant for it to sound more challenging, but the tremor in her voice gave her away.

"We're going to take a little ride. You may not want to be rushing to the next step after that."

As he was talking, he led her to his cruiser and shoved her into the backseat. Minutes later, he was back with Alex, who had a newly fattened lip and fresh blood on his chin.

Josh leaned in and smirked. "You two sit tight while we finish this. It won't be too long before I get to you."

With that ominous statement, he slammed the door on them.

CHAPTER NINE

SPASMS RAN THROUGH her muscles as a giant charley horse grew in the crick of her neck. Liz had lost the feeling in her fingertips a while ago. It was making her task even more difficult. Josh could walk out the door at any moment and this last small opportunity for escape would be gone.

She tried to drum all thoughts of doom out of her mind so she could concentrate on this one action. Liz grunted as the piece of plastic slipped from her grasp, marking another failed attempt.

"Shit!" Frustration and anxiety welled in her chest, threatening to overwhelm her with panic and despair. It was surprising how hard it was to detach the metal from the cap. She took a deep breath and forced herself to count to three before starting over again.

"What are you doing over there?"

"Trying to get us out of these handcuffs, what are you doing?" Liz replied grumpily. It was the third time she'd fumbled the pen cap and had to go fishing for it in the crack of the seat. If she could just get the angle right...

"What do you mean trying to get out of the cuffs? These are standard police issue."

Liz blew out a breath in exasperation. "Look, not to be rude, but could you be quiet for a minute? I've almost got it..."

Once again, she bent herself into an awkward shape, her hands behind her towards the door. If her survival wasn't at stake, she might have been more self-conscious, with her shoulders wrenched back and her chest thrust towards Alex. As it was, all she could think about was their present situation and the consequences of failing.

"Ah! Finally!" Liz blew out a big breath and rested for a minute.

"What'd you do?" His voice held a note of hope and curiosity.

She turned so her hands were facing Alex and showed him the little metal slide. "It's from the pen cap I managed to grab off the ground."

"I don't get it, how is that going to help?" She shot him an irritated look and he added, "I'm not saying I don't appreciate you trying to get out of these, but I just don't see how that piece of metal is going to help us."

"It's a shim. There's a gap where the arm of the cuff slides in, and if I can get this in that little hole, I might be able to jimmy them open." She closed her eyes, picturing what the cuff looked like in her mind and struggled to disregard the cramp in her neck. She could feel the weight of Alex's gaze on her, but did her best to ignore it.

Her shoulders were screaming in protest and she was beginning to wonder if the whole thing was stupid. Even if she was prone to it, which she was not, Liz didn't have the luxury of giving up. Finally, after a slight grunt, there was a metallic snick before she sighed in relief. Liz pulled her arms in front of her and groaned as she felt her tendons release their tension. The metal cuff dangled from her left wrist, but her right hand was blessedly free.

"Whoa! How'd you do that?!"

She immediately started working on her second cuff. Alex watched as she slipped the metal between the ring and the mechanism. The second one went a lot faster, now that she could see what she was working on. Alex eagerly turned his back to her. "Great, now do me."

Liz got started on his cuffs. "Keep an eye on the door and let me know if he's coming. We need to make sure he doesn't realize we're free from these things."

Alex spared a glance over his shoulder before turning forward to watch the door. He winced as she twisted his arm to a better angle. "Sorry," she muttered. "We're going to have to figure out how to get out of this cruiser once our hands are free. They're built to keep people in, remember?"

"One problem at a time." The determination in his voice fanned the small spark of hope in her.

*

Alex tried to hold still as she worked on his wrist. He could feel her warm breath on the back of his neck as she leaned forward to get a better look. He'd always known she was resourceful, but this was above and beyond.

"How do you know how to get out of handcuffs, anyway? This isn't the product of a checkered past, is it?"

He sensed rather than saw her shrug. "No, nothing like that. I just like tinkering and knowing how things work. Mason has left his handcuffs on the breakfast counter enough times that I've taken a look out of curiosity. Once you know how something goes together, it's not that hard. Basically, it's just another puzzle that needs to be solved."

As she finished her sentence, Alex felt the cuff on his right wrist release and heaved a sigh of relief. His fingertips felt like they were being stabbed with needles as sensation began to slowly return. "Let me turn around so you can get to this other one more easily."

He stared at the back of her head as she bowed towards the task at hand. The click of his second cuff releasing snapped him out of his reverie. He berated himself for losing focus when the situation was so dire. "Thank you."

Alex rubbed the soreness from his wrists and rolled his shoulders and neck a few times to ease the tension that had gathered there. A quick, cursory look at the car doors confirmed his fears. There was no way they were going to be able to get out of the backseat of the cruiser.

"Our best chance is probably going to come when he lets us out. If we're lucky, he'll come after me first. That way the element of surprise won't be wasted."

Liz nodded at him. "I guess the best thing we can do for now is keep our hands behind our backs and let him think he has us subdued."

Just then the other two men, both carrying large boxes, came out the back door. The one who had knocked Alex out lead the way, while the timid one followed with his head down. When she saw the second man, Liz leaned across Alex's lap and loudly cried, "Peter! Peter, it's me!"

At the sound of his name, the poor man jumped and dropped his box. Wrapped bags about the size of a cinder block fell to the pavement. The other man whirled around. "What the hell, Peck? Do you know what will happen to us if Josh sees you dropping the product on the ground?!"

"S-s-sorry, Jonesy." He quickly bent down to retrieve the box of drugs.

Jonesy said, "Ignore that bitch unless you want to share her fate. You're already on thin ice for losing this shipment in the first place."

Alex watched Liz as she focused on Peter, or what did that guy call him? Peck? Peck shook his head vehemently and stood up. She raised her voice even louder, daring him not to look at her in the window. "Peter! Don't you remember me? We used to hide out on the back steps and eat lunch together. I stood up for you against Josh that one time. How can you be working for him now?"

Jonesy shoved his face directly in front of her, effectively blocking her view of the other man. Liz flinched and dug her knee in Alex's thigh, causing him to wince. He nudged her with his shoulder as the man outside the window railed at her.

"Bitch, you better shut the fuck up right now. I don't know who you think this is, or was, but Peck's been my boy for the past five years. This Peter guy you're talking about? He's fucking dead. Just like you're going to be." He slammed his hand against the window for emphasis, causing Liz to startle and pull back further. Alex admired the way she had the wherewithal to keep her hands behind her back as if they were restrained.

The harsh reality of his words sounded like an inevitable death knell. Alex looked at the lovely woman leaning over him, her green eyes filled with a mixture of fear, anger, and determination. She wasn't going to die any time soon, not if he could help it.

He watched as she craned her neck and looked back towards Peter, who was once again standing with the box in his hands. There was nothing but mute fear and apology in his eyes before he scurried after Jonesy. Alex thought he saw him mouth the word "sorry" to her before turning away.

An expression of deep sorrow crossed her face. Alex regretted the way she pulled herself back to her side of the seat and resisted the urge to wrap his arms around her. "He recognized me. I know he did." She huddled by the door for a moment, lost.

"Did you know him well?" Alex had been quiet during the whole exchange, but was curious about Liz's reaction towards the other man.

"Maybe, one time I thought I did. We were never bosom buddies or anything. He was shy and didn't come out of his shell very often. But I used to share my sandwiches with him during lunch. I had no idea what became of him after school. We sort of drifted our separate ways after my parents died. For a moment, I actually thought he'd help us get out of the car…" Liz trailed off as she thought about that time of her life. Suddenly, she focused on Alex and shot him an enigmatic look. "Don't you remember him?"

The look of surprise on his face sparked indignation in Liz. "What? I've never met that man in my life."

"Yeah. You have. You and your buddies used to pick on him constantly during high school. He used to take the long way around to his second-floor classes so he wouldn't have to pass Josh's locker."

Realization dawned in Alex's eyes, followed by a look of remorse and regret. "That's *Pecker?*" He winced at Liz's furious expression. "Whoa, whoa. That's not what I meant. I swear, I'm not that guy anymore. It's just, I'm surprised to see how, um, Peter turned out. That's all."

Liz turned to look out the back window at the other car. The crack in her voice had his heart breaking as she said, "Me too." Neither of the men were visible from where they sat in the back-seat, but it didn't seem to matter. Liz was focused on something from her past.

Josh exited the back door and jolted Liz from her reverie. She faced forward and readjusted her hands behind her back as he barked last minute orders to the hapless pair. Alex saw her shake the memories from her mind and then carefully wipe her face clear of any expression.

Josh climbed into the driver's seat and gave them a smirk in the rearview mirror before pulling out of the alley. At the first traf-fic light, he turned away from the police station.

Liz asked, "Where are you taking us?"

Other than another quick glance in the rearview mirror, Josh didn't respond. Alex and Liz shot each other worried looks. They'd both been secretly hoping this was all a mix-up – or some kind of undercover sting operation. Given Josh's zealous use of violence, it had been a long shot at best, but even that remote possibility was squashed with the direction they were headed.

It only took a few turns and a few miles before they were surrounded by nothing more than trees. Alex watched with concern as the view outside became more and more remote, but soon realized that he recognized the area. One of his father's warehouses was located a few miles away.

Not that it would help if they couldn't get out of the car and away from the man driving it.

They turned down an unpaved road – hardly more than a dirt path –leading out into a field. The car stopped along the back perimeter, its headlights barely cutting through the deep shadows of the woods surrounding them.

Alex knew everything depended on Josh pulling him from the car first. Liz turned to him. He could see the strain in her shoulders as they both sat quietly, waiting to see what their captor would do.

Silence filled the car, interrupted only by the sound of their breathing. After a few moments, Josh sighed heavily. "Believe it or not, I never thought the situation would come to this, but I can't afford to leave loose ends. It's nothing personal."

At that, Liz scowled. But before she could say anything that would cause Josh to grab her first, Alex spoke harshly. "You murdering me is VERY personal."

Josh's shoulders tensed, the atmosphere turning colder. Without another word, he slammed out of the car. Liz and Alex both exhaled with relief as they watched him walk towards Alex's side of the car.

He flexed his hands, the muscles in his shoulder stiffening. There was only going to be one shot at this. If he failed, it would mean his and Liz's certain death. He tried to visualize himself as a cobra, coiled and ready to strike.

"I'll be right behind you," Liz whispered just before the door was yanked open. Josh gestured for him to get out of the car. Instead, Alex shot his legs out and hit him squarely in the stomach. Josh dropped his gun in surprise. A sharp exhalation and grunt filled the air as he fought to regain his balance. Before he could react, Alex slammed his fist into his nose.

He watched with satisfaction as Josh's neck snapped back and his eyes began to water. Josh's eyes widened when he realized his captive's hands were free, but a short moment later his police training kicked in. The element of surprise was gone; now it was just a matter of who could gain the upper hand.

Josh fell to the ground and reached for his gun. Alex lunged, grabbing his hand just as he pulled the trigger. A roar filled the air as the shot was redirected harmlessly into the night sky. Time stopped as both men grappled for control of the weapon, muscles straining, eyes bulging…a primal contest of will and survival. In a desperate burst of energy, Alex twisted Josh's arm and ripped the weapon from his grasp. It landed a short distance away.

Alex heard Liz rushing out of the car behind him right before he took a hit across the jaw. Stars momentarily filled his vision, and his head throbbed and rang in pain. He had to trust that Liz would be able to stay out of the way as he fought to stay focused.

Crouching in a stance with his fists raised, Alex didn't dare let his eyes stray from his target. The two men faced off. He watched Josh eye the gun lying on the ground a few feet away. They both dove for it at the same time, landing in the grass and mud.

"Liz! The gun!"

Alex jumped on top of Josh and began beating him around the head and shoulders. The advantage didn't last long. Josh bucked up with enough force to knock him off his back and they scrambled to their feet. The two men once again squared off, their breath sawing the air between them. Before either of them could re-engage, Liz silently stepped up behind Josh and swung the police-issue baton she'd found in the front seat with all her might.

CRACK!

Josh fell at her feet.

CHAPTER TEN

THERE WAS A brief moment of silence punctuated only by Alex's heavy breathing.

"Is he dead?" The baton dropped from her fingers as she fell to her knees beside the unconscious man. After a moment of careful examination, she let out an exhale. "There's still a pulse."

Liz shrugged at the unspoken question in Alex's eyes. "I may hate him, but I don't think I'm ready to add killing to my list of accomplishments." She gripped her hands tightly in front of her. Now that the immediate danger was over, they wouldn't stop trembling. She turned to Alex, hoping he was in better shape than she was. "Now what?"

He pressed a hand to his screaming ribs and fought to get his breath under control. "I don't know. He destroyed my phone – it had the recording of him in your garage. Right now, it would be a strictly he said/ she said situation." He gestured toward the body lying prone before them. "Add assaulting an officer to the mix, and I'm not sure we'd be the ones to come out ahead."

"But he was going to kill us!" A note of panic crept into her voice as the full scope of their situation came into focus.

Alex must have sensed she was on the brink of losing control. He came over and wrapped his arms around her. She tensed for a brief second before relaxing into the comfort he provided. "Liz. It was the right thing to do. To be honest, I don't think I could have held him off much longer. Most lawyers would argue self-defense...but that's assuming we can prove he wasn't acting in the interest of the law. Right now, we need to lay low and get to the bottom of this."

"We need Mason. He could help us."

Alex nodded but Liz could sense his hesitation. "Are you sure that's wise? We have no idea how deep the corruption goes in the police department. Josh being a cop means we have to consider this may involve more of the department than just him."

Liz tensed and pulled away from him. "Mason isn't dirty..."

Alex interrupted her. "I'm not saying he is, but he would be obligated to bring us in. Besides, he's new. He may not know who he can trust. We should call him instead of meeting in person. At least over the phone, we can give him some plausible deniability. If anyone asks, he hasn't seen us."

She didn't like it, but Liz had to admit he had a point. Before she could respond, a low groan came from Josh. Alex turned to her. "We need to get out of here. Liz, where did you put the cuffs?"

Liz ran to the backseat and grabbed both pairs of cuffs and the set of keys from Josh's belt. "Let's drag him closer to the car. I'll shackle him to the front grill." It only took a moment to secure Josh's hands on either end of the bumper. She looked up at Alex. "If I keep his hands separate he won't be able to get out the same way we did."

He gave her a wry look. "Remind me never to piss you off."

A wisp of a smile crossed her lips before she turned to the next hurdle. "Okay, so now what? We obviously need to find a safe place to hole up. I have to get ahold of Mason, and ultimately we need to figure out what the hell is going on with all those drugs in my garage."

Alex scanned the trees surrounding the clearing. Other than the shafts of light from the headlights, everything was shrouded in darkness. "What's the plan?" Liz asked. Another low moan came from Josh. Alex motioned for Liz to follow him a few feet away, out of earshot.

"I think we're close to a warehouse that my dad owns, but it's hard to tell which direction to go in the dark." He ran a hand through his hair. "We need to get away before somebody starts wondering where Josh is. All they have to do is check on the GPS in his squad car in order to find him."

She nodded towards the darkest part of the trees. "Let's get going, then."

"Wait, we need to take anything that could be useful to us. From this point on, our resources are going to be limited until we can figure this out." Liz watched as he took a flashlight out of the other man's belt and started pawing through his pockets, pulling a few bills out.

It was another stark example of their new status as fugitives. Her stomach knotted in fear. How the hell had this happened? Forcing herself to accept the situation for what it was, she grabbed the baton from where she'd dropped it earlier. She shrugged as Alex gave her an approving nod. "Just in case."

Liz looked at the gun and hesitated. Sighing, Alex reached down and picked it up. He checked the chamber and safety before stuffing it into the back of his pants "We can't afford to leave this behind. If drugs are involved, chances are we're going to be dealing with some unsavory people."

Liz grimaced. "Sorry. I know you're right, but guns were never my thing." She bent down and grabbed something else. "We should probably take his phone, too. He was talking about that drug shipment earlier, which means he's working with someone else. We need to know who."

"I agree, but keep it off and take the battery out until we decide to use it. We'll probably only get one chance before they're able to track the phone. Especially since we don't know if any other cops are involved."

"It still feels wrong not going to Mason about this." Liz protested.

"Think about it, Liz. His hands are going to be tied with something like this. No way would they let him take a case when there's obviously a conflict of interest. Besides, if there is another dirty cop on the force, how hard do you think it will be for him to get to us?"

Alex looked like he wanted to continue, but a squawk from the radio drew their attention. He impulsively grabbed her hand and gave it a squeeze. "Let's at least get ourselves someplace safe where we can talk about it further."

She nodded, surprised at the feeling of relief that flooded her. Liz didn't want to have to do this alone, but she hadn't realized just how much she was relying on him to watch her back. With a silent nod, they headed off into the woods.

CHAPTER ELEVEN

LIZ WOKE WITH an aching back and a couch spring digging into her side. They had both been exhausted when they'd found the warehouse owned by Alex's father. Breaking into the back office had been easy compared to breaking out of the handcuffs earlier.

The office stank of old fast food and stale cigarettes, a smell Liz found infinitely more offensive upon waking. She was surprised to find a musty blanket thrown over her shoulders and wondered where Alex had found it.

Craning her neck, she looked to where he had fallen asleep, upright in the office chair. His head was propped haphazardly on his hand and his hair had fallen across his forehead. There were quite a few bruises decorating his cheek and jaw from his fight with Josh, but they didn't detract from his male beauty. She hoped his ribs were okay.

He must have been as exhausted as she had been to fall asleep in such an awkward position. They'd spent hours walking through the dark woods, the flashlight a meager comfort, before they'd finally gotten their bearings and managed to make it to the warehouse. Scratches ran up and down her arms from stumbling through the brush and into tree branches, but it was her feet that had taken the worst damage.

Apparently, slippers weren't meant to be worn for a nighttime hike through the woods. Both her heels were bruised, the balls of her feet were swollen, and at some point, she'd sprained the little toe on her right foot. Of course, there'd been no way to know what she would come across last night when she'd run downstairs to grab her phone.

Liz reached up and found leaves stuck in her hair. Great. She probably looked as wrecked as she felt. Not that it mattered, considering everything that had happened the night before. Stifling a groan, she sat up on the couch, hoping she could sneak out of the office without disturbing Alex.

"Where are you going?" His voice was rough with sleep and sent sexy little shivers down her spine.

"I was just going to find a bathroom to clean up a bit."

"It's down the hall on the left. Are you hungry? I'll see if I can find anything in the breakroom."

"Sounds good, I'll join you in a minute." It was almost comical how mundane their conversation was. A part of Liz wanted to scream, to rant and rave and pull her hair out. A cop – her high school bully, no less – had tried to kill her. They'd found drugs in her garage. And here she was, sleeping on a beat-up old couch, with her old high school crush a few feet away. A man that, up until a few nights ago, probably didn't even remember she existed.

Liz clenched her hands so tightly that little half-moons were carved into her palm as she made her way down the hall. Fear and stress fluttered in her stomach and fought to overwhelm her. After using the restroom, Liz splashed cold water on her face and stood looking in the mirror, forcing herself to take deep breaths for control.

She wondered if Josh had been discovered yet. What could he say that would account for him being cuffed to the front of his bumper in the middle of a cold field at dawn? A flutter of apprehension had her clutching her stomach. One thing she knew for certain, he would be sure to paint her in the worst light possible.

There was nothing she could do about that now. Liz shook, took another deep breath, and forced herself to concentrate on what she could control. Anytime she was stumped by a puzzle, it helped to focus on the few pieces that were right in front of her. This was no different.

First things first – she had to get ahold of Mason and see if he could help her. There was a phone on the desk in the office she could use. She wondered how long it would take for them to track her phone call. Her stomach lurched. There might be police standing in her sister's kitchen even now. What if all their lines were already tapped, what then?

Stop. She had to at least try to contact them. But they should probably be ready to head out directly afterwards.

Which lead to her next thought. What was she going to do with Alex? It seemed like he was irrevocably tangled up in this mess, but she still wasn't entirely sure how it had happened. The timing all seemed a little too convenient – or inconvenient, depending on your perspective.

Liz made her way to the break room and found Alex standing by a Formica counter munching on a bag of Cheetos. A corner of his mouth turned up when he spotted her. "Breakfast of champions." He turned to the bright pile of bags. "You get your pick between Fritos and Lays."

"Hmm, corn or potatoes, huh? Sounds nutritious, either way."

Chuckling, he tossed her the Fritos. "Don't worry, we have plenty of chocolate candy bars for dessert." She could feel him eyeing her damp hair and face. "Feeling better?"

Liz sat down on a folding chair and popped open her breakfast. "Yeah, thanks."

"So, what's our plan?"

"Well, I know you have reservations, but I need to talk to Mason first. Maybe he can shed some light on the situation."

"Or, he could unintentionally lead them straight to us."

"It's still early enough that I think it's worth the risk. Whatever Josh was doing in my garage last night, it wasn't legal. Which means he'll want to keep it quiet. They might not even know what has happened yet."

Alex nodded. "Okay, but we still don't know how far this corruption goes in the police department. We'll need to make sure he understands we're not coming in, not yet."

"I'm not convinced hiding is the best course of action, but I'm willing to agree to it for now." She sighed. "You know, there are two things that keep niggling at me."

"What's that?"

She shook her head, trying to recall an old memory. "Well, for one, the fact that Peter was there took me completely by surprise. I got the feeling he would have helped us if he hadn't been around Jonesy."

"I don't know. He may have looked like he wanted to help you, but I doubt he'd have the backbone to actually do it."

Something about his tone irritated Liz. "That poor man has been terrorized his entire life. Can you blame him?"

Alex sighed. "No. I don't. And if I could take back the way I treated him in high school, I would in a heartbeat." He ran a hand through his hair, regret showing plainly on his face. "But that still doesn't change the fact that he's not the same guy you knew back then. Who knows what else could have happened to put him in the situation he's in? You can't make a guy grow a spine just because you will him to, Liz." After a brief moment of uncomfortable silence, he continued. "You mentioned two things bugging you. What was the other one?"

She pushed past his comment, not wanting to admit he was probably right. "I keep going back to the person on the phone with Josh. That is the person in charge. If we could figure out who he is, we'd be able to exonerate ourselves."

"Assuming we can get proof."

Right. Proof. Liz jumped up and started pacing. "We're going to need to be ready to leave the minute I finish the call."

"I've been thinking about that. I might have an idea where we can hole up, but it could be difficult to get to."

Liz headed back to the office and dialed Mason's number. She was surprised when he answered on the first ring. That couldn't be a good sign.

"Mason?"

"Liz." His voice lowered. "Are you okay?"

The question, asked so calmly, almost had her eyes welling. Instead, Liz ruthlessly tamped down her emotions and gave a mocking laugh. "I've been better."

"What the hell happened? I just got a call saying they found evidence of heroin at your shop. You're wanted for drug trafficking and dealing."

"That son of a bitch!"

"Who?"

"Josh! I went downstairs and caught him and two other guys breaking in, trying to retrieve a drug shipment hidden in a car that came in for service yesterday. He must have gone back and spread around evidence to frame me." Silence stretched on the other end of the line so long that, Liz wondered if they'd gotten cut off. "Mason?"

His voice lowered and something about his hesitation sent tendrils of dread through her chest. "That's not all. They're saying there are other vehicles they've confiscated recently that were associated with your garage. Apparently, they've been gathering evidence against your business for a couple of months now."

"Months?" Liz felt the world drop from under her feet.

"That's what I said."

"You knew about this?"

The silence answered her question more than anything he could have said. "Liz, I…"

"No. Don't. I get it." The frustrating thing was, she did. Logically she understood that Mason was duty-bound to remain silent. It still felt like a betrayal. Maybe Alex was right.

"Mason, I swear to you, I have nothing to do with this, but it's more complicated than just going in and telling my side of the story." Liz quickly filled him in, starting with going downstairs for her phone and ending with cuffing Officer Josh Carver to the front grill of his cruiser.

"Wait, let me get this straight. Alex Weston is with you?"

"Yeah, I wouldn't have been able to get away if it hadn't been for him."

"Hmm." Liz could tell Mason was deep in thought.

"What?"

"Nothing. Never mind." He sighed. "I can't say I'm too surprised about Josh. That guy is a wrecking ball in uniform. He's been trying to make detective for the last year and had no qualms letting me know he resented me coming into the department and taking lead. The problem is he's not even our biggest concern at the moment."

"What do you mean?"

"There's an MDEA agent named Matt Hagen coming in later this morning. He's been working the increase in heroin drug incidents throughout the region. He is highly motivated, and eager to make a name for himself. Rumor has it he's looking to make commander before forty. It's hard to say if he's just looking for an easy way to climb up the ranks or if he'll be open to hearing your side of things. Right now, because of the heroin found and previous incidents, Matt's under the impression that you may be the head of the drug ring in Maine."

Liz felt the tension in her stomach tighten. "I don't know what to do. Alex doesn't think we should come in until we know whether any other officers are involved."

"I hate to say it, but that may be the best course of action for now. I haven't been in this department long enough to get a sense of where everybody stands. I'll start investigating from this end, but until we know how deep the corruption goes, I can't guarantee you'll be safe if you come in to the station. How much cash do you have on you?"

"Nothing. I was in my pajamas when this all happened." She placed a hand on the receiver and turned. "Hey, how much cash do you have?"

Alex pulled his wallet out. "About a hundred bucks, including what I got off Josh."

Mason exhaled. "Damn, not as much as I'd like. You're going to need to stay under the radar. Remind Alex not to use any of his credit cards. Keep off the main road as long as you can and do your best to avoid any cameras. Do you have your phones?"

"Josh smashed Alex's last night. Mine is still on the workbench in the garage. I grabbed a phone number off of Josh's before I turned it off. Whoever he was on the phone with last night was definitely the one calling the shots. It's our best lead to finding out who's behind all of this."

"Give me the number and I'll try to track it. It may be difficult since my every move will be watched. Afterwards, you need to get rid of that phone. Better yet, take the sim card and battery out, then hide it. We may be able to use it for evidence later."

Liz gave Mason the number.

"Okay, got it. Listen, Liz. There's one more thing I have to tell you. Can Alex hear us?"

She looked up at Alex leaning against the office doorway. "Go ahead."

"Alex hasn't been officially implicated in this mess, and I'm not sure why. I was surprised to hear he's with you. Officer Carver didn't mention his name when he made it in this morning. Added to the fact that it's a fairly large coincidence he wound up being there right when everything started to go down. I'm just saying it seems a bit suspicious."

Liz chewed her lip. He was voicing every doubt she'd already had. She wasn't sure if she should feel more or less relieved by that fact. Mason continued. "What do you think? Could he be a part of the drug ring?"

She looked down at her hands. Liz felt Alex watching her, but couldn't bring herself to make eye contact. Could he tell they were talking about him? "Um, it's hard to say."

She could hear stress bleed into Mason's voice. "Watch your back and trust no one, Liz. For the time being, that includes Alex, ok?"

"It's going to be difficult."

"I know, especially since it looks like you'll be stuck with each other for the time being. I just don't want you to let your guard down. It won't be safe for you to contact me again. They're already watching us closely, and I wouldn't put it past them to tap our phone lines later today. Get a cheap burner phone, just in case you have to call again. You can find them at most convenience stores."

"Thanks, Mason."

"Just keep your head down."

Liz shuddered at the way those ominous words echoed in her mind as she hung up the phone and looked at the man standing in front of her.

CHAPTER TWELVE

MASON TUCKED THE phone into his back pocket. He could feel Olivia hovering in the doorway.

"Is she okay?"

Nothing about the situation was okay. "For now. It's a miracle, considering what she just told me."

"What do you mean?"

"Josh was at the garage last night. He's a part of the drug ring, although I have no idea in what capacity. Regardless, it's enough that he didn't want Liz to be able to testify against him. We're lucky she's alive."

"What?!"

Mason wrapped his arms around her. "That's not all. Alex was there last night, but I couldn't tell you why. She said if it wasn't for him, she wouldn't have been able to get away."

"Holy shit. We have to do something."

"*We* don't have to do anything. The department already knows of my connection to her and will be watching all of us closely to see if we make contact with each other. The best thing you can do is just sit tight."

"Mason…"

"I know. I know, it sucks. But if you find a way to talk to

Liz, you could be leading them – either the legitimate cops, or the dirty one – directly to her."

Olivia bit her lip and pulled away from him to pace the room. "Well, what are you going to do?"

"I'm going to go down to the department and try to figure out who I can trust." Mason ran a hand through his hair. He could feel the weight of the situation bearing down on his shoulders. "Dammit! I wish I weren't so new in the department. I'm still trying to build some rapport with the Chief, and I don't know the story with half the guys I'm working with. We're just lucky Brad was working the early morning shift and could give us a heads-up on what's going on. He said the Chief had to call the MDEA in on the case. Some guy named Matt Hagen."

"Is he any good?"

"I don't know yet." Mason stuffed his wallet in his back pocket and grabbed his keys from the basket by the door. "I need to get going. It'll look bad if I show up late, especially today. I'll let you know more when I find out."

"Promise me." Olivia joined him at the door. "I heard you tell Liz they've been investigating her garage for a while now."

"Livvy, about that…"

"No. Mason, I understand that you can't always tell me what's going on with your job, but you have to promise me that you're going to keep me informed about this."

Mason bent down and gave Olivia a gentle kiss. He still couldn't believe how perfect these last few months had been with her. "I promise. No secrets on this one."

"Thank you. Now, go save my sister."

CHAPTER THIRTEEN

ALEX STOOD IN the doorway and watched as Liz hung up the office phone. She then promptly started to dismantle Josh's cell. "So, what did Mason have to say?"

Liz's gaze never shifted away from the phone in her hand, "Well, he's just as confused as us. You were right, there's not much he can do for us at the moment."

"But he knew about what happened last night, right? That must mean they've found Josh."

She nodded, but didn't say anything further. With the phone disassembled, she began looking for places to stash the parts. She tucked a piece into one of the drawers in the file cabinet, then stashed another behind some books. He moved to stand beside her. "Liz?"

"Yeah, Josh managed to get away, and walked in to the station this morning to file a report. I'm now wanted for drug trafficking and dealing, as well as assaulting a police officer."

Alex let out a low whistle. "Shit. What are we going to do?"

With that, Liz pierced him with her gaze. "Well, Alex. That's the funny thing. Apparently, your high school buddy Josh never mentioned you. So, you can pretty much get out of here and no one would be the wiser. Any idea why he might have omitted your presence from the report?"

He raised his hands in defense. "What are you talking about?"

"You and Josh! For all I know, you two could be working together and this is all some big – I don't know – complicated plan. It wouldn't be the first time you guys have messed with me."

Her anger and distrust instantly put his hackles up. Indignation welled inside of him. "Hey, we're talking about life and death here. I think this is a far cry from a little high school teasing."

He took a step closer. "In case you've forgotten, I was handcuffed in the backseat of that car just the same as you. I stared down the barrel of a gun just the same as you. And when it came down to it, my life was on the line, just the same as you. Don't tell me I'm not as involved in this." He stopped and stood directly in front of her. "I'm right here, Liz."

Her eyes widened in shock at the ferocity of his response. Alex ached to reach for her, to show her how much he regretted the past between them, but stopped himself. She still didn't fully trust him. He could see the flicker of doubt in the depths of her gaze, but it was the fear in her voice that had him softening his tone.

He sighed. "I don't know why Josh didn't report me. Maybe he kept it back in an effort to draw me out. Or maybe he thinks he can tail me and I'll lead him back to you. Regardless of whether or not the legitimate cops know about me, the fact is the dirty cops *do* know I'm involved. There's nothing to prevent the drug ring from coming around and killing me. And what's worse is that no one would be the wiser."

Liz looked down and had the grace to blush. "I hadn't thought about that." She took a step around Alex, putting some distance between them, and tapped her chin. "You're right. We don't know why Josh has omitted your name…"

Alex noticed she didn't apologize for her earlier assumptions, but decided to let the matter drop. Instead, he leaned against the desk and waited for her to finish her thought.

"…but we may as well use his omission to our advantage.

Mason suggested we get what supplies we can without using our credit cards and go to ground. Since your face won't be plastered all over the news, it may be best for you to be the one to pick things up. I'll stay hidden in the trees, back away from the road."

"That works. I think our first priority should be getting you something for your feet. Your slippers aren't doing much good."

Liz looked down at her feet. "You didn't happen to see a spare pair of shoes around here, did you?"

"I didn't see any," Alex admitted.

She straightened her shoulders. "Well, then, I'll just have to make it work until we find an alternative."

He wished there were something else he could do for her. He'd seen the damage to her feet caused by their run through the woods last night. They had to be causing her a lot of pain. He was about to suggest they try wrapping her feet in duct tape, when he heard the faint wail of sirens. "Liz…"

Fear filled her eyes as her head shot up. "They must have tapped Mason's cell phone."

He grabbed her hand as they ran out of the office and sprinted across the open warehouse. "There's a trail behind the building that cuts through the woods. We may stand a chance if we reach it before they get within view!"

They burst out of the back door and into the early morning light, racing towards the shelter of the trees. Alex could hear Liz breathing heavily beside him. Even after they breached the shadow of the forest, it was a long time before either one of them felt comfortable enough to stop.

CHAPTER FOURTEEN

LIZ WINCED AS another twig caught her instep. After the initial flight from the warehouse, they'd had to slow down because of the rough terrain and her slipper-clad feet. Now, over an hour later, she was limping and wasn't sure how much longer she'd be able to go on.

As if sensing her pain, Alex stopped in front of her and turned. "We're nearly there. Do you want me to give you a piggy back ride?"

Liz couldn't help but smile at the image that entered her mind, but she knew there was no way he'd be able to carry her after the beating he'd taken the night before. "No. I can manage. Maybe I'll take you up on it if we're still out here in another hour, though."

He sent her a little smile of encouragement, but she could see he was worried. It would have been heart-warming under any other circumstance. As it was, all she could think about was getting her feet warm and dry.

Alex turned and started breaking the trail again. "For the most part, we've been running close to parallel to the road. Now we're going to need to cross Highway 1 and cut south."

Liz stopped and tried to get her bearings. "Isn't it more populated down there?"

"Yeah. Things are going to get tricky."

"Should we wait until it gets darker?"

He shook his head. "We need to keep moving. It's just a matter of time before my name gets out there, and then any movement we make in public is going to be twice as hard. We'd be better off being holed up by the time that happens."

Liz gestured ahead of them. "Lead the way."

Following Alex gave her a chance to think over what Mason had told her earlier. Liz tried to figure out how her garage could possibly have a history of being involved in a drug ring. Other than whatever Josh had left the night before, what evidence could they have?

Regardless of what the cops thought, she knew she wasn't involved, which only left Paul and Jimmy. But Jimmy was such a new employee, there was no way it could be him. Which left Paul.

She shook her head at the thought. No, that couldn't be right, either. Paul *knew* how much that garage meant to her. How many afternoons had she spent with him and her dad, fixing up cars? Hell, he was the one who had taught her how to take apart a transmission.

Her mind drifted back to that terrible night six years ago when her life had changed forever. It had been a quiet, rainy evening. Her parents had gone out to dinner for their anniversary and she hadn't expected them home until later. Fiona had gone to her room hours before, most likely to read in bed for a while before falling asleep.

Liz had been watching TV, but was feeling restless. She'd just gotten up to make herself a snack when the doorbell rang. She remembered wondering why someone would be coming by the house so late at night. Some deep-rooted instinct had her worried. When she opened the door and found Paul standing on her front step with a police officer, it was obvious something was wrong. His eyes were sorrowful and she remembered noticing that his hair was soaked and plastered to his head.

"Paul? What's wrong?" She stepped back to let the two men in and followed them into the living room. They both stood in the middle of the room as if lost.

After a brief moment of hesitation, the officer took his hat off. Liz watched as a drop of water slowly made its way from his hairline and slid down the side of his face. He cleared his throat nervously, his voice deep and rough with emotion. "Are you the only one in the house right now, miss?" She wrapped her arms around her stomach, as if her arms could be enough armor for what came next.

"My sister is asleep upstairs, but it's just the two of us until my parents get home."

Paul made a slight choking sound from where he stood by the mantle. "Liz, I..." He turned and gestured to the couch. "Why don't you sit down for a minute?"

She stepped closer to him and forced herself to stand up straight. "Just tell me what's going on."

"I'm so sorry to have to tell you this." Paul's voice caught. That's when she knew that whatever he had to say was truly bad. He wasn't exactly what you'd call an emotional guy.

Her gaze leapt back and forth between the two men who were obviously having a hard time with whatever they had to tell her.

Paul shook his head slightly at the officer and then paused to collect himself, searching her face as if he was trying to memorize how she looked in the last moments before he spoke. "Liz, there's been an accident..."

"An accident?"

"Your parents..." His voice cracked. "Liz, they didn't make it."

A great chasm opened under Liz's feet. It felt like the entire world was shifting on its axis. "What do you mean they didn't make it?" She didn't remember sinking to the floor. "Didn't make it? You mean, they're..."

Paul crouched before her, tears streaming down his roughened cheeks. "Dead. I'm so sorry, Liz. Your parents are dead."

He tried to put an arm around her, but she shoved him away, causing him to fall backwards in a sodden heap on the carpet. "NO!"

Jumping up, she paced the room, grabbing her hair as if trying to pull the words out of her mind. "No, no… there has to be some mistake. Paul, tell me you made some mistake!"

He stood and took her by the shoulders, forcing her to look at him. Her eyes pleaded with his, but she saw the truth in their depths. "Oh, Eliza girl. I wish I had. I wish it was."

That was the moment she knew it was true. He only ever called her Eliza when he was very serious about something. Usually when he was giving her a safety talk in the garage and he wanted her to pay special attention. He *never* called her by her full name otherwise. Her face crumpled in agony as the entire foundation of her existence crumbled in her mind.

"Liz? What's going on?" Fiona's sleepy voice cut through the fog of her grief. She stood on the stairs looking young and innocent in her polka-dot pajama pants, her hair messy from sleep. "Paul, what are you doing here?"

Liz wondered how she could possibly break such devastating news to her sister. She couldn't bear to be the one to deal the blow. Once again, Paul was the one who bore the heavy weight of responsibility and told Fiona what had happened.

The cop had stood in the living room with his hat in his hand for another fifteen minutes, but Liz hadn't been aware of anything other than her world fracturing around her. The two sisters had sat on the living room floor and clung to each other as they shared their grief. All the while, Paul had been there to watch over them, doing what he could to comfort them.

And he'd been there for all three sisters as they learned how to pick up the pieces of their family. Paul was a second father, a favorite uncle, and a mentor all rolled into one. There was no way he was involved in what happened at the garage.

Liz stumbled over a tree root and fell to her knees. Alex paused. "Do you need me to slow down?"

"No, I'm fine. I'm just not paying enough attention to where I'm going."

"Okay, but let me know if you can't keep up."

His comment made her bristle, even knowing he hadn't meant it as an insult. "I will." She took a moment to wish memories were as easy to brush off as pine needles before renewing her efforts to watch the trail. Her mind returned to her previous train of thought. If it wasn't Paul, then the only way this could have happened is if Josh had somehow managed to doctor the evidence to further implicate her. Liz felt a sense of relief. That must have been what happened. It couldn't be Paul.

She came to this conclusion just as they reached the side of a road. Alex stopped in the shadow of the trees and looked out over the open expanse of asphalt. Beyond was a parking lot and the back of a strip mall. He knew the gas station would be on the other side.

"This is it." He looked at Liz as she pulled up beside him. "How are your feet?"

"In serious need of a pedicure and some pampering."

His laughter startled her. He shook his head. "For some reason, I never considered you to be the pedicure type."

Liz slanted him a look. "What does that mean?"

He shrugged. "No offense, but you've always seemed more of a badass than that."

She wasn't quite sure how to feel about his assessment of her. Or the fact that he had thought about it at all. "I can be a badass and still like pedicures."

Alex turned, catching her with his gaze. "Clearly."

Liz felt her pulse spike at his undivided attention. It was ridiculous how much he could affect her with just a look.

Shaking her head, she took a step back and reminded herself she couldn't let Alex get too close. She still wasn't even sure she could trust him. "So, how are we going to get what we need? Should we just run over there?"

The sudden change of subject had Alex looking back out over the road. Liz thought there had been a glimmer of disappointment before he'd turned away. "No, I think running would make us more obvious. We'd do better just acting like we belong. Let's cut across and then skirt around to the back. I see some more trees over there. It'll be a good spot for you to stay out of sight."

Staying as close to the perimeter as possible without looking like they were sneaking, Liz felt self-conscious about her lack of shoes. It was nearly twenty minutes before Alex found a good location, slightly in the woods. At that point, all she wanted to do was sit down for a week.

"We have a decent view of that gas station from here. Why don't you sit on this rock while I go pick up a few supplies?"

"Are you sure you're okay to do this?" Liz asked. Now that the time had come, she was surprised to find she was nervous.

Alex stepped up to her. "Don't worry, I've got this. Just promise me you'll stay here until I come back."

Liz raised her arms and looked around. "Where would I go? According to Mason, I'm a wanted fugitive with the whole police force out looking for me."

He sent her a commiserating look. "Just rest here for a while. Once we have a few supplies, we can figure out the next stage of the plan, okay?"

It felt strange not being the one in charge, but for once, Liz was happy to let someone else take over. "Be careful. Your involvement may not have been reported this morning, but that was over two hours ago. Anything could have changed during that time and we wouldn't know."

Alex nodded and headed towards the building, but then turned and walked back. Liz had just gotten herself as comfortable as she could on the rock. She looked up. "What?" He bent over, his lips capturing hers in a firm, quick kiss. It was over before she'd even had a chance to respond.

Looking down, he stroked a finger along her jawline and smiled. "For luck."

He left her with her lips tingling and her eyes glued to his back as he walked away.

CHAPTER FIFTEEN

ALEX CHUCKLED AT the thought of Liz's stunned face when he'd planted that kiss on her, but then he pushed the thought away, knowing he'd need to pay attention for this next step. His long strides quickly got him across the field, his pulse racing with tightly leashed adrenalin. Slowing, he approached the back of the building and did one more scan to see if anyone was watching.

So far, the only thing he could see was the door to the bathroom and a spot for garbage. A bell chimed overhead as he went through the door. Alex nodded at the clerk, but noticed he was too caught up in his program to acknowledge him.

His stomach growled as he wandered down the aisle, and he suspected Liz was probably just as hungry as he was. The bag of chips they'd had for breakfast was long gone, but with only a hundred dollars, Alex knew he was going to have to prioritize.

Skipping the food aisles for the moment, he made his way to the side of the store where they kept cheesy tourist gifts and seasonal items like sunglasses and lip balm. Perfect. Just as he'd hoped, there was a bin of cheap plastic flip flops kept in the back corner.

He should have asked what size shoe she wore. Hazarding a guess, he found a bright orange pair in size 7. After another moment of looking, and coming up with another pair in equally offensive lime green, he decided the orange ones were the best option.

Now for food. Bright, colorful wrappers filled the shelves. Too bad there wasn't a great selection of actual sustenance available. Doing the best he could, he grabbed a bag of beef jerky, trail mix, a couple of granola bars, and some water. Checking the amount left in his wallet, he tossed in a cheap first-aid kit and some bandages he found in another aisle. As he walked up to the counter, he noticed the TV had cut to a breaking news story.

Glancing at the pile on the counter, the clerk asked, "Did you find everything okay?"

"Yeah, thanks. Hey, can you turn that up for a minute?"

The guy grabbed a remote and raised the volume. "Crazy, huh?"

"What happened?"

The guy looked at him, eager to be the one to pass on juicy news. "I guess there was a break-in at the garage downtown and they found some drugs. There was also a police officer injured before she made her escape. You think that broad has been dealing drugs out of her garage this whole time?"

"There's probably more to the story. Are they saying she's a suspect?"

"Well, technically they're calling her a 'person of interest,' – here he punctuated the term with air quotes – but it's easy to read between the lines." The clerk shook his head again. "Can you believe it? I used to take my car there for oil changes."

Alex wasn't sure how to respond to that. "So, what are they doing?"

His new friend shrugged. "They're looking for her now. I guess they think she was the head of some big drug ring."

"And they think she did this all by herself?" Alex hadn't really believed he'd been left out of the news cycle, but the proof was right there. What the hell was going on? Why would they not be gunning for him, too?"

"She's the only one they're talking about. But, who knows how she could have done something like that, y'know?"

Alex agreed with the guy and paid for his goods. "Well, thanks for the info."

"Yeah, no problem." The clerk turned back to the set, shaking his head.

Alex stepped out of the store and took a moment to adjust his purchases before making his way to the back of the building. Just as he was about to round the corner, the clerk opened the door. "Hey, Mister!"

His heart jumped and he tightened his hand on the bag's handle. How long would it take him to run across the field and back into the woods?

Instead, he turned around slowly. "Yeah?"

"You forgot your water."

Relief flooded over him as he took a step closer and accepted the water. "Thanks." He struggled to get his pulse rate back down to normal. Deciding not to take any more chances, he picked up his pace and jogged across the field.

Alex made it into the shadow of the trees and paused to catch his breath. A hushed quiet surrounded him and filled the air. The blanket of pine needles muted his footsteps, and he could see little patches of wildflowers pushing their way up in the dappled light. It would have been idyllic if they weren't currently running for their lives.

Where was she? Did he somehow get turned around?

He walked further into the stand of trees, trying to get his bearings. No, there was the clearing with the big rock he'd left her sitting on.

Afraid to make too much noise, he whispered loudly. "Liz?"

When there was no response, he scanned the area. "Liz?" he called a little louder. Shit, where could she be?

He checked the dirt for any signs of a struggle. If anything had happened to her...Alex shut down that train of thought.

A flash of color caught his eye. Bending down, he found a scrap of cloth that had gotten snagged. The small seed of fear in his stomach blossomed into full-fledged panic. Alex frantically circled the clearing, hoping to find any other clues. He'd just doubled back to the rock when he heard someone approaching from behind him.

Crouching down in the shadow of the rock, Alex waited.

CHAPTER SIXTEEN

LIZ GINGERLY PICKED her way through the trees. The pine needles were easier to walk on than other things she'd stepped on today, but they weren't exactly comfortable.

It was quiet. Quieter than it had been all day. Liz hadn't noticed how silent the woods had become until she reached the edge of the clearing. Then, it dawned on her what was missing.

All the birds had stopped singing.

Fear draped across her shoulders. The back of her neck prickled in warning. Squinting, she could just make out the shape of a man in the shadow of the rock. "Alex? Is that you?"

Instantly, he jumped up. Oh, thank goodness. If it hadn't been him...

"Where the hell did you go?" His harsh voice had her backing up. She crossed her arms. Maybe it wasn't so good to see him after all.

"You had me worried!" He reached for her, but thought better of it at the last minute. She still didn't budge. "Didn't we agree you were to stay put?" He brandished a scrap of her shirt. "I thought someone may have found you."

Damn. Hadn't she just been thinking the same thing? She took a step towards him, but her voice remained cool. "I was sitting here waiting for you and got to thinking. How are we going to get to the next location? I figured I could find some way to help, so I found us a car."

"Found a car?"

She shrugged. "Maybe temporarily liberated would be a better way to put it."

"Liz, don't you think stealing a vehicle is an unnecessary risk?"

The exasperation in his voice irritated her all over again. "Look, I'm not just some damsel in distress who is going to sit around and wait to be rescued. I'm perfectly capable of contributing to our way out of this mess."

"Not if it means risking your safety."

"You did it."

Alex protested. "That's not the same thing!"

"Why? Because it was you instead of me?"

"Well, actually, yeah. Your face has been shown on all the news stations. The entire police force isn't looking for me."

"And WHY is that again?"

Liz nearly winced as she watched her question hit home. Alex raised a hand and rubbed his chest, almost as if he could feel the pain of her words in his heart. The hurt and anger she saw in his eyes bothered her, but it was the resignation that had her apologizing.

She drew closer. "Alex, I'm sor-"

He stepped back and shrugged. "Don't worry about it." He shook the plastic bag in his hand. "I got some supplies."

Liz regretted the change of subject and the rift she had caused between them, but didn't know how to fix it. "Please tell me there are some shoes in there."

He dug into the sack and handed her the ugliest flip-flops she had ever seen in her entire life. Then again, anything was better than what she was currently wearing. Well, anything other than a pair of stilettos, maybe.

Eager to get moving, she sat on the rock and peeled the wet and muddy slippers off her feet. The big toe on her left foot was crusted over in dried blood from accidentally kicking a tree stump.

"Geez, Liz. Why didn't you tell me it was this bad?"

"There was nothing either of us could have done about it." She bent her head down to inspect her feet closer. "They weren't so bad this morning. This happened while we were running from the cops."

Alex reached over and touched a particularly sore spot on the sole of her foot. She sucked in her breath. "Sorry, there's a large and gnarly splinter here. I'm going to try to get it out."

"With what?"

After digging in the bag for a moment, he proudly brandished the first aid kit. "I thought this would come in handy. Just sit there for a minute and relax. I'll patch up what I can."

Despite the sorry state of her feet, this was pushing the bounds of intimacy a bit too much. She pulled back. "You don't have to do that. I can take care of it." It was embarrassing to think about Alex so close to her dirty feet.

A tingle of electricity raced up her inner thigh as she felt his fingers wrap around her ankle, warm and sure. He looked up. "Let me do it. I want to help."

Liz stilled, unsure of how to respond. Alex took out a disinfectant wipe and cleaned her various scrapes and scratches with long soothing strokes. Why had she never known how sensitive the arch of her foot was before?

She fell under the spell of his slow and steady touch, loving the way he traced the bones in her ankle and pads of her toes. Gradually, the pain in her foot was eclipsed by the gentle way Alex tended to her. She'd just started to relax under his ministrations when there was a slight pause. Liz opened her eyes right as she felt a quick tug and sting. "Ouch!"

"Sorry," he shot her a sheepish grin. "I had to get the splinter out."

"Maybe give a little warning next time," she grumbled.

He smiled and turned his attention to her other foot. "Yes, ma'am."

She shifted uncomfortably, aware of just how much she'd been enjoying his touch. "You don't have to do this, you know."

"I know, but it's easier for me to see where the damage is." As if sensing her impatience, he quickly cleaned and bandaged her other foot. "Okay, you're all set." He handed her the ugly flip-flops. "Hopefully you can walk on them a little better now."

Liz hurriedly put on her new footwear and stood up, ignoring the way her blood had heated at his touch. "Thanks."

"Sure." She watched as he packed up all the bandage wrappers and trash and stuffed them back into the plastic bag, eliminating any evidence that they had ever been there. He turned to her. "So, where is this car you liberated?"

"Not far. Follow me."

She led Alex through the strip of woods until they reached the back side of a grocery store parking lot. An older model Honda Accord that looked like it had seen better days sat on the far edges of the pavement.

It had been a huge risk leaving it. If the owner discovered it was missing the police could have been called. If they suspected Liz was behind the missing car, they could already be lying in wait.

She crouched down and scanned the perimeter of the parking lot before stepping out of the trees. Liz caught the expression on Alex's face as he took in the damaged back window on the passenger side and winced. "Believe it or not, I don't make it a habit of breaking laws."

He turned to her. "Where did it come from?"

She gestured towards the grocery store. "I saw them pull into the lot and make their way into the store, but we probably don't have much time." Sensing his reluctance, she added, "We're lucky there was a car old enough. Otherwise, it wouldn't have worked."

"Why an old car?"

Liz started walking towards the vehicle and opened the door before answering. She looked over the top of the car and noticed Alex seemed hesitant to get in. "Most of the newer models have anti-theft systems that make them nearly impossible to steal. The older ones can still be hotwired."

Alex finally opened the passenger door and got in as Liz reached down below the steering column for the exposed wires she'd left hanging there. It only took a few strikes with the starter wire to get the engine running again. With a sigh of relief, Liz sat in the seat and adjusted the mirrors before putting her seatbelt on. "We should probably get out of here before the owners finish their shopping. Which way?"

Alex pointed, then reached for his seatbelt. She quickly pulled out of the parking lot. Liz could feel his gaze on her and wondered what he was thinking.

"Well, I guess if I'm going to be on the run with someone, it might as well be with a car mechanic who can hotwire cars and break out of handcuffs. You really are something, you know that, Liz?"

The tone in his voice made it hard for her to know if he meant it as a compliment or not. "Uh, thanks…?" She glanced quickly towards him when he didn't reply, eager to change the subject. "So, where are we going, anyway?"

"It's on the outskirts of town. I figured you could hole up while I go pick up some groceries with the little money we have left. Who knows how long this ordeal is going to last or whether they'll eventually release my image to the press. It'll be better if we take advantage of the opportunity while we can."

"Good idea. I hate to say it, but we should also probably drop this car off before we get too close to our location. Eventually someone is going to come looking for it."

Alex reached for his own seatbelt. "Don't worry. I already have a plan for hiding it. Now all we have to do is hope we don't get caught on the way there."

CHAPTER SEVENTEEN

"CLARK! GET IN here!"

Mason raised his eyebrows. Chief Hamilton was on the warpath; he hadn't even managed to make it to his desk. "Yeah, Chief?"

"Shut the door, Mason." After the door was closed, he continued. "I want you to meet Matt Hagen. He's with the MDEA and will be working on the Liz Harper case. I'm assuming you heard what happened last night."

The man who stood up to shake his hand towered over the chief. Then again, Chief Hamilton looked like the human equivalent of a bulldog, one that was a bit stodgy and unkempt. Mason had yet to form a solid opinion of him. His clothes might be shabby, but he had the reputation of being punctilious when it came to reports. He was also said to be tenacious when he caught the scent of a case. At the moment, he seemed too busy fawning over the new arrival for Mason's comfort. He only hoped that he'd wait for all the facts to come to light before judging Liz guilty.

Matt Hagen, on the other hand, was tall and had a lantern jaw. There was a darkness about him that had Mason feeling like he'd just stepped out of Sleepy Hollow. His handshake was firm and perfunctory. He didn't bother to smile. "Detective Clark."

"Agent Hagen."

"I understand you are in a relationship with Liz's sister, Olivia."

"I am."

"I hope you understand that for the integrity of this case, you're going to need to steer clear of this investigation. That being said, I'm going to be asking you a few questions about Ms. Harper. In fact, I'll be interviewing her whole family."

It's not that it was unexpected. Mason would have been surprised if they let him work the case, but that didn't stop him from feeling the sting. "I'm familiar with the concept of conflict of interest. I'll do what I can to help. Although, I have to tell you, if you think Liz Harper has anything to do with those drugs you found, you're barking up the wrong tree."

The other man seemed to weigh Mason's words before continuing. "Thank you. I'll keep that in mind. That will be all for now."

Mason shot Chief Hamilton a look and headed towards the door.

"Oh, one more thing…"

Mason paused before stepping over the threshold. "Do you know where Liz Harper is right now?"

He turned to face the agent, thankful that he'd stopped Liz from divulging exactly that information on the phone call earlier. Mason made sure to maintain eye contact while answering. "No, I don't."

"And you'd tell us if you did?"

Agent Hagen might be a few years younger, but Mason could already tell he was a force to be reckoned with. He gritted his teeth, reminding himself that it would not pay to get on this guy's bad side. "I would, yes."

"Good."

Mason paused for a moment, making sure there was nothing more before he let himself out of the office. Helping Liz was going to be harder than he'd thought.

CHAPTER EIGHTEEN

ALEX DIRECTED LIZ to pull up to the curb in front of a modest lakeside cottage. "There's an old garage in the back. We can park the car in there once I return from grocery shopping."

This was one of the few furnished properties his father usually rented out during the summer. With his father's illness, Alex decided to keep it off the market this year for sentimental reasons. For the rest of the year it sat empty. Although the location felt secluded, he knew there were three separate exits from the immediate vicinity, and it was fairly close to two different highways.

He watched as Liz quietly assessed the place through the windshield. "It looks nice."

"When my mom was alive, we used to spend a couple of weeks here every summer. I haven't been back since she passed away."

"Are you sure you're okay with this?" It touched him that she would ask, given the strain of their situation. He noticed her shoulders drooping from exhaustion.

"Yeah. Come on."

"Wait. Before we go inside, I want to check the car. There may be something we can use."

"Well, I guess it won't do any harm, considering we've already stolen their car."

Liz shot him a resigned look before rummaging through the glove box. Reluctantly, Alex started checking the console.

"Got a flashlight here."

"There's nearly five dollars in change in this little container."

"That'll help. Although I've always hated paying for things with change."

Alex shoved the coins into his pocket. "Well, beggars can't be choosers."

Liz got out of the car. "Can you pop the trunk for me?"

After his search produced three stale French fries and a grand opening pamphlet for a local hair salon, Alex got out to join her. "Find anything good?"

Liz's response was muffled since her head was still in the trunk. "Well, I don't know if I would call it good, exactly." She stood up and showed him the sweatshirt she'd found, its front proudly sporting three wolves and a moon.

"Wow. It certainly makes a fashion statement, I'll give it that."

Sighing, Liz shook her head and slammed the trunk shut. "There's also a pair of jumper cables and a spare tire back there, but I don't think we need to take them out. As much as I hate to say it, this sweatshirt is probably the warmest thing I have right now."

Alex bit the inside of his cheek. "At least it will go well with the orange flip-flops."

"Yeah, yeah, yeah, yuk it up while you can. We both know I've never been into fashion. Let's just call this an extreme case."

Alex let them in the front door, locking it behind them. Glancing around, he was relieved to find the place in fairly good condition. Maybe the other property had been a fluke.

He looked at the woman beside him. Despite the terrible outfit, she still managed to look beautiful. It was a coincidence that he had happened upon this terrible situation, but he was thankful he had. Otherwise, he might not have been there to help Liz at the shop.

Suddenly, imagining a world without Liz made him feel very empty inside.

He took her hand. "Let me give you the grand tour."

The "grand tour" revealed a small, eat-in kitchen, a modest living room boasting a stone fireplace, and one bathroom. There were two bedrooms across the hall from each other, one with two twin beds, and the other barely bigger than the king-size bed. From the kitchen, a back door led to a path, which meandered through some trees to a dock on the lake.

Back in the living room, Alex pulled a dust cover off one of the chairs. "It's still too early in the season for us to have hired a cleaning service, but it shouldn't be too bad. At least it means we'll have some privacy to plan our next move."

"Do you think there's a towel I could use to freshen up?" Liz pulled a second cover off the couch, folding it before tossing it into the coat closet.

"Absolutely, help yourself. I wish I had a change of clothes for you, but I'm afraid you're stuck with what you have. The sweatshirt is ugly, but at least it will help you stay warm."

Liz gave the offending garment a glance and shot him the first genuine smile he'd seen from her all day. "Hey, you never know. This sweatshirt might be good luck."

Silence filled the room between them. Up until that moment, they'd been so preoccupied with getting somewhere safe that it had been easy to set aside what was actually going on. He watched as her expression popped like a soap bubble and the gravity of their situation reasserted itself.

Sensing she would rather be alone to break down, Alex pulled a key off his ring. "This is to the house, just in case."

Liz shook her head. "Thanks, but you keep it. I don't plan on going anywhere."

"Keep the door locked while I'm away, okay? Is there anything else you need before I take off?"

She glanced around the room as if lost. "I don't think so."

Satisfied she'd be safe for the time being, Alex turned towards the door. "Remember to lock up behind me."

"Alex." The quiet way she said his name had him turning. She circled her arms around his neck and leaned in, her body flush against his. His arms wrapped around her waist as she stood on her toes and pressed a kiss to his lips. She lingered for just a breath, keeping the exchange sweet and simple, before stepping away. "Be careful."

He wished he could pull her back and explore the moment more fully, but knew it wasn't the time. Instead, Alex forced himself to go through the door. He waited to hear the click of the lock before walking towards the car.

CHAPTER NINETEEN

LIZ WATCHED THE car pull away and looked at the orange flip flops and sweatshirt again. It was hard to reconcile his thoughtful gestures with the man Mason had cautioned her against trusting. If Alex wasn't trustworthy, would he be so worried about taking care of her?

Besides, who was Mason to talk about trust? Despite him practically being her brother-in-law, he'd never once let on that they were investigating her garage for drug activity. Not even a single hint! How was that for loyalty?

Logically, she understood that it was his duty as a police officer that had kept him quiet, but knowing that didn't help her emotionally. She wasn't sure whether she was more hurt or angry by his omission.

Then it struck her. Had Olivia known about any of this? She and Mason were so close, it was hard to imagine him keeping it from her. Then again, Olivia was her sister. They'd been a team since long before Mason had come around. No, she would have said something if she'd known.

Liz spun around in the room, plagued by doubt. A few months ago, had someone asked if she could trust her sister, she would have laughed in their face. Now...?

Liz hated having doubts about her family like this! No. She

had to believe Mason kept it from Olivia the same as he had from her. In fact, it appeared that the only one in this situation who'd been completely up front with her was Alex.

She was beginning to trust him, despite Mason's warnings otherwise.

With the weight of her doubt starting to lift, Liz felt lighter than she had in a long time, regardless of recent events. Gradually, she became aware of her surroundings.

The silence of the house had settled around her. It felt strange and foreign after spending the whole day hiking through woods, sneaking through parking lots, stealing cars, and running from the cops. She suspected the momentary peace was like smoke and could dissipate any moment.

Deciding to take advantage of the opportunity, Liz picked up the plastic bag and headed towards the bathroom. The moment got better after she rummaged through the linen closet and found shampoo and conditioner.

Her feet stung when they first came into contact with the hot water and reminded her of the scene earlier that day. Even then, after she'd just questioned his integrity, he'd been determined to take care of her.

Why was she so stubborn when it came to him?

Liz ducked her head back and let the warm spray of the shower comfort her. She thought about her hesitation with Alex. It was more than the fact that he'd just happened to be at the garage during the robbery. Why hadn't Josh included him in his report? It didn't make sense. Liz couldn't think of a single good reason why he would be omitted. But even that wasn't the real reason she was struggling to trust Alex. Liz knew it was greater than the entire situation she found herself embroiled in at the moment.

If she was being honest with herself, she could admit that it had more to do with her own personal insecurities, from being the brunt of everybody's jokes back in high school. Could someone like Alex Weston truly be interested in her?

Liz shook her head and stepped out of the shower. She looked at her blurry reflection in the fogged mirror. It seemed ludicrous to be thinking about such frivolous things, considering the life and death stakes she found herself in.

Yet, despite how desperate things were right now, Liz couldn't help but have faith it would sort itself out. She was innocent, after all. She knew it, and had to believe the system would eventually catch up to the truth, especially if she helped it along.

It was that last bit that got her back on track. So far, all she'd been doing was reacting to someone else's moves. Her life had become some invisible puppeteer's play thing. It was time to change the rules.

And that started with figuring out who was in charge.

The problem was she didn't have much to go on, other than the one phone number. How was she supposed to hunt this person down?

Liz changed into her new ugly sweatshirt, grateful that it was large and nearly came to her knees. She went through the house and found a washing machine and dryer in the basement. Her yoga pants, tank top, and cardigan had seen better days, but since they were her only clothes, it was worth taking the time to wash them.

As she climbed up the stairs and back into the kitchen, a wave of fatigue washed over her. It would probably be a few more hours before Alex would be back, so she decided to take a nap.

Within minutes, Liz had slipped into a dark, dreamless sleep.

*

Night had fallen by the time Alex got back to the cottage. He let himself in and stood just inside the doorway, listening for any movement that didn't belong. None of the lights were on in the house and everything was silent.

Carefully avoiding the lumps of shadowy furniture, Alex made his way into the kitchen and set a few grocery bags down on the counter. Other than a water glass by the sink, there was no evidence of Liz anywhere in the room.

He could smell the shampoo she had used in the shower earlier as he passed the bathroom. Alex poked his head into the master bedroom and found the bed still made. Nothing had been changed.

He knew she'd been struggling to trust him, but when she'd kissed him, he'd taken it as a sign they'd turned a corner in their relationship. Had she left him, after all? A deep sense of disappointment began to form in the pit of his stomach at the thought.

He crossed the hallway and slowly cracked open the door to the second room. Relief flooded him as he spotted a figure beneath the covers. Stepping closer, he looked down at the peaceful expression on her face. His eyes roved over every contour, detailing the way her lips were slightly parted and her lashes looked like lace against her cheek.

She was so tough that it was easy to overlook her fine, delicate features. Her high cheekbones, the arch of her brow, the way her bottom lip was slightly fuller than her top lip...

Gradually, he became aware of the fact that he'd been watching her for a few minutes and reluctantly took a step back from the bed. If she truly had begun to trust him, then the last thing he needed was to have her wake up and find him looming over her like a creep.

Shaking the moment off, Alex left the room and retraced his steps to the kitchen. Making dinner would be a much more endearing and productive use of his time.

CHAPTER TWENTY

LIZ WOKE TO the smell of something delicious. Her stomach growled in response, and she wondered what Olivia was making. Shadows crouched in darkened corners and stretched across the room. Pulling the covers up further on her shoulder, she turned and almost fell off the bed.

What?

Startled, Liz looked around the unfamiliar room. It took a few moments to remember everything that had happened.

Not Olivia, then. Alex must be cooking.

At the thought, Liz immediately sprang from the bed, cursing the moment her feet hit the floor. *Owww.* She'd forgotten the state of her feet. Using a little more caution, she gingerly made her way down the hallway. "I must have passed out. How long have you been back?"

"Only about forty minutes."

"Did you run into any problems?"

"Nope. Just a typical trip to the grocery store, although I've never bought a burner phone before. You should have seen the dirty look the clerk gave me when I pulled out all that change."

Liz laughed. "I can imagine."

"I hope you like spaghetti."

"I love it."

"Great. There's also garlic bread in the oven and I managed to find a bottle of wine left in the pantry. Can you open it? I think there's a corkscrew in the drawer over there."

Happy to have something to do, Liz got the tool and set to work. After looking in a few cupboards, she found the wine glasses and poured them both generous servings.

"Thanks." Alex turned and let his gaze roam over her. Liz felt her heart stutter in response. She became painfully aware of the fact that all she wore was a sweatshirt, even if it was longer than most dresses.

She stepped back. "It's after six. Do you think it's safe enough for me to call Mason?"

"I don't know. I know that calling from a disposable phone is supposed to help, but I think they still have ways of tracking them. Just promise to keep it short, okay?"

"I will. I'll squeeze it in before dinner."

"Sure. The sauce is fine to simmer for as long as we need. We can hold off on the pasta since it doesn't take very long to cook."

She turned and sat on the couch in the living room, knowing it was well within Alex's hearing. The phone rang three times. She was just about to hang up when there was a response from the other end. "Hello?"

"Olivia?"

"Liz! I'm so happy to hear your voice. Things are crazy around here." And then, quieter, "Are you okay?"

The lump of tears that welled up in Liz's throat made it hard to talk. She hadn't realized just how stressed she was until she heard her sister's voice. "Yes, I'm okay for now, but we have to keep the call short."

"I can't believe this has happened. Mason is doing everything he can to get to the bottom of it."

Liz brushed the tears from her cheeks. The enormity of the

situation hit her. "I can't believe they've been investigating the garage for months!"

"And you had no idea there was anything going on?"

"No, I swear! Did Mason tell you about the investigation?"

"I just found out about it this morning, Liz. It killed him not to tell you. You have to believe that. Have you seen anything strange happening around the garage? Anything at all?"

"No, Livvy. That's just it. I've been wracking my brain trying to remember any little details that might have escaped my notice, but there's nothing."

There was a beat of silence as Olivia thought about what Liz had said. She lowered her voice. "Do you think Paul might have seen something?"

Liz's stomach sank. "What? Olivia, there's no way! Paul loves the shop as much as I do."

Relief and regret infused Olivia's voice. "I'm sorry, I had to ask. They've had him answering questions down at the station practically all day and only just let him out. Mason said they've been grilling him hard. They even brought Jimmy in, but his interview barely lasted an hour."

Liz felt awful. "Poor Jimmy. I'm sure this wasn't what he was expecting with his new job. Who else could have been transporting drugs through my garage without my knowing?"

"I don't know. Mason did say that the Chief is gunning for you. Your disappearing act has him convinced you're involved. Agent Hagen seems to be keeping an open mind, so far. I'm not sure which is worse – you being on the run, or being at the mercy of dirty cops."

"Do you think it would be better if I came in?" The thought put a bad taste in Liz's mouth. She couldn't think of anything much worse than being locked up in a jail cell with Josh holding the key.

"No. Mason still hasn't been able to find anything out about that phone number you gave him." There was a knocking in the background and she could hear Olivia's muffled response before she came back on the line. "Listen, Liz, I have to go. I'm assuming Alex is still with you?"

"Yeah."

"Huh. Seems kind of odd, considering his name hasn't come up in the investigation. Do you think you can trust him?"

Liz looked through the open archway between the living room and the kitchen. Alex had just opened the oven and was pulling the garlic bread out. Her heart melted a little watching him. "Yeah."

Olivia sighed. "I hope you're right. Okay, let's try to talk again soon. Evenings around this time will probably be best. Love you, Liz. Stay safe."

"I'm trying to. Love you, Livvy. Tell Fiona I love her, too."

The minute she hung up the phone, Liz felt a vast hollowness in her chest. A void so great it threatened to swallow her whole.

"You okay?" Alex stood in the doorway, his face shadowed by the light streaming in behind him.

"Oh sure, just peachy." Setting the phone aside, she stood up. The stress of the situation was overwhelming and making her feel antsy. She needed a way to blow off steam. "Is dinner ready?"

Alex handed her a plate. "It is."

The two of them filled their plates and sat down at the kitchen table. For the first time since being attacked in the garage, neither one of them seemed to know what to say. Instead they concentrated on the first few bites.

Silence stretched between them.

Unable to stand it anymore, Liz looked up from her plate. "This is good. Thanks for making dinner."

She watched as Alex reached for his wine glass and took a sip. "Glad you like it." He held her gaze. "I think we need to figure out what to do from here. This is a nice opportunity to regroup, but we won't be able to hide here forever."

With such an unpleasant topic to discuss, Liz almost regretted the loss of the quiet. Unwilling to let it ruin her meal, she took another bite and chewed slowly, thinking about what he'd said. "Do you have any suggestions about what our next step should be?"

"Actually, I've been thinking about that. I know you're still unconvinced we shouldn't be going to the police. Ordinarily, I would agree with you. The main flaw with that plan is that it's our word against Josh's. I can't help thinking we'd be on the losing side of that scenario."

"Right. If it makes you feel any better, Mason and Livvy agree. Which is why we need to find some proof of his involvement," Liz said.

"Or a way of tipping the scales further in our favor. What if we introduced another witness into the mix?"

"Okay, but how do you propose we do that? We're the only ones who saw anything."

Alex shook his head. "That's not true. Peter and Jonesy were there, too."

"Yeah, but you saw how they were under Josh's thumb! Not to mention that they're drug addicts. I hardly think they'll be considered credible witnesses." Liz set her plate aside.

"True. On the other hand, Peter is probably familiar with some – if not all – of the operation. He might be able to direct us towards other avenues of proof."

Alex leaned forward. "Think about it, Liz. You were probably the closest thing to a friend he had in high school. He may not have helped us out of the car, but it was obvious he recognized you and felt bad about what was happening. Maybe we can play on that."

Liz gnawed on her bottom lip as she considered Alex's idea. She'd been appalled to discover the path Peter's life had taken.

"Okay, it's worth a shot. Although I don't know how much good it will do. He seemed lost to me."

"Me too, but we have to try." Alex looked down at his plate with regret. "I wish I had known back then what I do now. I never would have given him such a hard time."

She appreciated his self-reflection. Liz took a moment to reach across the table and give his hand a squeeze. "It's true that it wasn't right to bully him, but you can't take full responsibility for his actions, either. In the end, it's our choice whether we let those experiences tear us down or strengthen us. There were a lot more factors working against Peter than just a couple of jerks at school."

She shot him a quick smile to soften the blow of calling him a jerk. His hand felt good in hers. His fingers were long, his palm lightly calloused from working in construction. A thought of what it would feel like caressing sensitive skin had her blushing and pulling away.

"I guess that's one good thing that came out of me being sent away to school. I'd hate to think how I would have turned out if I'd stayed here."

"Everybody was shocked when your dad sent you away. I don't think the football coach ever fully forgave him for that."

Alex chuckled. "Hell, it took me forever to forgive him for sending me away, too. It was years before we were able to have a conversation that didn't end in yelling or a cold silence that dragged on for days. And even when we did start talking again, I was so angry with him. My life had been good here. Comfortable. It's easy being a big fish in a small pond.

"It wasn't until after I left that I started to get a sense of how small the pond was. I resented him for taking me out of my comfort zone. I felt abandoned. It was further proof that he didn't want me after my mom died."

"Oh Alex, I'm sure he was trying to do what was best for you."

"I figured that out eventually. Although I'm ashamed to admit how long it took me. By the time I was old enough to set my resentment aside, we'd both become used to the distance between us. I don't think either one of us knew how to close the gap."

"What changed?"

Alex leaned back in his chair, giving up the pretense of eating. "One day, I got a call from him. He told me he was sick and needed my help. That's when I decided to come home."

"That must have been hard for him, and you."

"I'll admit, it's been an adjustment. I never realized just how much I'd acclimated to big city living until I came back. It makes me wonder if Bath was always this small, or if it was me all along."

"Oh, it's small," Liz smiled, "but that's not necessarily a bad thing. The town rallied around my sister during everything that happened to her this past winter. I can't imagine the same thing happening in a big city. Just because we live in a small town doesn't mean we're small-minded."

"You have a point. I always assumed this move would be temporary, but the longer I'm here, the more I'm tempted to stay." He seemed to shake himself out of his reverie. "What about you, Liz? It seems like ever since I've known you, you've wanted to be a mechanic. Now you've taken over the shop your dad owned. How'd that happen?"

Liz thought back to those days, remembering what it had been to like to go to school with Alex. By the time she was a sophomore, she'd already been working at the shop for years, and had been familiar with the flow and feel of the place. "I guess that's one thing I've never had to doubt. Even after my parents died and everything was in such a state of upheaval, I knew that I was meant to work on cars."

"Not everybody finds that sense of purpose, especially at such an early age. You're lucky to have that."

She shrugged. "Well, you know how awkward things were for me at school. Anything to limit my interactions with people was welcome. Being able to climb under a car or stick my head under a hood and shut out the rest of the world was everything to me. After my parents died, that urge to push the rest of the world away grew even sharper. I was lucky that Paul stepped in and helped me direct my energy towards something productive."

"You two seem close."

"We are. I mean, he's always been like an uncle to me. Even when I was younger, Paul always knew when I'd had a bad day. He'd tug on my ponytail, then offer to teach me something new. I think in some ways he understood where I was coming from, even better than my dad did."

"How so?"

Now that the subject had changed, Liz found she was still hungry. She took another bite of pasta, thinking about her answer for a moment. "I don't know if you ever met my dad, or how well you remember him, but he had this way about him that people naturally responded to. He was the kind of guy everybody could relate to and liked instantly. Actually, you're a lot like him in that way."

Liz paused, a little surprised by her own observation, but at the same time realizing it was true. It was an aspect of her dad that she'd always admired, so it shouldn't be a wonder that she'd gravitate towards someone who shared that same quality.

She pulled herself from her musings and continued. "On the other hand, Paul and I would much rather limit our interactions with others. Partly because we're uncomfortable with people we don't know well, but also because neither one of us has any patience for the majority of them.

"After my dad died, Paul made sure I knew I was still welcome at the garage. When everything felt out of my hands and became overwhelming, he gave me a safe place and something useful to do. I was able to regain my sense of control when working on a transmission or rebuilding an engine. It gave me a chance to positively influence the world around me and made me feel like I could contribute something worthwhile."

"Wow. I never thought about it like that. I imagine that would be a heady feeling considering everything else was in turmoil."

"Exactly. Dad had already stipulated in his will that his half of the garage would go to me, to be held in a trust until I turned eighteen. After my birthday, it reverted directly into my ownership. But it was Paul who made sure I had the skills I'd need in order to honor it."

"I can understand why you feel so much loyalty to him. I've only had a chance to talk to him a few times, but he sounds like an amazing man."

Liz mulled over that time in her life for a moment before answering. "You know, for someone who never had kids, Paul managed to step into a parental role seamlessly. Not just for myself, but for both of my sisters, too. Now I see him doing something similar for his nephew, Jimmy, and it's remarkable watching it happen from the outside. Especially since I know how it feels being on the receiving end of that kind of attention." Talking with Alex about the shop and how much it meant to her reminded her of their current situation.

Her brows grew furrowed. Seeing the direction her thoughts had taken, Alex said, "You know this is only temporary. At some point, the truth will come out and you'll be able to get back to work."

"I just wonder how much damage this will do to my business in the long run. It's taken me a long time to build up a good reputation. It was especially hard both because it's a male-dominated field and because I'm young. It pains me to know my reputation may never recover."

"You said yourself, this is a small town. Once people know you didn't have anything to do with the drugs, they'll rally around you."

Feeling restless and wanting to change the subject, Liz stood and began gathering their plates. "I hope so." The long-term ramifications of this situation were just another thing she had no control over. What she could do was make sure the kitchen was clean. With that thought in mind, she methodically began washing the dishes. After a moment, Alex got up and started putting the left-over food away.

For a few moments, they were each content to concentrate on the chore at hand, but too soon Liz turned the water off. "This faucet drips."

She heard Alex move directly behind her. "I'll make sure it gets taken care of before we rent it out."

Warm, strong fingers gripped the spot where her shoulders met her neck, kneading the knots he found there. She couldn't stop the low groan that escaped as she bent her head forward, encouraging him to continue.

After a moment, Liz shuddered and fought the urge to lean back into his arms. It would be so easy to bury her head in the sand and forget the predicament they were in.

But then what would happen tomorrow? Or the next day? They had no way of knowing how long this was going to last. Sure, he may be willing to help her now, but what about a week from now? Or months?

The fact was, Alex's name hadn't been reported to the authorities. Best case scenario was that, he had a chance to go back to his life and pick up where he left off.

Worst case scenario was that, he was involved somehow, and she was a fool for starting to trust him. The scene at the café between him and Cynthia flashed in her mind. Even if he wasn't behind the drug ring, that didn't mean he wasn't romantically involved with someone else.

The last thing she wanted to do was rope him in any deeper than he already was. She knew that if they pursued the attraction between them, he'd feel even more obligated to help her.

Oh, but his hands felt so good on her shoulders, his fingers just the right combination of strong and gentle. She could practically feel the stress draining from her body and being replaced with something needier.

With a sigh of regret, she straightened and turned. She stared at his chin, hesitant to meet the question and awareness in his eyes. "Thank you."

"My pleasure. Well, I don't know about you, but I'm exhausted and could use a shower."

"I took that nap, but I'm still feeling tired myself. I might go see what books are on the shelf in the living room and retire early. If we're going to find Peter and convince him to testify, it's going to be a long day tomorrow."

He briefly stroked his thumb across her cheek before letting his hand fall down to his side and taking a step back. "Good night, Eliza."

It was only after she was safely tucked into her bed that she admitted she'd liked hearing her name on his lips.

CHAPTER TWENTY-ONE

THE NEXT MORNING dawned bright and clear. Despite being hyper-aware of the sexy man sleeping in the room across the hall, Liz had managed to get a decent night's sleep, and was eager to get something constructive accomplished.

At six-thirty, Alex walked into the kitchen, yawning, and automatically grabbed a coffee mug out of the cupboard. "Mornin'."

Liz sat at the dining room table, eating a bowl of cereal. "Hey. How'd you sleep last night?"

"About as well as can be expected, I guess. You?"

"Same."

He poured some cereal into a bowl and sat down next to her. The morning domesticity felt a little too cozy. Liz quickly finished her breakfast. She felt his gaze follow her across the room as she got up to rinse her bowl in the sink.

Fifteen minutes later, they were both walking out of the house. "I'll drive."

She shot Alex a deadpan look. "She who hot-wired the car, drives."

"Shit."

Liz laughed. "That's what I thought."

The levity was short-lived. Backing the car out of the driveway, Liz hesitated to pull out onto the street. "So, how do you propose we find Peter? I'm not exactly familiar with where the local heroin addicts are hanging out nowadays. Not to mention, we don't even know if he's still in Bath. The way our luck is going, he could be down in Portland by now."

"I don't know. Maybe we can just drive around to some of the rougher parts of town and see if there's anyone we can ask. There have to be clinics or places that addicts congregate, right?"

"I can't think of anyplace like that in Bath. But I'm guessing hospitals might have some information. The closest one is in Brunswick, which isn't too far from here."

Alex put his seat belt on. "Do you think we can get there without being spotted?"

Liz shrugged. "It depends on how quickly the owner of this car discovered it was missing and reported it. The sooner we head over there the better, I think."

"Okay, let's do it."

They managed to hit the road before morning rush hour, glad that the traffic was still light. Since the lakeside cottage was on the outskirts of Bath, it only took them twenty minutes to pull into Brunswick. It was a far cry from the shoeless trek in the woods the day before.

Liz pulled into the parking lot of Mid-Coast Hospital, careful to stay towards the perimeter and near the exit. Putting the car into park, she turned to Alex. "Now what? I think we both know I can't go in there."

"Leave the car running. I'll go in and pose as a concerned family member looking for my brother. Hopefully, someone will be able to direct me where to go from there."

Liz gripped the wheel nervously. The shadows had already started to shrink in the morning light and she could hear birds chirping in the trees nearby. It was a new day, and yet it felt like they were no closer to clearing her name than they had been yesterday. If anything, she was afraid running had made her look guiltier.

"I don't know about this. What if you walk into the hospital and they recognize you? You may have been implicated by now. Your face may be all over the news just like mine."

Alex reached over and took her hand, forcing her to meet his gaze. "Then the hospital employees will call the police. Chances are, we'd still be able to get out of here before they arrive. Worst case scenario, I'd be taken in. If that happens, I'll tell them my side of the story and hope for the best. But, Liz, I don't think that's going to happen."

"But…"

"Look, I know it's a long shot, but I don't know how else to find him. This is a risk we need to take. If we can find another witness to corroborate our story, it would be huge. I promise to be as fast and discreet as possible. Just give me half an hour to see what I can find out. Take off if I'm not out in thirty minutes."

Liz nervously plucked at her newly washed, if somewhat battered, yoga pants. "You'd better make it back, Alex."

Taking her face gently in his hands, Alex leaned forward. She could feel his breath feathering her lips, but it was his eyes that had her pinned. "I will. But if I don't, I need you to promise me you'll leave and head back to the house."

His lips brushed against hers, as light as butterfly wings, yet the energy that crackled between them was anything but fragile. He was like a flame, drawing her into his light. All the restless energy that had kept her awake the night before came rushing back.

She leaned towards him to deepen the kiss just as he shifted back in his seat. His expression was a mix of regret and promise. The car door creaked as he pulled on the handle.

He turned to her. "Remember, thirty minutes. If something happens, I'll try to meet you back at the house."

Liz felt her lips with her fingertips. It was almost as if the kiss had been the last vestiges of a dream, one quickly fading in the harsh reality. "I promise. Please be careful."

He nodded, then strode across the lot towards the brightly lit double doors of the hospital.

*

Thirty-five minutes later, Liz tapped her fingers on the steering wheel and quietly drove herself insane. She was not the kind of person to just sit on the sidelines and wait for things to happen, and she hated having to rely on someone else.

Where was he, anyway?

She checked the time on the dashboard clock for the third time in a minute and debated how much longer she should give him before taking off. It didn't feel right leaving him, despite her promise.

Liz flicked the radio on and scanned the stations, wondering if there was any news being reported about her and the garage. After making her way through the dial, she turned it back off. No news was good news in this case, right?

The digital display clicked past another minute.

She was just about ready to call it quits when she noticed his tall frame striding out of the building. Relief and a shock of something deeper filled her chest as she noted his naturally confident gait and broad shoulders. At least he didn't seem to be under duress.

As a boy, he'd always had a certain charisma about him. But now, as a man, she realized he'd found a way to harness it. He exuded more than just charm. There was also an element of power and confidence that was incredibly sexy.

Liz shook her head. Of all the inappropriate times to be attracted to somebody, this had to take the cake. Here she was, on the run for her life, accused of drug trafficking, assaulting an

124

officer, and who knew what else, and she was lusting after a guy like a cat in heat.

Alex scanned the parking lot before making his way over to the car. She couldn't tell if he looked relieved or peeved that she was still there. He climbed into the passenger seat. "I thought I told you to take off."

Peeved. His tone of voice instantly doused all of the uncomfortable feelings she'd been harboring for him. "Don't pretend you weren't happy to see me."

"I always am. But that doesn't mean you weren't taking a big risk."

He always was? What did that mean? She brushed the comment aside, afraid to attach too much weight to his words. "So, what'd you find out?"

"Well, a lot, actually. Did you know this hospital actually runs its own addiction resource center?"

"What? I had no idea."

"Yeah, that's why it took a little longer than I was expecting. Instead of just asking for directions, I ended up going to the clinic and talking to the woman in the intake department."

"So, did you ask her about Peter? Does she know who he is, or where we can find him?"

He gave her a rueful smile. "She's not actually allowed to divulge that kind of information because of doctor/patient confidentiality. She wouldn't say much even after I told her he was my brother."

Liz let out a disappointed sigh. "Now what?"

"Well, she wasn't allowed to give any specifics, but she did suggest I go check out a certain apartment building. Told me to ask around. I think we should head over there and see if anybody is willing to talk."

"Okay." Liz leaned forward and put the car in gear, happy to have something to work with.

Before she could get going, Alex placed his hand on her arm. "Liz, it's not the best part of town. Are you sure you don't want to hang back and just let me go?"

She shot him an incredulous look. "Not a chance. If we're in this together, then we do this together." Pulling forward, she added under her breath, "Besides, I'll go crazy if I have to sit here alone again."

The tone in her voice dared him to laugh at her, so she was relieved when he didn't argue. "Fair enough. Hang a right at the next light."

Chapter Twenty-Two

ALEX ASSURED HER that it wouldn't take long to get to the area the nurse had specified. As they followed her directions, Liz became increasingly baffled.

It was nice. The wide, tree-lined road wound through neighborhoods filled with well-maintained older homes, with friendly front porches, and clean lawns. Sedans were parked in the driveways, and flags hung by the front door.

In fact, the most remarkable thing about the place was that there was nothing remarkable about it.

"Are you sure we're in the right place?" Liz asked for the second time in as many minutes.

Alex didn't even bother to look at the address he held in his hand. "She did say it would start to get seedier a few blocks from here. Apparently, the town has been trying to gentrify this area, but it's obvious where their efforts have stopped.

Sure enough, in another five minutes of driving they were looking at a combination of gas stations, car dealerships, thrift stores, and empty buildings. They pulled up to an apartment building that looked like it had seen better days.

Liz parked in the side lot and got out, taking a look around. Salsa and hip hop tumbled out of the front door and warred over the air waves. As Alex and Liz approached the entrance, they noticed the door was propped open with a half empty bottle of what looked like urine. So much for building security.

There was a small manager's plaque hanging on the first door to the right.

"This seems like a good place to start. Are you ready?" At her nod, Alex rapped on the scarred wood. A loud thump sounded from within the apartment, as if someone had fallen off a chair. The banal banter of a morning talk show was abruptly cut off before muffled footsteps approached the door.

They cast each other a glance, realizing that someone must be looking at them through the peephole. A moment later, they heard a deadbolt release and the sound of a chain being removed.

The woman who opened the door wore a polyester pink bathrobe that barely came down to the middle of her thighs. Her hair was a washed-out brown, streaked with gray, and wound haphazardly in a bun. Eyes the color of faded denim peered at Liz, squinting slightly as she scanned her face. Liz fought the urge to fidget under her perusal. After an uncomfortably long moment, the woman settled her gaze on Alex.

"If you're looking to sell something, I'm not buying – religion or otherwise." She had a deep throaty voice that would have been better suited singing the blues. Clutching a cigarette in her right hand, she took a long drag and waited for their answer.

"Oh, um..." Liz looked towards Alex, unsure of what to say. What if they were in the wrong place? How did one go about asking after a heroin addict, anyway?

Alex stepped forward and shot the lady his most charming smile. Liz watched with fascination as the expression on the woman's face visibly warmed. "We're sorry to bother you, ma'am. My name is Al and this is...Beth. We're looking for my brother and were told he may be in this neighborhood. Could we ask you a few questions?"

A shrewd light entered the woman's eyes, but she stepped back from the threshold and gestured for them to enter. "Your brother, huh? I doubt that. But you have nice manners, so we'll see what I know. I'm Marsha, by the way."

The two followed her into the tiny living room and sat on the old couch she indicated. Liz noticed it was covered with a patchwork blanket that had faded over the years. Marsha may not have much, but it was obvious she'd done what she could to make her home comfortable.

The woman groaned as she sat in the only other chair in the room. "So, who is your brother and why do you think he might be here?"

Once again, Alex took the lead. "His name is Peter. He's about 5'9" and has blue eyes."

Liz leaned forward. "Some of his friends may call him Pecker, or Peck."

Up until that moment, the woman had been shaking her head, but when she heard the name Peck she nodded. "Did you say Peck? Sure, I know Peck." She reached over towards the coffee table and tapped her cigarette into the overflowing ashtray. "Nice guy. He carries my groceries in for me sometimes. Even fixed my sink about a month ago. He's a good sort, when he's in his right mind. What do you all want with him?"

"What do you mean when he's in his right mind? You mean when he's not high?" Liz couldn't help the note of disappointment that crept in her voice.

The other woman narrowed her eyes. "Don't you be judging him, missy. We all have our demons to fight. Some of them are just more socially acceptable than others."

Alex cleared his throat. "Well, that's why we're here. We'd heard he's been having some trouble. We thought he could use some help fighting those demons."

"Oh honey, some demons can't be slayed by anyone but the one that's cursed." The woman gave him a look of pity and took another drag. "If you are his brother, why haven't you tried to help him before?"

He looked down at the floor. "I'm ashamed to say that I was so eager to shake this small town I failed to keep in touch after I left. If I had known what kind of trouble he was in, I would have tried to help him sooner. Jonesy let me know what was going on when I ran into him the other day."

"You know Jonesy?"

At Alex's nod, she stopped for a moment, as if trying to make her mind up about something. Silence stretched between the three of them to the point of discomfort before she cleared her throat. "He's usually upstairs in apartment 306. If he's high, he'll be passed out in one of the back bedrooms."

Alex and Liz both thanked the woman and stood up. Once again Liz found it hard to believe how far Peter had fallen since their time in school together. Marsha walked them towards the door. She placed a hand on Alex's arm, taking a moment to squeeze her fingers and revel in the muscle she found there. "Don't get your hopes up. You probably won't like what you find. But if anyone ever deserved some help, it's him. I wish you luck."

Liz watched as Alex patted her hand in reassurance. "Thank you for your help. I'll do what I can."

Without sparing a glance at Liz, she gave him a final nod and shut the door. Liz gave Alex a rueful look and let out a deep breath. "Well, for some reason I get the feeling I'm not her favorite person."

Alex grinned and took her hand. "If it makes you feel any better, you can be mine." Before she could respond, he began walking down the hall. "Let's go see if we can find Peter."

CHAPTER TWENTY-THREE

MATT HAGEN CROUCHED down and inspected the pattern of heroin dusting the concrete floor. He looked up at the man looming over him in a clumsy attempt at intimidation. There was no reason for him to be standing so close.

Matt stood, allowing his full frame to unfold until he was once again standing a couple of inches taller than the other man. He had to squash the small part of him that felt satisfied when Josh took a step back.

"You said you found this scene at," he checked his notes unnecessarily, "a little after six yesterday morning?"

"I did, yeah."

"And what brought you here?"

"While I was out patrolling, I noticed the door was ajar. It seemed odd, so I thought I'd check it out."

"And it's been undisturbed since?"

"Other than my initial walk-through. I was checking for any victims. You were very specific about leaving the crime scene intact. Nobody else has been here since."

Matt nodded. That was what he'd expected to hear. Still, something seemed off. It was a little too neat and tidy for him. His internal bells were ringing. The question was, what was his subconscious sensing?

He'd been in situations like this before and knew that a part of him was picking up on a small detail that his conscious mind hadn't clued into yet. But it would. Until then he'd just have to follow the evidence and feed as many facts as he could into the equation.

Whatever it was, it may or may not be relevant. More often than not, it was the little details that got missed that would lead to solving a case. On the other hand, sometimes it was just the impatience and territorialism coming from local law enforcement that triggered his instincts. Time would tell.

"Okay, let's go check out her apartment."

"You don't want to check out the car?"

"No. I think I've seen what I need to here. I'll come back down for a more thorough look later. Right now, it's more important that I get a sense for who Eliza is."

"Liz."

"Excuse me?"

A sneer crossed Josh's face before he had a chance to school his features. "Nobody calls her Eliza. It's just Liz."

Hmm, interesting. Matt gave Josh a nod. "All right, Liz then. Time to go see how she lived."

A loud, obnoxious ring emanated from Josh's pocket. He gestured to the device in his hand. "Sorry, new phone." Matt watched as the other man hesitated before answering. "Why don't you go on ahead and I'll catch up." Josh turned away. "Hello?"

Matt paused to observe for another moment before heading through the back door and climbing the stairs to Liz's apartment. His first impression was that the place was spare, but tidy. There weren't a whole lot of personal affects around the apartment. A fact that was surprising since, in his experience, women had a tendency to fill their homes with knickknacks and throw pillows.

He calmly circled the perimeter of her living room, noting the blanket over the back of the couch and the phone charger set up on the table nearby. He sat down on the cushion that seemed to be her favorite and looked around. The remote control was on the table in front of him, and he turned the TV on.

After scanning the buttons, he checked the programs on her DVR. Unsurprisingly, he found three different car shows. There were also a couple of unwatched episodes of a crime / detective show and an older recording of a Foo Fighters concert in London.

His suspect was quite the rocker, judging by this latest evidence and the musical choices on the stereo downstairs. He sighed and stood up. Nothing illegal about that.

Matt stepped into the adjoining kitchen and opened a few drawers before finding the silverware. The handles were simple and plain, easily found at any department or big box store. He deftly fingered through the spoons, noticing none of them were misshapen or burned on the edges. If he included the one sitting in the sink by the dirty cereal bowl, there was a full set of eight.

After confirming that little fact, he searched for and found the trashcan and recycling bins under the sink. Reaching in, he grabbed the first soda can he found and shook it. Empty. The second and third ones were, as well.

With that, he walked out of the area and gradually made his way down the hallway towards her bathroom. In there, he checked the medicine cabinet and the trashcan. Nothing unusual to note other than the fact that she seemed to rarely wear makeup and flossed regularly.

So far, there hadn't been any of the typical indications that an addict lived in the apartment. Opening the door to her bedroom gave him pause. For the first time in his career, he felt like he was intruding on someone's private space. Here, he finally felt like he was getting a sense of who Liz was.

And here are the excess throw pillows, he thought, a bit wryly.

Feeling a little relieved on some level to have his assumptions confirmed, Matt proceeded to move through her bedroom. On the dresser, there was a photo of her with an older man, standing in front of the building he was currently in, the name of the garage clearly visible. The man had his arm slung around her shoulders and they were both sporting ear-to-ear grins. She appeared to be fourteen or fifteen years old in the photo, and it was obvious they were related. This must be the father she inherited the shop from. Setting the frame down, he continued with his assessment of Liz's life.

He noticed the half-read mystery and the nearly empty glass of water on her nightstand. There was a pile of dirty clothes tossed into one corner by the dresser. She didn't appear to be a fan of doing the laundry. He rummaged through her drawers. Other than a couple pairs of beat up jeans and a large collection of band shirts, there was nothing to discover. No needles in the nightstand, no rubber hoses or belts or anything else that could be used as a tourniquet. No bent or burnt spoons used for dissolving heroin in the kitchen. Not even something as innocuous as any laxatives in the medicine cabinet. Nothing.

From everything he'd seen, Liz was simply a single woman living a rather sparse and solitary life. He got the feeling that she was a private person. In fact, he already knew through his research that she didn't keep any profiles on the usual social media sites. And, even though she was single, he'd yet to find any online dating accounts.

All of which didn't prove she wasn't dealing. However, in Matt's experience, people who dealt with the world of heroin tended to get sucked into using their own product or, at the very least, were surrounded by people who did. If Liz had managed to avoid that pitfall, she'd be a member of a fairly small group. It would speak towards her self-control and discipline. It also contradicted the impression of panic and disarray left down in the garage, with the residue of drugs tossed all over the place.

He rubbed his forehead. So far, nothing about this case was

adding up. He walked over to the window and gazed outside, trying to sort out the pieces of the case that he had so far. He was surprised to find a well-groomed blonde woman in a heated discussion with Officer Carver down in the parking lot. Despite her professional attire, she was barely keeping her cool. On the other hand, it could have something to do with the long sleeves she was wearing. Seemed like an odd choice, given the hot summer day.

He watched as Officer Carver shook her hand off his arm. Josh looked up and became visibly shaken when he spotted Matt in the window. After a few terse words thrown at the woman, he opened her driver's side door and insisted she get in.

She rolled down her window to get in a final parting shot. Her tires kicked up dust from the gravel lot, leaving Josh fuming in a cloud of dust. Minutes later, Matt could hear the other man enter the apartment.

"Everything okay?"

Josh gave him an unconvincing smile and shrugged. "Ex-girlfriend. What can I say? She can't get enough of me." He laughed. When Matt didn't respond, he cut his amusement short. "Find anything useful up here?"

Unwilling to divulge his thoughts, Matt said, "I don't know yet, but I'm getting an overall impression of who she is."

He raised an eyebrow at the derisive snort that came from Josh. "We won't know anything until the tech guys come through. Speaking of which, if you're done in here, we can get that started."

It wasn't worth arguing about. "I'm finished here. Go ahead and let them know they can come in now." He'd learned what he needed from Liz's apartment. Figuring out how it all fit together would come in due time.

CHAPTER TWENTY-FOUR

ALEX KEPT LIZ'S hand in his as they made their way towards the front door. He knew she was perfectly capable of handling herself, but he regretted that she was there. It was bad enough to be on the run, but to thrust her in this precarious situation made it feel even worse.

When they neared the entryway, they saw that someone had placed a large pile of boxes in front of the elevator, indicating it was out of order. Flyers, for sale, and help wanted signs were posted in the hallway. Spray painted graffiti was scrawled across every surface and wall as they climbed the stairs. The whole place held an underlying feel of neglect and danger.

Alex hadn't let his guard down since they'd left the house, but in this building, he felt an even greater urgency to stay alert. Stress sat heavy on his shoulders and his eyes constantly scanned their surroundings.

Despite the sense of danger, life permeated the building. The smell of fried onions, garlic, and garbage pervaded the air. They heard a man in one of the apartments yelling at the TV as they passed. Two kids came barreling down the stairs in front of them, laughter trailing after them down the hallway until it was abruptly cut off by the door slamming behind them.

It dawned on him that he had a lot in common with many of

the people in this building. If not for the circumstances of birth and opportunity, he could have found himself living in an apartment just like this. The thought was humbling.

Together they climbed the stairs to the third floor and made their way down the hallway. He noticed Liz's hand had grown steadily clammier in his as they approached the last door on the right.

"3-0-..." Alex flipped what looked like a nine upright from where it had been hanging by a nail, "...6. This is it. Ready?" Now that they were standing in front of the door, they realized it was slightly ajar. She pulled her hand from his grasp and wiped it against her jeans. He noted the deep breath she took to steel herself and admired the determined look projected.

"Here goes nothing." She reached up to knock on the door, but Alex stilled her and nodded towards the open door.

"Let's not announce ourselves, just in case. I don't want him to take off running before we've had a chance to state our case. We need him to testify."

He waited for her nod of consent before reaching for the doorknob and giving it a push. Sure enough, the door swung open easily.

"Are you sure this is a good idea? Peter might not be the only one living here. It could be dangerous, sneaking up on a person, especially if drugs are involved. I'd rather not get shot."

Alex hadn't thought of that possibility. He shrugged. "Well, there's nowhere for him to run now that we're in the apartment. I guess it wouldn't hurt to let him know we're here."

"Peter? Peter, are you here? It's me, Liz." She hesitated in the doorway and waited for a response. Growing bolder, Liz moved further into the room. "Peter?" She turned to Alex. "What do you think? Should we go back into the bedrooms?"

Alex felt uncomfortable, but figured they'd gone this far.

Resigned to see their course of action through, he said, "Stay behind me. Who knows what we'll find."

Liz trailed so closely that she accidentally stepped on his heels. She sent him a sheepish look. "Sorry."

The first bedroom was empty but for a stained mattress lying in the corner of the room. Alex hesitated to look too closely at the dark brown marks and backed out of the room. "Not there."

They moved to the other bedroom. This time, they opened the door, and discovered a lump under a pile of blankets. Liz pushed passed Alex to get a closer look. "Peter?"

Alex leaned over the prone form and shook his foot. "Is he breathing?"

The low groan that came from beneath the covers startled them both into jumping back. Liz laughed unsteadily as she pulled her hand away from her throat. She peeled the blankets away from the sleeping man's face and gasped. "Peter!"

The thin man rolled over at the sound of her voice, his blood-shot eyes barely open a slit. "Oh God! No…" He whimpered, pulling the covers over his head. "Please, I didn't know what to do!"

Liz gave the blanket another hard tug, trying to get a better look at him, but it only caused him to protest louder. "No! Please don't haunt me! There was nothing I could do to stop him. I'm sorry he killed you, but if I protested, he'd have killed me too." Whatever else he said was lost in a babble of sobs and incomprehensible sounds.

A confused look crossed Liz's face, before understanding dawned. "He thinks I'm a ghost come back to haunt him."

Alex tamped down the urge to yell at the guy. This was taking too long. They needed to get going before anybody else happened upon them.

Alex reached over and shook Peter's shoulder, forcing him to roll back over and acknowledge them. "Peter, wake up. I need your help."

"Please, forgive me! What have I done?!" the man wailed.

Exasperated, Liz ripped the covers from the man's trembling fingers, her patience as limited as Alex's. "Peter, dammit. Would you listen to me? I'm not dead! Pull yourself together. You are the only hope I have of staying alive and I need your help."

At her declaration, Peter's eyes widened even further. Reason dawned across his face. It was obvious from the way his pupils were dilated that he was still feeling the effects of whatever drug he was on, but Alex had to give him credit. At least he was attempting to be lucid.

He let out a watery hiccup. "Liz? Is that really you?"

Rolling her eyes, Liz gave him a brief smile. "Yeah, it's me. I'm still alive, for now."

"No thanks to you." Alex would have said more, but it felt a bit like kicking a puppy.

Liz shot him a disapproving look. "You're not helping." She turned back to Peter. "Can you get up? We need to talk."

Fifteen long minutes later the three of them stood in the postage-sized kitchen while Peter searched for a clean mug among the dirty dishes in the sink. Peter's hand shook as he poured the coffee. "I'm sorry, Liz. It's not that I don't want to help. I just don't think I can do it."

"But, Peter, without you, it's just our word against his. And since Josh is a cop…"

"That's right, he is. And if he knew I was talking to you right now," the man gulped, beads of sweat beaded on his forehead. "Look, you were always a good sport. You've treated me fairer than I deserved. But Liz, he'll kill me. I know my life is shit, but it's still better than the alternative."

Alex gritted his teeth. Even he could see the man was scared out of his mind and barely keeping it together. It would be a miracle if Peter's testimony would be worth anything in court, assuming things did go to trial. Maybe this whole idea had been a mistake.

Liz must have been thinking the same thing, because she decided to try a new tactic. "What if you didn't have to testify? If we can get enough evidence against him without your statement, it could work just as well. What do you know about this drug ring? Who was Josh talking to on the phone?"

Before Liz had finished talking, Peter had started to shake his head. Alex came to the realization that Peter wasn't going to be much help. He fought the urge to wring his neck.

Blissfully unaware of the dark thoughts running through Alex's head, Peter took a sip of coffee and winced when it was still too hot. "All I can tell you is what Josh told me when I got the call to come to your garage. He said the large shipment I lost had been recovered and I had to help retrieve it. I didn't even realize it was your place until you showed up!"

Before Liz could respond, Alex leaned in. "Why did he call you?"

Up to that point, Peter had been focused on Liz, barely acknowledging Alex's presence. He shot a glance towards Alex before directing his answer to Liz. "Sometimes I don't make as much money as I think I will on the street, so they give me odd jobs to make up the difference." He rubbed his hand on the back of his neck. "I was in charge of delivering the shipment when I got pulled over."

At Alex's sound of disgust, Peter's shoulders hunched. "What? They would have killed me if I didn't help recover the drugs I'd lost. I had no idea what Josh had planned, I swear!"

"Do they usually let people work off debts like this?" Liz asked, warning Alex with a look to stay quiet.

"I guess. I've been a client for a long time, so they know me. It's not the first time they've had me run an errand for them in exchange for payment." He rubbed the back of his neck. "Never anything this involved, though."

"And you have no idea who Josh was talking to? You're sure? Please, think back. Any small clue could be important."

Peter took another gulp of his coffee while he thought about it. "I'm sorry, Liz. I swear I don't know anything else. Other than the fact that someone told Josh about the car being in your shop..."

"Someone fed him that information." Liz turned to Alex. "You were there in the office with me when that vehicle came in. Who else was there?"

Alex thought about it. "Just you, me, Paul, that kid..."

"Jimmy."

"Yeah, Jimmy, the client..."

"And Cynthia came in at the end," she added.

"Right, and Cynthia. I forgot about her." He thought for another moment. "I think that was everybody, don't you?"

The answer didn't seem to please Liz, but she nodded anyway. "Yeah, that's what I remember, too."

"Unless someone saw the vehicle being pulled into the parking lot and knew what they were looking for." Alex didn't think that was the case, but he couldn't help but throw her an alternative explanation. He knew it worked when her eyes lit up at the possibility.

"Oh, that could explain things, right?" Even as she said it, Alex could tell she didn't actually believe it. Instead of dashing her hopes, he decided to pursue another line of questioning. "Peter, was it you I chased out the front door of the house a few nights ago?"

Peter began to cough, choking on the sip of coffee he'd taken. After a few moments, he asked, "Was that you?" At Alex's nod, he continued. "I had no idea, man. All I knew was that someone was chasing me and I had to get out of there fast."

"But why were you there in the first place? Were you the one who trashed the house?"

At that, Peter grimaced. A flush crept up his neck and across his face. "What can I tell you? We were told it was a safe place for us to use. We were sent there to help with the distribution. They gave us a couple blocks of junk and we had to measure it out and stick it into little baggies for resale. In exchange, we earned a few samples for ourselves. It was safer than being on the streets and we're less likely to get caught."

Rage grew in Alex's chest. The thought of that type of activity happening in one of his father's properties felt like a violation all over again. "Who?"

"What?"

"You said you were told it was a safe place to operate. By whom? Who told you?"

Hearing the tightly held anger in Alex's voice, Peter grew visibly more uncomfortable. "Man, I dunno. Jonesy is the one who told me, but I have no idea where he got the information from. I swear! The only reason I was there a couple of days ago was because I was a little light and was hoping I'd be able to scrounge up a fix."

Alex crossed his arms, mainly to prevent himself from throttling Peter's neck. "Well, where does Jonesy hang out? Maybe we can ask him where he's getting his information."

Horror filled Peter's eyes before his gaze slid away and became intent on the dust-filled corner behind the television. "Jonesy? Um, well...he has a way of moving around between cities. He's originally from Boston, but I dunno know where he's hanging out these days."

"How convenient for you." The sinister tone must have hit a nerve because Peter flinched, even though Alex hadn't made a move towards him.

Liz, who had been observing the two men during the exchange, stepped between them. She placed a hand on Alex's chest, afraid of how close to the edge he was. Peter looked at the two of them, clearly uncomfortable with the direction the conversation had gone.

"D-d-o you think you guys could take off now? It would be bad if someone came and found you here."

"Why? Are you expecting somebody?" Alex moved towards him.

Liz held her ground in the small space between the two men and sent Alex a quelling look. "Sure, Peter. We'll be going." The encouraging tone Liz used grated on Alex's nerves. This guy clearly did not deserve her kindness. She spontaneously grabbed Peter's hand. "Please think about testifying for us. I promise we will do everything in our power to keep you safe." She looked around the dingy, empty apartment, her disappointment clearly showing on her face. "We could help you."

Peter's expression softened as he looked down at their joined hands. "You know, I used to have the biggest crush on you? You were the only person who ever gave a damn about me." He sighed, his shoulders rounding slightly. Whether in defeat or fear, Alex couldn't say. "I'll think about it."

Liz nodded and gave his hand a quick squeeze before letting go. "Thank you. I'm not sure how long it'll be before its safe enough to go to the police, but we'll try to come back in a few days."

"Okay." Peter escorted them towards the door, as if he'd begun to remember manners long forgotten. As they stood in the hall-way, he hesitated. "Be careful. There might be more than one force at play here."

Liz cocked her head. "What do you mean?"

Peter looked down at his feet, unable to meet Liz's gaze. "After I lost the shipment, Josh acted more than just stressed and angry, he was scared. I think he was getting more pressure than usual. Then I came across Jonesy getting ready to make a run down to Boston. I asked him about it, but he told me to mind my own business."

"So, you think we're dealing with a larger drug ring?"

His crossed his arms. For a moment, Alex didn't think he'd answer, but then he said, "I think there's more than one group of people who are interested in what happens to the drugs here. I'm not sure how everything is related, but you should know you're probably dealing with more than just a small-town drug ring."

"Great. The stakes are higher than we thought. How does this knowledge help us? Alex asked. He didn't mean for it to sound confrontational, but given how he'd been acting earlier, he wasn't surprised at the look Liz gave him.

Again, Peter shrugged and seemed to shrink into himself. "I dunno. Maybe it doesn't."

"Is there anything else you can think of – no matter how minor it may seem – that could be useful? Something we can follow up on?"

Peter started to shake his head no when he paused. Seeing that he'd thought of something else, Liz leaned forward, but it was Alex he turned to. "Well, again, I don't know if this makes any sense… but your dad's house isn't the first time we've used a vacant house or rental as our base of operations."

Alex sounded incensed. "You're kidding me! I would have thought a rash of houses being broken into would have made the local news."

"We don't usually stay more than a week, and we're supposed to clean up after ourselves when we're finished. You showed up right after we moved on to the next place but before we cleaned it up."

Peter's voice had become taken on a whining tone that set Alex's teeth on edge. He took a deep breath and strove for patience. "Could you tell us where some of the other locations have been?"

Peter hesitated before nodding. He turned and scrounged up a scrap piece of paper from the living room table, a delivery flyer for a local pizza place. After another moment, he found something to write with and scrawled three other addresses down before handing it to him.

"That's all I can remember."

"How long ago did you use these places?" Alex asked as he looked down at the information.

The other man shrugged. He gestured to the first one on the list. "That one was about a year ago. The other ones were more recent. Like I said, we never stay at any of them for long and I've never gone to the same one twice."

Liz turned to Alex. "Sounds fairly sophisticated, if they have access to all these places and are smart enough to clean up after themselves."

"Yeah, it doesn't sound like your typical druggie – no offense." Alex gave Peter an apologetic look but Pete just shrugged the comment off. He looked like he was trying to slink back into the apartment.

Liz continued. "Plus, you have to take into account that they have Josh working for them. A cop on the force is advantageous. The person leading this group is smart and keeping their distance from the action, using Josh to do the dirty work."

Alex grimaced. "And smart makes them even more dangerous."

"Exactly." Liz asked Peter to consider what they'd discussed and assured him they'd be back in a few days no matter what. Whether it was the topic they'd been discussing or the events from the night before, they weren't surprised to hear the lock slide into place from the other side of the door.

Neither of them noticed the shadow that moved across the peephole of the door across the hallway as they left.

CHAPTER TWENTY-FIVE

"WHAT DO YOU mean you can't find them?"

"Exactly what I said. We almost had them a couple of days ago, but since then they've disappeared."

"Have you been monitoring all her contacts?"

Josh let a sliver of irritation creep into his voice. "Of course. The entire police department has been watching all known associates, including Detective Clark. I'm telling you, she made that initial phone call yesterday, but they'd already left the warehouse by the time we got there. There's been nothing since."

"Maybe he has another phone on him."

He shrugged. "It's possible, but I don't see how unless he had it before this whole incident began. He hasn't stopped into any convenience stores that I know of, and all his movements have been accounted for."

The sigh that came over the line had Josh gritting his teeth. "Stay on it. They have to slip up at some point, and when they do we need to get to them before the cops."

"What are you going to do?"

"I'm going to bring our little birdie in and see if he knows anything."

"Won't that blow your cover? Right now, he has no idea who you are, just that you exist."

"Oh, he won't be sticking around long enough to tell anybody, don't worry."

Josh looked at his phone after he heard the click. Poor guy. He *almost* felt sorry for him.

CHAPTER TWENTY-SIX

LIZ STALKED DOWN the hallway fuming. Misreading her anger for frustration, Alex reached for her. "Don't worry, Liz. We'll figure something out." She pulled her hand back before he could hold it.

"You didn't exactly help the situation, did you? Or did you think bullying him would be the fastest way to get what you wanted?"

Alex stopped mid-stride and stared at her. "What are you talking about?"

"Seriously? I'm talking about the way you went in there and tried to coerce Peter into helping us. The entire point of going to the apartment was to enlist his help, not harass him further. Did you actually think the best way to get his cooperation was to throw your weight around?"

"Throw my weight…? Liz, you're forgetting the guy left us to die! What did you expect? That'd I'd pat him on the head and assure him it was all water under the bridge?"

"No, but I did expect you to appreciate the precarious position he's in and try to have a little empathy. Especially considering the fact we were asking him to put his life on the line and testify on our behalf." She turned and kept walking. "It's not as if he got in this situation in a vacuum. It was exactly this type of behavior that set him on this road in the first place."

Alex's jaw tightened. "I don't know who you think I am, or what I've done, but I'm getting tired of being typecast into this role you seem to have made for me. I'm not the bad guy here, Liz. In fact, I think I've proven time and again that I'm on your side. Honestly, I don't know what more I can do to convince you of that."

She wished she knew what it would take. Not knowing how to respond, Liz continued down the stairs and stepped out of the front entrance. She inhaled deeply trying to release her frustration and anger. The fresh air was a relief after the smells permeating the hallway they'd just exited.

They were back to square one.

Alex looked like he wanted to continue their conversation, but stopped when he noticed flashing lights down the block. "Looks like we may have lost our ride." Her pulse jumped to a staccato of panic and adrenaline.

Grabbing her elbow, he quickly steered her in the other direction, back behind the apartment building. They both picked up their pace. Alex cast her a sideways look. "How fast can you get us another vehicle without being obvious?"

They walked a few blocks, making their way over to the next neighborhood. All the while, Liz scanned the cars parked around them. "I'm not sure. It's not like I've had a lot of practice boosting cars. A lot depends on the type of car we can find."

Two blocks over, Liz found what she was looking for. She led Alex towards an old, dark-green Chevy Citation. "Keep an eye out for me, would you?"

While Alex turned his attention towards the windows looking down at them from all sides, Liz cast about until she found a rock from one of the nearby lawns. Three sharp raps shattered the rear driver's side window. She swept the broken glass aside with care and reached in to unlock the door. Stealing another car left a bad taste in her mouth. She regretted there wasn't an alternative.

Crouching down by the curb, she pulled the wires from the steering wheel base. A moment later, the vehicle was running. Alex leaned into the open driver's side door. "Maybe you should let me drive; that way you can stay hunched down in the seat and out of sight."

Liz would rather have been the one in control, but realized he was right. For the first few minutes, all they could think about was getting away unseen. Alex made a number of turns before finally reaching the main road.

With the immediate danger behind them, an awkward silence descended upon the car. Nearly being caught had paused their argument, but now her mistrust had her shifting uncomfortably.

Instead of addressing it, she turned her thoughts to their larger problems, mentally cataloguing what they knew so far. Other than Peter, there was Jonesy, Josh, and one other person that they knew was operating the drug ring in Maine.

That unknown person must either spend a lot of time in the area or is locally based, otherwise they wouldn't know what houses were available for their distribution operation. "You know, the amount of properties involved has me thinking they have to have a real estate agent or property manager on the payroll. Didn't you say your dad's agent was Cynthia?"

She watched as Alex clenched his jaw. "I don't see it." Of course, her implicating his ex-girlfriend would bother him. The image of the two of them talking in the café floated through her mind.

She would have continued to make her case, but the shake of his head cut her off. "Look, I know you two have history, but there are a couple of reasons why I don't think it's her," he said. "First, why would she leave a house that she's representing in the state

I found it in? Wouldn't that just expose her? If she was dealing drugs, you'd think she'd want to keep a lower profile."

Liz didn't want to admit it, but he had a point. If the name of the game was to fly under the radar, leaving a house that was obviously being used for drugs didn't make sense. On the other hand, having a real estate agent involved would help insure the house wasn't shown to customers until it was put back in order. "Okay. You might have a point, but having a real estate agent could work both ways. What's your other reason?"

Alex gripped the wheel. "You know Josh. Do you honestly think he'd allow himself to be in a position where he answered to Cynthia?"

The minute he said it, Liz knew he was right. There was no way a male chauvinist like Josh would answer to a female. Maybe the fact that she disliked the woman really was clouding her judgment.

Hell, Peter said this group was most likely connected to a drug ring based in Boston or an even larger city to the south. Maybe the person they were looking for wasn't even local. They'd seen how relieved Josh had been to find the car in Liz's garage, which means they must have been under quite a bit of pressure from the bigger group.

Desperate and dangerous did not sound like a good mix, especially where Josh was concerned. Back in high school, she knew that he'd always played fiercest when their team was down a few points and he was backed into a corner. A life and death situation involving drugs would only make his response more cutthroat.

What she needed was more evidence, preferably a witness that could and would be willing to testify against a police officer, and a way of bringing this all to the authorities in such a way that they would be willing to listen before arresting her and throwing her in jail.

No sweat.

Liz must have chuckled at the dark turn her thoughts had taken because Alex glanced down at her. "What's so funny?"

"Honestly? Nothing. I think my fatalistic sense of humor is getting the best of me." She winced as she shifted and tried to rub the knot out of her calf. "How much farther, anyway?"

"Well, I had a thought about that. Think you can handle being down there for a while longer?"

Liz bit back her disgruntlement. "Why?"

"I thought we could go check out the locations on this list. There might be a commonality between them."

She was still frustrated with him. The last thing she wanted to do was spend a couple of cramped, uncomfortable hours in the car driving place to place, especially while sitting on the floor. On the other hand, how could they afford not to?

"Fine."

"We don't have to. It was just a suggestion."

"No, you're right. Let's get going."

CHAPTER TWENTY-SEVEN

MATT MULLED OVER the facts in the case. He stepped back from the board, hoping something would be illuminated from the new perspective. The problem was, everything felt like conjecture at this point. There just wasn't enough information to formulate a clear picture of the situation.

"Sir, you wanted to see me?" Josh glanced around the room before settling on the photo of Liz Harper pinned up in front of him.

"I did. I was looking through the department's cases concerning suspected drug activity. I noticed your name came up on a recent one. What can you tell me about it?"

"Not much more than what I recorded, sir. I got a call to investigate a house that had been broken into and vandalized. When I arrived, there was evidence that it had been used by a couple of druggies. Some paraphernalia, a couple of sleeping bags… the usual."

"Is that sort of thing common here in Bath?"

"I wouldn't say common, but it happens more every day." Josh hovered in the doorway. Matt could feel the other man watching as he rifled through the papers on his desk. He waited and let the silence fill the room.

"Can I ask you a question?"

"Sure…" Matt's pulse picked up. Now they were getting somewhere.

"Why has the MDEA been investigating the garage to begin with?"

He debated just how much to tell him. There had been enough incidents in the past few months that he'd begun to suspect a leak in the department. On the other hand, he still needed the local law enforcement to trust him.

Deciding to relay the facts already on record, Matt said, "In the past eighteen months, we've confiscated three other vehicles that had hidden compartments in them. We suspected they were being used to transport drugs, but didn't find anything at the time."

"What did you find?"

"All three had the same quality of workmanship. Whoever had built those compartments knew what they were doing. Then we lucked out. One of the pieces used still had a part of a serial number on it. From there we were able trace it back to a delivery made to Bath, ME. Since there are only two mechanics working in and around this town, we were able to narrow the search significantly.

Seeing an opportunity, Matt decided to ask Josh a few questions. "What are your impressions of Liz Harper?"

"Sir?"

"Liz Harper. I noticed you corrected me earlier about her name. I'm assuming you're familiar with our main suspect."

"It's a small town. We went to high school together. She's always been a social outcast. Has lived and breathed that car shop for as long as I can remember. Her parents died a few years back, when she was a junior or senior. Can't remember the exact timing."

"Do you think she could be guilty of this?"

"Absolutely."

At that, Matt looked up from his notes. "Really? That certain?"

"I have no doubt in my mind, sir."

A warning bell went off in Matt's mind. Something was off about the other man's conviction. Taking pains to conceal his thoughts, Matt continued. "What about Mason? What do you think about him?"

"You mean other than him being some hot-shot city slicker who has the Chief convinced he's God's gift?"

"Not much of a fan, huh?"

"Let's just say, he never would have been hired if it hadn't been for that little incident this past winter."

"You mean the one where he caught the stalker that killed his partner and saved the woman he's currently dating? The one who also happens to be Liz' sister?"

"That's the one."

"From what I understand, there was an investigation into the matter and he was cleared of any wrongdoing."

"The suspect died, and it wasn't even his jurisdiction. If you ask me, Mason got off easy. Some judge probably had a pity party for him." Josh leaned against the doorframe and crossed his arms. "Still doesn't negate the fact the guy is a pompous dick. Excuse my language, sir. I wouldn't be surprised if he knows a lot more than he's letting on."

"I see. It does seem like the Harper sisters have had a lot going on recently. Well, thank you for providing me with your insight, Officer Carver."

Josh gave Matt a smirk. "Anytime."

CHAPTER TWENTY-EIGHT

HOURS LATER, LIZ threw herself down on the couch. "I don't get it."

"Get what?"

"As far as I can tell, none of those locations had anything in common."

"Yeah, I don't know what I was expecting. I was hoping something would pop out at us."

It was the most words they'd spoken to each other in hours. The argument they'd had earlier still sat between them, sucking all the air out of the room. Despite spending all day in the car with each other, things hadn't gotten any easier between them. Their conversations had been stiff and overly polite. Neither one of them seemed capable of talking about anything more than the weather, traffic, or the case.

After another moment, Liz groaned and got up from the couch. "My back is killing me. I'm going to go take a hot shower. Maybe it will help get some of the knots out of my muscles."

"Fine. I'll get dinner started."

Forty minutes later, Liz assessed the soup and sandwiches and sat down at the table. "Looks good."

"Nothing fancy. Would be nice to have Olivia here with us. Bet she could cook up a feast while on the run."

"I'm sure." Liz took a huge bite of her BLT and slowly chewed.

For the first few moments, neither one of them said a word. Finally, Alex sat back in his chair. "Look. I'm sorry if you think I was too hard on Peter."

"You were."

Frustration flashed in his eyes, but he forged ahead. "I was doing what I thought was best."

"What you thought was best was to mock and berate him? You thought jumping on him was the best way to convince him to help us?"

"Dammit, Liz! The man left us sitting in the backseat of that car knowing full well it was a death sentence."

"But it wasn't. I'd already gotten our hands free."

"He didn't know that. I was trying to play on his sense of guilt, get him to agree to help us."

"I guess we can both see how well that worked out. Peter was so afraid of you, he was trembling when we left."

"Oh, and I'm sure that had nothing to do with the drugs in his system."

Liz shot up from her chair. "You know what? You're impossible. I'm going to bed."

"We still need to discuss what our next move should be."

"I want to go back and try to talk to Peter again. He'll come around after he's had a chance to sleep on it. Also, I think I should go by myself to speak to him."

"Liz…"

She washed her dishes and set them in the rack to dry. "If you have any other bright ideas, you can let me know tomorrow. For now, I'm going to bed."

Alex sighed. "Fine."

*

The sharp edges of her frustration kept her awake long after she'd climbed under the covers. Liz knew her words had created a chasm between her and Alex. It was a gap she wasn't sure how to bridge, or even if she wanted to. In some ways, keeping Alex at a distance felt safer.

The droning sounds of the television filtered in from the living room. It was midnight before she heard Alex close the door to his bedroom. By the time Liz finally dropped off to sleep, it was mercifully dreamless. The next morning, her anger had dulled enough that she could think clearly about the situation.

Logically, she knew it wasn't fair to lay Peter's drug addiction at Alex's feet. In the calming light of day, she could admit that his aggressive behavior had stirred a purely visceral reaction in her. In fact, now that she'd had a chance to sleep on the matter, she felt a little embarrassed about her response to the previous day's events.

It was tempting to drag her feet and hide out in her bedroom a little longer, but what good would it do? At some point, she was going to have to see him. Pulling her shoulders back, Liz took a deep breath and made her way to the kitchen. The scene that greeted her from the doorway stopped her in her tracks.

Alex was taking slices of bacon out of a skillet and placing them on a plate. That done, he began beating a bowl of eggs into a frothy mix before turning and catching two slices of toast as they jumped from the toaster.

A curl of desire slowly unfurled low in her belly. What would it be like to wake up to this every weekend? She shook the idea from her mind before it had a chance to take root. "Smells good."

He turned as she entered the room. "Oh good, I was just about to wake you. There's a fresh pot of coffee. I wasn't sure how you took it."

Still bleary-eyed, and a little overwhelmed by the morning domesticity, Liz moved on auto-pilot towards the coffee pot. "Just black." She filled a mug for herself before sitting down at the table. He plated the food and placed it in front of her.

Liz took a bite of eggs and toast. "Mmm, this tastes great. Thanks for making breakfast."

Alex sampled his own meal before he gave her a boyish grin. "Well, you've officially experienced the other half of my cooking repertoire. Scrambled eggs are part of my specialty."

"What's the other half?"

"Spaghetti and garlic bread."

Liz laughed. "Well, that was good, too. I usually order out or eat something from a can." She sobered when she remembered it was her desire to order a pizza that had started this whole adventure. "I want to apologize for how I reacted yesterday. I know it wasn't right to blame you for Peter's addiction."

Alex gave her a long look over the rim of his coffee before setting the mug down. "I appreciate you saying that. I'll admit, I could have handled the situation better."

"I'm not going to give up on him, Alex. Peter said he'd think about testifying for us. Maybe now that he's had a chance to think about it, we'll be able to convince him it's the right thing to do."

"I agree we should go back, but I don't think he's going to change his mind. We need to plan for the worst-case scenario and figure out another way of proving our innocence."

Liz knew he was right, but still wanted to hold out hope for her old friend. Somewhere underneath all those years of addiction and abuse was the boy she had once known. She'd caught a brief glimpse of him when he'd told her of his old high school crush. If she could appeal to that part of Peter, there was still a chance he'd do the right thing.

Glad that they moved to more even ground, Liz took a deep breath. "We didn't get a lot of information to work with yesterday. Where do we go from here?"

"I don't know. There is another thing that I've been worried about, though. My dad isn't in good health. At some point I'm going to need to check on him. I usually stop by at least once a day. If I don't show up soon, he's going to wonder what's going on."

Liz hadn't even thought about that. Sure, she was cut off from her family, but at least she knew they weren't depending on her. She could see the weight of his responsibility weighing heavily across his slumped shoulders. It made her even happier that his image hadn't been plastered on the news the last few days.

"Are you two close?"

"We didn't used to be, no. When I was younger, my dad was a hard, cold, and distant man. I used to wonder if he was warmer and more affectionate when my mom was alive. What kindness did he show her to make her fall in love with him? Whatever ability he had to share his emotions must have died with her."

"I'm sorry, that must have been difficult for you."

"It wasn't easy." Alex put his fork down and looked around the kitchen. "Strange that we ended up here, actually. This is where I've always felt closest to my parents. We'd come here during the summer for two weeks. After Mom was gone, I could see her when I watched my dad looking out at the view, or when he'd take me to their favorite restaurant. It was the one time of year he connected with me. It was as if this was the one place he could tap into that side of himself."

"He must have loved her very much." The idea of loving someone that much scared her. But to lose them? That was terrifying. After losing her parents, she didn't think she could put herself in that kind of position again. "Let's look in on him this afternoon. Like you said, the cops aren't looking for you yet. As long as we're discreet…"

Alex shook his head. "I was thinking along the same lines, but I don't think it's a good idea for you to come. Even if I'm not on the news, the officials could still be looking for me. Or, at the very least, Josh could be. It occurred to me that he might resort to using my father as bait."

"So, what? You think I should stay here while you go out and take all the risks?" Liz didn't like the sound of that at all. It was her garage that been broken into. He wouldn't be in this situation if it hadn't been for her. Unfortunately, she couldn't think of any other option. "You know, sneaking back to see your father more than once isn't going to be a viable option. We're going to need a long-term solution."

"I agree. I'm hoping this situation won't last for much longer and alternatives become a moot point. If nothing else, do you think one of your sisters would be willing to look in on him?" As if reminded of their original quandary, he shifted the conversation. "Have you thought any more about talking to Paul?"

Liz sighed. "I have. Other than going back to Peter and convincing him to testify, I think that's my only option. It's still hard to believe they've been investigating my garage for the last couple of months. How could that be? What have they witnessed? I've been trying to figure it out, but honestly, I haven't seen any unusual activity. If Paul and I can compare notes, something might pop out at us."

"Talk about walking into a potential trap. I'm guessing he's under as much surveillance as your family at this point. We should hold off on trying to talk to him until some of the initial interest has died down."

Even though she knew Alex was right, it didn't make it any easier to accept. She got up to clear the plates and start on the dishes. As the sink filled, she let her gaze wander through the kitchen window and out over the view of the lake. There were worse places to be holed up for a few days. At least she could be thankful for the safe retreat.

"Are you sure we'll be able to stay here for a few days? Will anybody notice it's occupied and think it odd?"

"We should be fine for a few weeks, at least. Like I said, this cottage wasn't rented out this year. There are only a few other residences along the perimeter of the lake, and most of them are rentals like this one. There shouldn't be many prying eyes. In fact, feel free to go for a walk while I'm out today. The path around the lake isn't quite three miles and it's beautiful along the water."

Three miles. The distance was barely less than what they had traveled the day before, but for some reason it didn't sound nearly as daunting as it had the other day. Funny how context could change a person's perception about something.

Liz contemplated Alex as he leaned against the kitchen counter. She supposed the same could be said about people. After having had a chance to get to know him better, she was finding Alex to be a much more interesting person than the one she'd known in high school.

"You know, I might do that. It wouldn't hurt for me to get familiar with this place, anyway." She could see the relief on his face as she agreed. He must have been worried she'd argue about coming with him to his father's house. "Promise me you'll be careful at your dad's place. If anything seems suspicious, get out of there."

"Promise. I'll take the car and drop it off away from here. My dad has a sedan that he can't drive anymore. Don't worry if I'm not back until later this afternoon, or even early evening."

"Okay." Liz handed him the dishtowel she'd been using to dry the dishes. "Try to leave the car somewhere it will be found, and wipe it down with this. I feel terrible for its owners. I've already taken their names and addresses off of both registrations. Maybe I can repay them for the inconvenience once all of this blows over."

"Free maintenance for life."

Even after the strained conversation they'd had, Liz managed to crack a smile. "You know, that's not a bad idea."

Alex hesitated at the door, almost as if he was afraid to leave. "Are you sure you're going to be okay?"

"I'll be fine, I promise. Now hurry up and go check on your dad."

CHAPTER TWENTY-NINE

ALEX DROVE PAST his father's house a second time, trying to get a closer look at the unfamiliar car parked in the driveway. He debated whether he should stop and go in, or hold off and wait until the visitor had left.

Ultimately, his concern for his father won out. He was painfully aware that whoever was operating within the drug ring knew of his involvement, despite his name not officially being reported to the police. There was no way he could risk not knowing who was inside, and maybe leave his dad at the wrong person's mercy.

On the other hand, he didn't want to draw any undue attention to the house if it was a wholly unrelated matter. Deciding it would be better to park the stolen vehicle away from anything connecting it to him, Alex drove another five blocks before ditching his ride.

He made his way back to the house and let himself in the back door. No reason to announce his arrival if something fishy was going on. Pausing in the kitchen, Alex strained his ears to detect anything unusual. A high trill of laughter came from the living room, followed by his father's own raspy chuckle.

With his curiosity piqued, Alex walked down the hallway, and stopped in surprise when he saw who the visitor was. Cynthia? What the hell was she doing here? Liz's words from the previous day echoed in his mind. Could she be on to something, after all?

"Alex!" His father's voice boomed in greeting. It sounded more robust than Alex had heard in a long time.

Realizing he'd been spotted, he moved into the room. "Hey, Dad."

"Good to see you, son. Where've you been?" Without waiting for an answer, his dad continued, "You remember Cynthia, don't you?"

"Yes, of course. Cynthia, how are you?" Alex reached to shake her hand right as she stepped in for a hug.

"Oh, come on, Alex. Is that all you have for your old girlfriend? It's not as if we're strangers, y'know."

Alex relented, giving her a perfunctory pat on the back before extricating himself from her grasp. Despite the way she smiled up at him, he noticed there were dark shadows lying under her carefully applied makeup.

"I didn't realize you were going to have company, Dad. What brings you by, Cynthia?"

She took a moment to fluff her hair back into place before including both men in her smile. "I was following up about that little issue you'd brought to my attention. I wanted to come by and assure your father that I was taking care of everything and it would never happen again."

The older Weston cleared his throat and shot his son a disapproving glance. "Imagine my surprise when she mentioned what had happened and I had no idea what she was talking about."

Well, hell, Alex thought. The last thing he needed was to get in trouble with his father. It didn't matter how old he got, his dad had the uncanny ability to make him feel like a snot-nosed kid all over again.

Alex ran a hand along the back of his neck. "I didn't want you to concern yourself with it. I brought it up with Cynthia and figured I'd handle it. Everything is under control."

"Now don't be giving your son a hard time, Mr. Weston. Alex did mention it, and we are going to schedule an appointment to talk about the matter further."

Alex watched as his dad gave her an affectionate pat on the hand. "You're too good to me, dear." Rod turned to his son. "Isn't she a peach?"

Cynthia smiled sweetly at the older man before sending Alex a direct look, not bothering to mask her open interest. Unsure of how to react to her unspoken invitation, Alex was about to excuse himself when his father groaned in pain. "Dad? Are you okay? Is it time for another painkiller?"

"No, Cynthia here got me one a minute ago. I'm sure it will kick in any moment." Rod winced, but gamely tried to smile through his discomfort. "I think I'm just a little overtired, that's all. You'll have to excuse me, dear. Alex, I trust you'll work with Cynthia to come up with a security plan?"

"You got it, Dad."

He nodded. "Good. Why don't you two take off and let this old man rest for a bit? Alex, can you tour the rest of my holdings and make sure they're doing okay?" A sly look entered his eye. "It will give you both a chance to catch up. After so many years, I'm sure you have a lot to talk about."

"Oh, um, Dad…right now isn't a good time."

At the same moment, Cynthia beamed at him. "That's a great idea! In fact, I don't have anything planned today. Why don't we go right now?"

The timing was terrible, but there wasn't a good way to politely decline the suggestion. Amazing how his dad still had a knack for getting what he wanted and manipulated the situation as he saw fit. It was part of the reason why he'd been such a successful businessman. It was also one of the reasons their relationship had been strained for so long.

Worse, he knew his father's suggestion was valid. Alex did need to check on his various properties. He wondered how he could wiggle out of the situation. "How long do you think it will take?" Maybe he could give her an hour and then beg off.

"Oh, only a few hours or so." She stood and gave Rod a light kiss on the cheek. "You take care of yourself. I'll be back in a few days to give you a report on that sale we talked about."

"Bye, Dad. Take it easy this afternoon, okay?"

"Sure, sure, son. I appreciate you helping me out with this."

Alex rolled his eyes as his father gave him a wink over Cynthia's head. The poor guy actually thought he was doing him a favor. It made it hard to hold it against him, even if he had been neatly outmaneuvered.

As they both walked out the front door, Cynthia flashed him a brilliant smile. "Won't this be fun? Why don't I drive, since I'm probably more familiar with the area?"

"Fine." At least he wouldn't have to explain where his car was.

Alex slipped in on the passenger side. Despite the roomy, luxurious leather seats, he felt confined. Had Cynthia always had that predatory gleam in her gaze, or was that something she'd acquired in their years apart?

He supposed she'd always been this ruthless. However, that facet of her character had never been fully focused on him before. It was obvious she'd set her sights on resurrecting their old relationship, and he knew she was not a woman used to being denied.

An image of Liz's clear, sea-glass green eyes popped into his mind. While direct and piercing, they never had the same air of calculation that was ever-present in Cynthia's. He hoped she wouldn't worry about him taking so long to get back.

Cynthia climbed into the driver's seat. "Well, let's get started! Your father has six properties, so it will be a full morning. Actually, a couple of the houses are not far from here."

At her tone, Alex felt relief course through him. If she decided to maintain this level of professionalism things wouldn't be too bad. "Sounds good."

It only took them an hour and a half to tour through three of the places on their list. With each house Alex tried to convince her to stop the tour, but she seemed determined to follow through with it. Cynthia was able to tell him the price and specifics of each property, what the comps were for the area, the average time it took for other similar properties to sell, and the quality of the local schools.

He noticed she carried a portfolio with information about each place, but rarely had to reference it. She even knew the people who lived in the neighborhoods and would share tidbits of their lives, what they did for a living, the names of their kids and what age they were, even who she had sold a house to in the past.

The situation he'd found at the first house turned out to be an anomaly. Cynthia was actually quite good at her job. He began to understand why his father had hired her. As they left the third property, Cynthia reached into her bag and pulled out a tissue.

"Excuse me," she said as she wiped her nose. "I think I may be coming down with something."

He noticed that she did seem a bit more flushed than she had that morning. "Are you okay?" Finally, here was an excuse he could use. "Why don't we stop for the day? Every place you've shown me has looked to be in good order. I'm sure the problem at the other house was an isolated incident.

"Oh, I'm fine. Just a bit of that cold that's been going around. Nothing too bad, I'm sure." She quickly stuffed the tissue into a small trash bin she kept in the backseat of her car, then turned towards him. "Sorry about that. Anyway, this next house isn't for sale, but your father rents it out every summer. It's a bit of a drive, but the area is lovely."

Up to that point, Alex had nearly convinced himself that things would be okay. Now, her words dropped tension into the pit of his stomach. The heavy weight of stress he'd been feeling the last few days landed firmly back onto his shoulders.

There was only one place she could be referring to, and he had left Liz there a few hours ago standing in the kitchen.

CHAPTER THIRTY

"MIND IF I sit here?"

Mason looked up from his sandwich, and kept looking up. Matt Hagen was so tall that he stood out no matter where he was, which was saying something, considering Mason wasn't exactly a small guy.

He gestured to the empty seat across from him. "Sure. If you can get your legs to fit under the table."

After making himself as comfortable as possible, Matt folded his hands on the table. He watched as Mason took a bite of his sandwich. "I suppose you know why I'm here."

Mason nodded and swallowed. "To be honest, I thought I would be seeing you sooner or later, although I've been staying out of the investigation as you asked. What's on your mind, Agent Hagen?"

"Please, call me Matt."

"Okay. What can I help you with, Matt?"

The agent looked around the dining room at the other tables. "So, this is the café that was burned to the ground?" His attention shifted back to Mason. "The one Olivia used to own?"

Mason wiped his hands and leaned back in his seat. He took a sip from his drink. "There have been a few changes, like the name, and Jackie and Tom own it now." He paused. "But you already knew that."

Matt nodded. "Seems like everybody has made a full recovery from this past winter."

"Not quite, but we're close. Once Olivia's new restaurant is opened, we'll be able to put the rest of it behind us. We're all eager to move forward."

"Recovering from something like that must have cost quite a bit." Matt watched as the other man's expression hardened.

"What are you trying to imply? If you want to look into our financials, all you have to do is ask. All you'll find is that the money came from insurance, savings, and a small loan from my family trust fund."

Actually, Matt had already looked into it, but he'd wanted to gauge Mason's reaction. "I walked through the crime scene, and checked out Liz's apartment."

"Oh yeah?" Mason leaned forward and began eating his sandwich again. "I'm guessing you didn't find more than a few pairs of grease-stained jeans and a couple of beers in the fridge."

Matt had to hand it to him – that wasn't altogether inaccurate. He decided to play it straight. "That's about right. I have to admit, it's difficult for me to pin down why someone like Liz would get into the illegal drug business. Unless, of course, she got tipped off that her garage was under investigation and cleared out anything indicating otherwise. The captain tells me you knew about that."

Mason's right eyebrow winged up at that last statement, but he kept chewing. The only other indication that he was offended by Matt's insinuation was the way his jaw tightened and his eyes turned frosty. "I know it may be hard for you to believe, but I didn't mention it to her, much to Olivia's dismay. Trust me, when she found out I was keeping something like that from her, I had to do some heavy-duty groveling. I have a feeling I'll be in the doghouse for quite a while over that."

Matt would have responded, but Mason continued. "Look, man. I know you don't have any reason to believe me, but you're wasting your time if you think Liz had anything to do with those drugs."

"What makes you so sure?"

"You know that the Harper sisters lost their parents a few years back?"

"Yeah, I've read something about that. It was a car accident, right?"

Mason nodded. "Yes. The other driver involved was hopped up on a combination of alcohol and pain meds – OxyContin. Granted, the poor road conditions were also a contributing factor, but the fact remains that none of those girls would touch something like heroin, given the events surrounding their parents' death."

"Ah. Hmm, I didn't realize that. Thank you for the insight." Matt sat back in his seat and mulled over this new piece of information for a moment. "So, who do you think is behind all of this?"

Matt could tell the question caught the other man off-guard. Mason watched him for a moment, carefully weighing his words. "You need to understand something about Liz. She's a very pragmatic, methodical type of person. She would need to have a very good reason not to come in to the police station, especially since she knows I have every intention of becoming her future brother-in-law. You should be asking yourself why running from the cops looked like a better option."

"Now look who's doing the implying." Matt narrowed his eyes. "Are you saying that it was an officer that broke into her shop?"

Mason set his empty plate aside, his face carefully devoid of any expression. "Not without proof, I'm not." He threaded his fingers and leaned over the table. "But it bears looking into. I think you might be surprised by what you find regarding the first officer on the scene."

"Did she tell you it was Officer Carver when you talked to her?"

A flash of defiance and frustration crossed Mason's face before he regained control of his features. "I don't know what you're talking about."

Matt gave him a knowing look. "I'm sure you don't." He got up from the booth. "Well, I hope for her sake as well as yours that you're telling the truth. If I find out that you've been aiding and abetting a wanted person, I will come after you. I've looked through your files, Mason. You're a damn good detective. I'd hate to see it all thrown away over something like this."

Mason had grown very still at Matt's warning. He leaned back and put his arm on the back of the booth, appearing as calm and confident as ever. Matt would have bought it, too, if it hadn't been for that split second where his shoulders had tensed up. "I can promise you that I have not seen Liz and I don't know where she is. You will be the first to know if I find out."

"See that I am." Matt walked towards the door. Damn, he hated working in small towns. Everybody was connected with everybody else. The sooner he could solve the case, the sooner he would be out of there.

CHAPTER THIRTY-ONE

FEELING AT ODDS with herself after Alex left, Liz cast about for a way to keep herself occupied. It didn't take her long to finish straightening up the cabin. The few dishes from breakfast were already washed, dried, and placed back in the cupboard. Moving into the bedroom, she grimaced at the gaudy sweatshirt in her hands before quickly folding it and placing it in a drawer. That done, she began to cast about for something else to do.

Less than half an hour later, she set the book she'd been attempting to read aside in disgust. Pacing the living room created more tension than it eased. Being idle was going to drive her nuts. Vacations had never held much allure for her, and this was a far cry from a vacation. She'd much rather work nine or ten hour days than deal with this terrible waiting.

Liz remembered coming across a toolbox in the basement while doing the laundry and headed downstairs. She could use this time to fix that leak in the kitchen faucet. The sound of a car door slamming startled her as she lugged the box back upstairs.

Was Alex back so soon?

She nearly flung the front door open before coming to her senses. Deciding to play it safe, she drew a small part of the curtain aside. An unfamiliar silver luxury car sat in the driveway.

Shit!

The toolbox she was carrying fell to the floor. Her hands became clammy as panic thrummed through her veins. For a moment, indecision kept her planted in the entryway while her mind quickly inventoried every item that indicated her presence in the cabin. There was nothing to be done about it now. Hopefully nobody would be able to connect any of it back to her.

Liz slipped out the backdoor just as she heard the key turning in the front door. There'd been no time to hide the toolbox sitting on the floor. Racing across the backyard, she hoped nobody would spot her through the kitchen window. Rough bark scratched the palm of her hand as she ducked behind a tree. Who could possibly be in the house right now? What were the odds that somebody would just show up?

Her heart raced as her thoughts turned sinister. Had she been caught? How had they been able to trace her to this location? Did Alex have something to do with this? Was it possible he had turned her in? Could he have been playing her this whole time?

She shied away from that thought. No. If so, why did it take him so long to report her? He could have done it when he'd gone grocery shopping. Liz shook her head. She couldn't afford to jump to conclusions.

Gradually, the deep-seated, animalistic fight-or-flight instinct eased, and her mind turned towards observation and logic. There weren't any sirens in the distance, no flashing lights. In fact, no indication of any police presence at all. If Josh had found her, would he report her to the police or – more likely – the drug ring he was working for? On the other hand, if Josh had discovered their location, would he be bold enough to park in the driveway?

A shadow crossed the kitchen window, and Liz instinctively crouched a little lower. Somebody was definitely in the house. Then she remembered. During breakfast, Alex had mentioned borrowing a sedan from his dad. He could be in there wondering what had happened to her.

Feeling like a fool, Liz was just about to make her way to the door when she heard a high trill of laughter. Of all the people Liz had been prepared to see, Cynthia hadn't been even a remote possibility. And yet, there was no denying the shining gleam of her blonde hair reflecting the afternoon sun as she stepped out the door.

A complicated twist of regret, mistrust, and what felt disturbingly like envy lodged in her chest. Her suspicions were confirmed when she heard Alex's deep voice respond to a question Cynthia had posed. She watched from the shadows of the trees as he turned and locked the door.

Cynthia stood with her head tilted up towards the sun in what she must have felt was an attractive pose. Tossing her hair over her shoulder, she snaked her arm through his, leaned close and smiled up at him before walking back towards the car. Alex took a few steps with her before extricating himself from her grasp. He paused and scanned the backyard. It was obvious he was looking for her, but Liz was too stunned to give him a signal. In fact, it took her a few minutes after they drove away to gather her wits and head inside.

She was glad she'd taken the time to do her laundry and put her meager belongings into the dresser. It only took her a couple of minutes to grab everything and stuff them into a plastic grocery bag. Yet, as she reached for the doorknob, her complicated reality reared its ugly head.

Where was she supposed to go?

And *how* was she going to get there?

Going back to her family wasn't an option. Relying on Paul wasn't an option. Who else could she turn to? Pride and necessity waged a battle in her mind and left her feeling impotent.

The practical little voice in her mind whispered that Alex hadn't betrayed her. Neither one of them had discussed the kisses they'd shared earlier, nor was there any real commitment between them.

In fact, continued that sobering voice, he had already gone above and beyond what any normal person could be expected to do, given the situation. He'd helped her escape and stayed with her, even when they'd discovered his name hadn't been reported. This despite the fact that his father was ailing and dependent on him.

Wasn't it her bruised pride and ego making her want to leave now? Wasn't she smarter than that?

Liz sighed and put her pathetic plastic bag down. Logically, she knew that staying was the best thing to do, but she still felt apprehensive. Once again, she found herself pacing back and forth in the living room, filled with a restless energy. Her eyes alighted on the toolbox, still sitting by the front door.

Well, if nothing else, the kitchen faucet would get fixed.

CHAPTER THIRTY-TWO

ALEX DIDN'T THINK the afternoon could drag on any longer. From the moment he'd followed Cynthia through the front door of the lakeside rental, he'd been on edge. Relief at not finding Liz in the house or on the property had been fleeting. He only hoped she was out on a walk and nothing bad had happened to her.

During their walk-through, he had practically squirmed at all the evidence that the house had been recently occupied. None of the dust covers were on the furniture in the living room. The air in the bathroom felt faintly humid from his shower that morning, and the kitchen still smelled like coffee.

As they reached the back door, Alex hazarded a look at Cynthia to see if she was noticing any of the details that were screaming at him. She seemed mercifully oblivious. Standing in the yard, he began to hope that he'd dodged a bullet with her, but then she turned and he noticed her expression had grown dark.

She sighed and pulled out her phone, her lips pursed in irritation. "I swear, this new cleaning company is just as bad as the last one." Covering the phone with one hand, she sent him an apologetic look. "I'm sorry about the state of the house. I promise I will make sure it's up to standard by the time I put it up for rent."

Shit, he was going to get people fired if he didn't say something. "Wait." Alex put a hand on her elbow, urging her to pull the phone down from her ear. "The truth is, I've been staying here. I was hoping you wouldn't notice."

One of her carefully plucked eyebrows winged up. Before she could say anything, Alex continued, "Look, I know I probably should have said something earlier, but I didn't want my dad to feel guiltier than he already does. The truth is, I'm happy to be able to take care of him. But every once and a while, I need to get away and unwind."

Cynthia's expression softened. For a brief moment, Alex could see the young girl he had once dated. She stepped closer, placing a hand on his chest. "I know it's been hard. You don't have to go through this alone, you know."

Alex stepped back and ran a hand through his hair. Here was the tricky part. He didn't want to piss her off, but he also didn't want her to think there was any chance of them getting back together.

He headed back to the car. They'd both put their seatbelts on when she sniffled, then let out a huge sneeze. He was thankful that it broke a potentially awkward moment between them. "It looks like your cold is getting worse. Why don't we skip the last two property tours? It's obvious you aren't feeling well, and I'm afraid I've already taken a large portion of your day."

"Oh, that's very kind of you, but I promise you I'm fine. If you're not up to seeing the last two properties today, maybe we could just stop for a late lunch or something. We could go over a few more details..." She reached across the console and placed her hand on his knee. "Or, we could just unwind after a long day of work."

Alex coughed and shifted a little more towards the door, dislodging her hold on him. "No, I'm sorry. I appreciate you taking the time out of your busy day, but I actually had a few other things planned before Dad roped me into this."

Cynthia moved to grip the steering wheel with both hands

and he wondered if he'd just offended her. He remembered that up until the cottage, they'd actually been getting along fine. He grimaced and ran a hand through his hair. "Look, I didn't mean for that to sound…"

She shot him a huge, painfully fake grin and shook her head. "Nope, no need to apologize. I'm glad we could put your father's mind at ease. Hopefully I've managed to convince you that everything is under control, recent events notwithstanding."

Her voice had cooled considerably and there was a barely concealed edge in the undertone. The least he could do was reassure her of her job. "You have, Cynthia, and I appreciate it. It's a relief to know it was just a fluke. Obviously, you know your stuff. In fact, you have me thinking I may be jumping the gun by insisting Dad should consider selling his properties."

Her next smile seemed to be a little more genuine as she pulled up to the curb in front of his father's house. "I'm glad to hear it. I know it must be tough watching his health decline, but I hope you reconsider your stance. It wouldn't be too much work for you to manage these properties, especially with me here."

Alex pinched the nose of his bridge and closed his eyes for a moment. It didn't help knowing other people were noticing his father's health declining and could see the way things were going. "I have to admit, it was never my plan to stay in Bath permanently, but lately it hasn't been as hard picturing myself settling down here. I'm not sure this is as temporary a move as I'd originally thought."

He didn't notice the satisfied gleam that entered Cynthia's eyes at his announcement. "I'm glad to hear that I may be able to convince you to stay in town longer."

The implication of her words had Alex feeling cramped. Suddenly the front seat of her car felt too small and intimate. He'd been thinking about Liz as the reason why he'd started to think about establishing a life here in Maine, not implying Cynthia had anything to do with it. Unfortunately, there wasn't any way to clarify what he meant without making the conversation more difficult than it already was. He couldn't reveal the fact that he wanted a relationship with the Bath police department's "person of interest."

Suddenly, it felt imperative that he get back to her.

Alex reached for the door and exited with hardly a glance in her direction. "Thanks again for taking me to see the properties. I'll discuss things with my father and see you later." He barely heard Cynthia say good-bye before he closed the door and was sprinting up to the house.

*

The shadows were already stretching across the street by the time he'd settled his father in for the evening. He was relieved when he was finally able to pull his father's sedan into the garage and make his way up the front path to the lake house.

All the curtains were pulled tight across the windows. The place looked empty from the outside. He let himself into the front room and was relieved to see the light on in the kitchen. A muttered curse drifted towards him, followed quickly by a bang.

What did it say about him that finding Liz lying on the floor with half her torso under the sink wasn't even surprising? In fact, standing there looking down at her sneaker-clad feet, it felt nearly normal.

"Whatcha working on?"

Liz squealed and sat up, smacking her head on the edge of the cabinet. "Owww, dammit! You're not supposed to sneak up on me like that!"

He chuckled, which earned him another scowl. "Sorry. Here, let me help you up."

Liz rubbed her forehead and climbed to her feet. "No, it's fine. I didn't realize how late it had gotten."

"What are you doing down there, anyway?"

She shrugged and gestured weakly towards the sink. "Just thought I'd see if I could do anything about the faucet dripping, which then led to me taking a look at your garbage disposal."

Damn, she looked good. All day Alex had been thinking about coming home to her. Now, it was all he could do not to wrap his arms around her. He took a step closer, but stopped as she pivoted away from him and turned the water on.

"See? All fixed." She stared at the water like it was the most fascinating thing in the world.

"Liz?" He reached out to her, but again she turned and sidled away from him.

She grabbed for a glass and filled it with water. "So, how was your day?"

Alex frowned. It was so hard understanding her moods sometimes. One minute they seemed fine, then the next...he shook it off. "It went well enough. My dad cornered me into touring his properties with Cynthia, which was fine up until she headed for this house. I about lost my shit when I realized where we were going."

The tension he had sensed in Liz evaporated instantly. Her stiff shoulders and back sagged slightly in relief. "I know."

He paused. "You knew we came by today? Damn, Liz, I was so afraid she'd discover you were here. When we didn't see you, I assumed you'd gone for a walk around the lake like we'd talked about."

"Another five minutes and she probably would have found me. I was just coming up from the basement when I heard the car door slam outside. Did she say anything about the toolbox by the front door?

"I told her I was staying here."

"Alex! Why would you do that?"

"I didn't have much of a choice. She noticed something was up the minute she walked through the door. I told her that, with my dad being so sick, I was using the place to unwind once in a while. I'm sure she bought it.

"Where were you? I half expected to see a pair of sneakers poking out from behind the curtains or under the bed."

"I ran and hid behind the tree in the backyard. After about fifteen minutes of crouching there, I started feeling silly. In fact, I began second guessing myself so much that I almost walked back into the house. It's a good thing you came out when you did."

He winced. "That would have been terrible timing."

"Tell me about it. You mentioned picking up your dad's car this morning, but we never discussed what kind it was. I thought it might be your and felt foolish for hiding."

"This business of running from the authorities is hard, huh?" The comment had been meant to lighten the mood, but wound up having the opposite effect.

Liz crossed her arms and leaned against the counter. Alex could tell she was debating whether or not to say something more. He waited her out. She gave her attention to the table, to the stove, to the sink, and then finally to him. "So, um...that's all today was with Cynthia? Just property management for your dad?"

Alex had to admire the courage it had taken for her to ask him that, despite the thread of underlying vulnerability in her voice. He took a step forward, his body mere inches from hers. "That's all it was. Just property management for my dad."

She sucked in a breath and held it for a moment before slowly releasing it. "And you and Cynthia..."

Alex placed both hands on the counter to either side of her waist and slowly leaned closer. "There is no me and Cynthia."

Liz opened her mouth to ask another question, but he was done giving her words. Alex swooped down and covered her lips with his, capturing her tiny gasp of surprise and letting it feed his own desire. For once, he'd let his actions do the talking for him.

Gratification swept through him when he felt her respond,

eagerly molding her body to his own. Her arms snaked around his neck and he could feel her fingers weave into his hair. Clenching his hands at her hips, he drew her closer, willing her to feel how much he wanted her.

CHAPTER THIRTY-THREE

HIS KISS COMPLETELY took over her senses. Instinct had her reaching to control the situation or risk going up in flames. She pressed herself more firmly along the length of him. He was so tall that she had to stand on her tiptoes in order to reach his mouth. Liz ran her hands through his hair and pulled him back, letting him know that she was going to set the pace.

Her lips brushed softly along his, moving from one corner of the mouth to the other. Other than his mouth parting on an inhale, he didn't move. His willingness to let her take control was all the invitation she needed. Deepening the kiss, she let her tongue tangle with his. Moaning, he pulled her roughly against him. His strong fingers trailed up the side of her waist.

Deciding they'd do better sitting down, Liz grabbed him by his shirt and led him into the living room. She pushed him down on the couch. Alex reached for her, drawing her between his legs. "Wouldn't it be better if we moved to the bedroom?"

She acknowledged to herself that it probably would be, but knew she couldn't afford to get too comfortable with this man. Her body was already at risk, she wouldn't let him near her heart. "Shh." Leaning down, she kissed him again before grabbing the hem of his shirt and ripping it over his head.

Yes. This is what she wanted. He looked like a golden Greek god. Slowly, she sank down between his legs, kneeling on the floor in front of him. Her hands spanned his broad shoulders before roaming over his hard muscles. Unable to resist any longer, she leaned forward and licked one hard, male nipple, exalting the way his breath caught in his throat. Her tongue traced along the pectoral muscle in his chest. Liz could feel his heartbeat race beneath her lips and smiled. She loved being able to affect him like this.

Alex sent shivers through her body as he gently traced the curve of her cheek before following it down the length of her neck. Delicious heat pooled at her core as she felt his bulge against her belly.

Need was combustible.

Hers had been lying dormant for years, waiting for that one moment to ignite her entire system. The spark of his awareness was intoxicating and revved her entire being to full throttle. Previous encounters were mere wisps of smoke compared to the all-consuming fire currently heating her blood.

His muscles tensed as she slowly made her way down to the ridges along his abdomen. She massaged his thighs, enjoying the way his legs spread further for her. His arousal pushed proudly against the inside of his zipper, begging to be released. She pressed her mouth against the prominent bulge and blew hot breath through his jeans. Alex groaned, his head falling back to the couch.

She had the power to make him lose control. She, Little Lizzie, the-flat-as-a-board, grease monkey, could hold the heat and strength of his desire in her hands.

Her fingers fumbled at the waistband of his pants. "Alex."

"Hmm?"

"You're wearing too many clothes." He chuckled and lifted his hips, letting her drag his pants and boxers off of him in one fell swoop. His erection sprang forward, unapologetically eager.

"Better?"

Liz soaked in his broad shoulders, the contours of his chest, and the proud, jutting proof of his desire. The thought of tasting him had her licking her lips. She looked up to find Alex watching her with hooded eyes. She could see that he knew what she was thinking and watched him swell even more.

Liz sat up and, never breaking eye contact with him, opened her mouth. Alex sucked in a sharp breath as his cock jumped in anticipation. Leaning forward, she gently – almost delicately – sampled him.

Wetting the palm of her hand, she carefully gripped his base, holding him directly in front of her lush mouth but not – quite – touching. The moment stretched until neither of them could stand it anymore. Ever so lightly, she brushed the soft inside of her lips over the head of his cock, letting him feel her breath on his sensitive skin. Teasing him until he was straining towards her, his flesh begging for her full attention.

She was greedy for the taste of him, eager to feel him filling her wet, hot mouth. Wrapping her lips around the head of his dick, she slid him fully in, moaning as he hit the back of her throat.

Looking up through her lashes, Liz was gratified to see his head had dropped to the back of the couch. His Adam's apple bobbed as he groaned her name. He blindly threaded his fingers through her hair, pleading for her not to stop.

Oh, she wasn't going to stop.

Liz began gently stroking him in a long, slow rhythm. She made her way back up the length of him, sucking him the entire way, flicking her tongue along the sensitive spot just under the tip of his head.

His hips jerked. Need urged him to take control. One hand gripped the edge of the couch while his other pressed harder on the back of her head. Liz reached up with her other hand and grabbed his hips. She held him securely in place and seated him more fully in her mouth before repeating the motion over and over again.

His back arched. After a few more hard, sure strokes she could feel his powerful thighs begin to vibrate. Her own sex throbbed for him. She loved knowing she could make him lose control and reveled in the way she affected him.

"Oh god, Liz..." Raw passion edged his voice as he tensed. She was so close to pushing him over. Giving his length another long suck, she swirled her tongue around the head. He shuddered before abruptly pulling away. Startled, she reached for him again. "Wait," he ground out. "I need to feel you."

She hesitated for a split second before reaching for the hem of her shirt and pulling it off. Liz stood, slid her pants off, then straddled his lap, eager to feel him inside of her. She took his face in her hands and let him see her desire, gratified to see it reflected back at her.

He leaned forward and kissed her neck before nipping at the delicate flesh there. Her breath caught as he trailed his mouth down and nuzzled the line between her breasts. His magical fingers traced the line between her hip and shoulder, then around her back.

Reaching down between them, she grabbed his base and positioned him. Her thighs burned as she hovered over him and teased them both by rubbing his tip around, dipping it just inside her entrance. Liz was wet and ready, she didn't know who was being tortured more, him or herself.

Steadying herself with one hand on his shoulder, Liz guided him fully into her. Lower and lower she sank until she was deliciously impaled on his shaft. She could feel him growing even harder in her. It took her a moment to adjust to his size, but she relished the way he filled her so completely.

His hands palmed her ass as she rocked her hips. Her body tingled at the friction between them. Shockwaves shot up through her core to her nipples. Her system revved, every nerve ending pulsing and throbbing. Panting filled the air as she picked up speed. He reached up and pinched her nipple between his thumb and finger, just hard enough to border on pain.

She bucked like a racecar coming off the mark.

"*Jesus*, Liz." He pistoned his pelvis up against hers, stoking the heat and tension built up in her. "Is this what you want?"

"Yes…" Her answer turned into a throaty purr as his lips moved down her jawline. He traced the sensitive tendons of her neck, pausing to lick at the sweat that had pooled in the hollow of her throat.

Pleasure and pressure built to a dizzying pitch as passion took over. Their combined desire had taken over and neither one of them were in control. Every part of her being, every molecule of her existence, was redlined as they barreled towards climax at a fever pitch.

*

Alex had never seen anything as hot as Liz in that moment. Her head thrown back, her body arched, her breasts twin points thrust up at attention. He could feel the bite of her nails in his skin as her hands gripped his shoulders for balance and she gave herself over to passion.

She was so long and compact, with whip-lean hips and the subtlest curves. He'd wanted to explore them further, to take his time with them. But then, he hadn't been expecting the way she'd taken over. Her silken thighs wrapped around his waist, securing him more than any restraint ever could.

He was at her whim, at her mercy.

And he was loving every second of it.

Thought fled as Alex felt her inner muscles begin to tighten around him in a vise grip. Her heat and scent were everywhere, surrounding him, intoxicating him. He thrust his hips up, driving himself into her, needing to fill her with every part of himself.

Together they pushed the throttle and strained towards the

finish line. With a final burst of speed, her greedy little clutch milked him for every drop as they crested the hill together and soared for one shining moment.

Liz collapsed against Alex's chest, her breath tickling the side of his neck. Her nipples dragged along the sensitive skin of his chest and kept time with the rhythm of their breaths. He wrapped his arms around her and lightly stroked her back down to earth, following every dip and hollow of her vertebrae.

A sense of bliss and well-being filled his mind, the first he'd felt in months. She raised her head to look at him and he shot her a cocky grin. "Wow." Her eyes lit up at his reaction. "We've come a long way from high school, haven't we?"

He watched as a hint of caution and wariness filled her eyes. It was in direct contrast to the way she brightened her smile. "Things were different. I don't think you said more than two words to me back then."

Liz sat up and carefully began extracting herself from him. His skin chilled in her absence and Alex fought the instinct to drag her back into his arms. There was a sense of vulnerability in her that he wasn't expecting. Before he could explore it further, she was pulling back.

"Thanks for the stress relief. I'm going to go clean up."

Stress relief? He could practically see the walls being resurrected around her as she retreated back into her inner sanctum. The intimacy they'd shared moments earlier vanished. Even standing before him naked, she suddenly felt miles away.

"Um, okay. I guess I'll go get dinner started."

She barely acknowledged him with a nod, then wordlessly gathered her clothes and walked away.

Alex was left sitting on the couch confused. Despite the fact he'd just had the most mind-blowing sex of all time, he couldn't help feeling a little empty inside.

CHAPTER THIRTY-FOUR

HE SHOULDN'T HAVE had sex with her.

It's not that he hadn't wanted to. He'd wanted to ever since he'd walked into Olivia's kitchen and seen her taking the dishwasher apart. But he should have realized it would further complicate an already complicated situation. If he were smart, he would have waited until this whole situation was resolved. That way, he could have asked her out on a proper date, the way normal people did.

Irritated with himself, Alex rolled over and thumped his pillow into submission. Minutes later he was flopping onto his back. The clock on his nightstand said it was a little past three in the morning. If he didn't get to sleep soon, there was no way he'd be able to function tomorrow. The stakes were simply too high to be walking around half comatose. Staring at the ceiling, he thought about ways out of the mess they were in.

A muffled crash broke into his brooding. Every hair on the back of his neck stood at attention. Alex jumped to his feet and climbed into his pants. Slipping his shoes on, he grabbed a t-shirt before pressing his ear to the bedroom door.

The house was hushed and sleeping. Silence stretched out just long enough that Alex wondered if he'd dozed off and dreamt it. Knowing he'd never be able to rest until he confirmed everything was okay, he slowly turned the handle. The soft click of the door-knob made him wince. He stopped, listening for any indication there was someone in the house.

It was probably Liz, he thought. Some part of him was relieved to think she might be as restless as him after the events of the evening. As it was, they'd each gone to bed alone after a stilted conversation that had felt lacking on both sides.

Still. Better safe than sorry.

Alex eased the door open, thankful when the hinges didn't squeak. He paused in the doorway, letting his eyes adjust to the dimmer light in the hall. That's when he heard it, a quiet shuffling noise of careful feet stepping on carpet.

There was no reason for Liz to be walking with such caution, even factoring in the hour.

Going with his instinct, Alex crossed the hallway and carefully opened the door to Liz's room. He could barely make out the lump of her body under the covers. Taking care to fully close the door, he hunched his way to her side.

Whatever they were going to do, it would have to be quick and silent. He knew it wouldn't take long for whoever was in the house to locate the bedrooms. By then they needed to be out of there.

He hesitated for a split second before placing his hand over Liz's mouth. He could feel her lips open in protest and imagined the alarmed look on her face, but before she could struggle in earnest, he put his mouth to her ear. "Shh. There's someone in the house. We need to get out of here."

He was relieved when she nodded her head, indicating she understood. Crawling from the covers, Alex noticed she'd gone to bed dressed in her yoga pants and tank top.

Instead of trying to go out the bedroom door, Alex led her to the window. They were on the first floor and shouldn't have any trouble getting out. As they lifted the sash, they heard the door across the hall slam open.

Speed took priority over silence. Alex shoved Liz out the window. She crashed through the screen and fell into the shadows below. He hoisted himself onto the sill right as the door behind him opened. A sound, like a nail gun on steroids, chased him from through the opening. The frame burst into splinters as he jumped.

It barely registered. "Liz!"

"Over here!" She called from the left, towards the garage. Good – if they could get the car… He raced after her dark silhouette. "Shit. I don't have the keys."

They circled around, hiding behind the garage. Liz panted out the questions that were tormenting Alex. "Who was that? How did they find us?"

"I don't know. We'll have to worry about it later." He pulled her towards the path around the perimeter of the lake. "Come on. Let's keep moving."

"Wait!"

"There's no time!"

They ducked into the trees. Liz slipped off the trail and stopped. "Alex, wait!" She whispered loudly. "Don't you think he's going to assume we went down this path?"

"What do you suggest?"

Before she could answer, a dark shadow came flying out the back door. They shrunk back against a tree trunk and watched as he started towards the lake dock.

"Does this path meet up with the street?"

It was so dark that Alex could barely see Liz. He leaned closer to catch her question. "Yes. It runs around the lake. On the other side is a swimming area with a parking lot."

"Can you get there quickly?"

He didn't know what she had in mind, but he suspected he wasn't going to like it. "Why?"

"We don't have time to talk about it." He sensed rather than saw her crane her neck as she tried to figure out where the intruder had gone. "Can you do it or not?"

"I can."

"Okay. I'm going to circle back around and grab the keys to the car. You lead him down the path. I'll pick you up at the parking lot."

"Are you nuts?!" Even his whispered response sounded like a shout, but before Alex could argue further he watched as Liz crouched low and ran through the trees.

What the hell was she doing?

Helpless to do anything but follow her instructions, Alex ran. He tried to make enough noise to attract the attention of the shadowy figure who was slinking through the backyard. It was a relief when his attention turned towards the trees.

Great, now all he had to do was make sure he wasn't caught. Alex sprinted down the edge of the path, relying on his instinct and muscle memory to guide the way.

CHAPTER THIRTY-FIVE

LIZ STEPPED OVER a log and slowly made her way around the side of the house. She could hear the sound of twigs snapping as Alex drew the man's attention away from her.

This was such a stupid idea, but hopefully it was so dumb it would work. She hesitated. If she miscalculated, or the man lost interest and doubled back, then she would be screwed the minute she left cover. After glancing both ways, Liz ran for the front of the house, holding her breath the whole way.

The front door was hanging open, having been broken in. She hadn't even considered how she'd get back into the house. Slipping over the threshold, she dashed in to the kitchen and grabbed the keys off the kitchen counter.

After a brief moment of debate, she rushed back towards the bedrooms. She'd been on the run without shoes once before, and even flip flops were better than nothing. Slipping into the cheap pair of shoes, she also grabbed the cheesy sweatshirt out of the drawer.

Getting out of the house was more nerve-wracking than she expected. There was no way to know whether the intruder was still chasing after Alex or if he'd given up and come back.

No choice. Liz was going to have to chance it. She peeked out of the doorframe and strained to hear anything out of place.

Familiar night sounds of crickets and frogs filled the night air and reassured her. Liz left the doorway in a crouch and followed the edge of the driveway to the garage.

These next few steps were going to be the most dangerous. Biting her lip, she winced as the sound of the garage door opening filled the air. No going back now. Liz rolled under the door as soon as the gap was high enough. The car doors beeped as she unlocked them.

Come on, come on... she watched in her rearview mirror as the door took forever to raise. Finally! Liz threw the gear into reverse and hit the gas pedal, passing under the door with less than an inch of clearance. Looking behind her, she kept one hand on the steering wheel and sped out of the driveway.

A pop and a loud crack reverberated throughout the car. Liz instinctively ducked. "Holy shit!" She barely glimpsed a dark shadow racing across the back yard towards her. Blood and adrenalin surged as she slammed the car into gear and sped away. The whole right side of the windshield was a spider web of glass. Where the hell had he come from?

She didn't have time to wonder. Her heart hammered as questions raced through her mind. What if he'd managed to catch up with Alex? What if Alex was lying in the trees bleeding out? What if...? Liz ruthlessly silenced her train of thought. None of that would matter if she got caught. She had to get to the parking lot and hope for the best.

Headlights swung wildly in her rearview mirror. "Damn." Liz gasped. It was a matter of seconds before she'd miss her opportunity to lose her pursuer. Taking the next left, she wound her way through the neighborhood streets.

There was a darkened driveway up ahead that curved behind a garage. Making sure no one was in her line of sight, she pulled the car as far back from the road as possible and shut off all the lights.

The sound of her own heartbeat filled her ears as she peered out the back window. Her knuckles blanched as her fingers gripped the fabric of the seat. The heavy weight of quiet anticipation surrounded her. It was surreal how peaceful the world was outside her bubble of fear. Worst of all, waiting gave her time to think.

Having sex with Alex had been a mistake.

Dinner last night had been a tense and overly polite affair. What conversation they managed was forced and uncomfortable. She cringed at the memory of it. How many times had she answered 'nothing' when he'd asked her what was wrong? Enough times that he'd finally stopped asking and they'd sat in strained silence.

She knew it was her fault.

The problem was, there *wasn't* anything technically wrong. They'd been amazing together. Better than Liz could have ever dreamed. Which is saying something since she'd done quite a bit of dreaming in that department.

The chemistry between them was explosive. Maybe a little too combustible, actually. That was part of the, well...if not a problem, then certainly her discomfort.

He was too close to breaching her walls. And too strong. And too kind. Not at all like the bully of her past, the role that she'd designated for him in her mind.

And she couldn't keep her thoughts in order around him. Or control the feelings he invoked in her.

She didn't like not being in control. She didn't like not knowing how things worked, especially in herself.

Liz had instinctually tried to get some perspective on the situation before diving headlong into it, but her willpower had failed her. Afterwards, she'd pulled back. Of course, Alex being Alex, he'd called her on it. Which left them sleeping across the hall from each other and both going to bed, if not angry, then certainly irritated.

*Please be okay, please be okay...*the image of him being chased through the woods tormented her. Had she made a mistake?

Should they have stayed together? At the time, all she could think about was not losing the meager resources they'd managed to find while on the run. But was a car and a cheap pair of flip-flops going to cost Alex his life?

Liz bounced her knee impatiently and forced herself to count to five hundred. She was about to turn the key and head to the parking lot when an engine's deep rumble approached. The shadow of a vehicle skulked past. He'd turned off his headlights, but the son of a bitch was still hunting her.

Who the hell was this guy? How had he found them? Liz thought back to the events of the day. Maybe they'd been too quick to dismiss Cynthia's involvement. She was the only other person who knew Alex was staying at the house. The fact that this intruder had shown up on the same night was too great of a coincidence to ignore.

Holding her breath, she holed up a while longer as he passed by the driveway again. He never stopped or paused. Hoping she'd waited long enough, Liz started the car but left her own lights off.

It only took a few minutes to reach the parking lot. The gravel crunched under her tires as she swung around the perimeter, taking cover by the trees. She was about to get out and search for Alex when a figure stumbled into view.

The moonlight glinting off his blonde hair was all the confirmation she needed that it was Alex rushing forward. Relief stabbed her in the heart. He wrenched the door open and climbed into the passenger seat.

"You damn fool! You had me scared to death!" Before she could respond, he kissed her, plunging into her mouth and possessing her completely. The whole night – which had become impossibly crazy, confused, and dangerous – stopped. Here, for one brief, shining moment was peace and reprieve. It felt like standing in the eye of a hurricane.

Alex held her face in his hands and leaned his forehead against hers. Neither of them spoke. He traced his finger along her cheek-bone and down along the length of her jaw before pulling back. He gazed at the windshield, assessing the damage there. "When I heard the gunshot..." He ran a hand through his hair and turned back to face her. "Promise me you won't do that again."

"I reacted and did what I thought I had to do. I'm sorry." She gestured to the ruined glass before checking the rearview mirror and pulling out of the parking lot. "Things got a bit out of control."

He scoffed. "A bit? If I wasn't so happy to see you alive I'd strangle you. Dammit!" Alex slammed his hand on the glove box. "How the hell did he know where to find us?"

Liz hesitated to verbalize her theory, hoping he would come to the same conclusion she had. She didn't have to wait long.

"Cynthia."

She sighed with relief, glad that he was going to be reasonable. "I'm afraid so, yes. She and Josh must be connected in some way. I still have a hard time believing she's the one calling the shots, though. Josh answering to any woman seems unlikely."

Alex blanched. "She was at my dad's house, Liz."

"Do you think she would harm him? Should we go there right now?"

His shoulders hunched, the anger and stress vibrating off of him. He took a deep breath. "I don't think she would harm him. I'm guessing she was there to keep an eye out for me. In fact, it may be safer for all of us if I keep my distance from him at this point."

"Okay." Liz checked her rearview mirror. "If it makes you feel any better, Cynthia may be a raging bitch, but I don't think she's the type of person to turn violent."

Alex nodded. "I think you're right. Our best bet is to get to the bottom of this and figure out who is in charge. So, what's our next move?"

"I've been giving it a lot of thought. I think we should go back to Peter and see if he's changed his mind about testifying."

"Come on, Liz. Do you really think that's going to accomplish anything? I know he's your friend, but he's a wreck."

"He's also our best hope!" Liz gripped the steering wheel and took a moment to consciously ease her foot off the gas pedal. Being pulled over for speeding wouldn't help matters.

Alex didn't respond to her outburst. After counting to ten, Liz tried again. "Why are you so sure it won't work? Peter's had some time to think it over. I'm sure I can get through to him this time."

Exasperated with his continued silence, she asked, "Fine, what do you think we should do?"

"I'm not saying going back to Peter is a terrible idea, but we have gone that route once. Let's try a new approach. Don't get mad, but I was thinking we should go to Paul and see what he has to say about the whole situation."

Her shoulders and neck tensed, but before she could open her mouth to argue, Alex raised his hands. "Wait, now…hear me out, Liz."

The words she wanted to say burned on her tongue, but she let him continue. "I'm not saying he's involved in all of this."

"Good, because he's not." Liz's chin jutted out into a stubborn point. "Besides, Olivia said they've already questioned him."

"True, but if you could talk it out together, compare notes about what you've seen, and add the details of what we've been through, we might all be able to come up with something new. You two know that garage better than anybody else. If there was any evidence that something had been going on, you'd be the ones to recognize it."

She relaxed her defensive stance and considered his words for a moment. "Okay, that's not a terrible idea. But how would we even get ahold of him? If the police are looking at him that closely, it won't be easy to avoid detection."

"I don't know. I think we should go to his house and then assess the situation."

She wasn't entirely convinced going to Paul was the best course of action, but she knew part of that was because she couldn't believe he'd have anything to do with the situation she currently found herself in.

Maybe Alex was right. Maybe she was letting her own biases cloud her judgment. On the other hand, she was worried about her old friend, Peter. He hadn't looked good the last time they'd talked. This would give her an excuse to check in on him. "Let's try Peter first." She raised her hand as Alex began to protest. "If I can't get him to come around, we'll do it your way and go talk to Paul."

CHAPTER THIRTY-SIX

ALEX DIDN'T BOTHER to reply, knowing not to push his luck. He was relieved she was willing to consider his plan. Well, at least for the time being. He'd never met another person that could be so damn exasperating. Her moods were as fickle as the New England weather.

Speaking of which, he reached up and flipped the radio on, hoping to catch the forecast. If they were going to be running around, it would be good to be prepared for once.

"To recap this breaking news. Police are searching for two "people of interest" in connection with the death of a white, male in his mid-twenties, who was found today at an apartment complex in Brunswick. Investigators say the male and female are wanted for questioning. If you have any information about their whereabouts, you are urged to contact the authorities immediately. We'll update you with any new developments as soon as they are available."

It took him a moment to register the words, but when he did, they seemed to echo in his mind. "Damn."

"You don't think..."

Alex shook his head and turned the dial, hoping to catch another news segment. Moments later it was confirmed. "Earlier this morning the body of a man was found at an apartment complex located here in Brunswick, Maine. His death is suspected to be a homicide. Ordinarily a quiet college town, there has been a notable rise in drug-related crimes over the last year. Two suspects are wanted for questioning by the police. One is thought to be related to a drug case from earlier in the week; the other is thought to be an accomplice. If you have any information regarding this case, contact police immediately. We've posted a link to the security footage captured from a building across the street. Please check our website for more details."

The tears running down her cheeks twisted something deep in his chest. She swiped them angrily away. "I'm sorry, Liz."

Her shoulders were bowed. It took her another moment before she managed to respond. "Do you think they killed him because we were there?"

"No." He shook his head vehemently, as if to strengthen his assertion. When Liz didn't respond, he shook it again. "No, Liz. I think Peter was running with a dangerous crowd and it finally caught up with him. Whether we visited him or not, they would have considered him a loose end."

At her gasp, Alex winced. "I'm sorry. I know that wasn't all he was. But that's how these guys – whoever they are – would think of him."

Some part of her must have come to the same conclusion, because for once, she didn't argue. Drying the last of her tears, she sat back in her seat and glanced in her side mirror.

He did the same. "Is anyone following us?"

"Not that I can tell." She squared her shoulders. "Well, I guess we only have one option now."

"I'm sorry. If there was any other way…"

"No, I know." They drove for a moment in silence, each lost in their own thoughts. Suddenly, Liz said, "I hate this. How did my life spiral so out of control? After my parents died, I told myself I never wanted to feel that helpless again. I've spent my whole life solving the problems around me and repairing what needed to be fixed – maintaining order. But this!

"This is beyond anything I could have expected. Everything we've done the last few days has been a reaction to some guy in charge of a drug ring, of all things. How can we defend ourselves when we don't even know who is calling the shots? We need to figure out a way to get a handle on this situation." Her fingers flexed on the steering wheel. Under her breath she added, "Because, I don't think I can stand playing defense like this for much longer."

"I know the feeling."

She shifted in her seat to face him, before returning her focus back on the road. "You know we do have one other option."

"Liz."

"I could turn myself in. Something Olivia said has me wondering if we've been going about this all wrong. Running only serves to make me look guiltier."

"No, you can't do that. What if there are more dirty cops? The stakes are even higher than they were before. It's not just drug trafficking and distribution. This is murder."

She shuddered. "That's exactly my point. Alex, we've been in over our heads since the beginning, and that was before they killed anybody.

"I have to believe that Mason and this MDEA agent, Matt whoever, will be able to protect me. I need to tell him my story, and trust he'll understand why I didn't come in right away."

"That's assuming you even get a chance to talk to him. What if they throw you in a holding cell and something happens before you have the opportunity to meet with him?"

"Mason is there, he knows the situation. I know he'll do everything he can to protect me. Besides, this is the biggest case the department is working on right now, I'll be a priority."

Alex mulled her words over in his mind. As much as he wanted to, he couldn't fault her logic. "I know it doesn't make sense, but my gut is telling me it would be a mistake to surrender right now."

"I realize turning myself in would affect you, too. It'll be even harder now that they're trying to pin Peter's death on us, especially if the security footage shows you entering the building with me." She paused, measuring her words. "I'd understand if you wanted to hang back until this is all cleared up."

Her words sliced him to the core. He stiffened. "What is it going to take for you to realize I'm in this until the end?" His hands lay fisted in his lap. "I'm not saying this because I'm worried about my name being dragged in the mud. Judging by that newscast, we're long past that point. I'm. Not. Leaving. You. You should know this by now."

Her eyes softened before gripping the steering wheel a little more firmly. "I wish – I wish things could be different..." She shook her head in confusion. "How could I have missed all of this happening right under my nose?"

"You're not the only one," Alex pointed out.

An edge of doubt seeped into Liz's voice where there had only been frustration. "Could Paul have seen something and not tell me? Maybe he was trying to protect me."

"Don't you think we should ask him?"

"You mean before we go to the police?"

"I don't see how waiting a few more hours to turn ourselves in could do any more harm, do you? It might be our only chance to get the unvarnished truth from him without our lawyers present."

"Fine. Let's give it a shot."

CHAPTER THIRTY-SEVEN

PAUL TURNED INTO the quiet neighborhood and pulled his car into the cracked driveway of a small ranch house. It had been another long, harrowing day at the police station. All he wanted to do was go inside and bury his head under a pillow.

They had held him for hours, asking him the same questions over and over again. About the garage, the cars coming in, their customers, what his involvement was with the heroin they'd found, and if his nephew was a drug user. Even Mason had doubted some of the answers that he'd given.

That had been bad, but it had been far worse once their inquiry turned to Liz. The MDEA agent had demanded to know what her role in the drug ring was. Paul's heart broke, knowing her name was being dragged through the mud. He wondered if her reputation would ever be able to recover from an experience like this.

He truly hoped so.

Paul unlocked the door and let himself into the dark house. After fifty some-odd years, it was still hard to believe he was finally a homeowner. When his nephew had come to stay with him a few months ago, it had become readily apparent that his apartment was too small for two people. Providing Jimmy with a place to stay had been the best decision he'd made in a long time.

With the sparse furniture, and the giant television taking over one wall, it was obviously a bachelor pad. But at least, with the shoes by the door and the coats in the closet, it was also starting to feel a little more like a home.

He flipped on the hall light and took a moment to hang up his jacket before making his way to the bathroom. It was only after he emerged that he noticed a chair in the kitchen was lying on its back. Milk dripped across the table from where a half-eaten bowl of cereal was upended. He watched as it pooled on the cheap linoleum floor.

Fear coursed through him, his hands damp with sweat. "Jimmy?"

The only answer was the sound of the refrigerator turning on and humming into the quiet. Paul's heart dropped at the implications. Quickly, he made his way to the back bedroom, telling himself not to jump to conclusions.

His nephew's room felt like a cave on the best of days. When he'd moved in a few months ago, he'd immediately installed blackout shades. Large glass and chrome desks covered two walls, dedicated to his computer equipment and monitors. Almost as an after-thought, a twin-sized bed was shoved into a corner. It was hard to tell if any violence had happened from the sheets tossed in disarray, since Paul knew the bed was hardly ever made.

The first notes of "Welcome to the Jungle" pierced the silence. It was his custom ringtone for his nephew. Jimmy had programmed it into his phone as a joke. Paul fumbled the device out of his pocket.

"Jimmy?"

"No. But if you want to see him again, you'll do exactly as I say."

Paul's worst fear loomed before him, taking the shape of stark reality. "If you lay a hand on him…"

"That," the caller interrupted, "will be up to you." Whoever was on the other end was using a voice modulator to mask their identity. The cold electronic tone further infused the exchange with sinister overtones.

Panic grew in his chest. "Please, don't hurt him. Just tell me what I need to do."

Paul grabbed a pen and wrote down the address given to him. Two minutes later, he was once again rushing out of the house. The slowly drying pool of milk was the only witness to his passing.

CHAPTER THIRTY-EIGHT

LIZ WOVE THROUGH various neighborhoods and tried to stay away from the main streets. A route that would normally take twenty minutes took closer to an hour. Light had already begun to blossom on the horizon before they neared their destination. She pulled the car to the side of the road about a mile away. Neither of them talked as they made their way through the woods towards Paul's place.

Hidden in the trees, they monitored the house for a while. The air was dewy with fresh promise. A few birds were chirping in the branches above them, greeting the morning with optimism. Liz let her eyes wander over the small, postage stamp-sized front yard that she knew Jimmy mowed weekly. His car was in the driveway, but all the windows were dark.

After another moment of quiet observation, she asked, "Now what?"

Alex watched the area for another heartbeat before he answered. "Well, I don't see anybody." They both continued to crouch in the shadow of the trees, straining their ears for anything suspicious.

She couldn't see or hear anything unusual, but Liz had a bad feeling. "I don't like this, Alex. It feels too risky."

He turned to her, his eyes intense. "We need answers, right? This is how we can get some."

She shook her head. "But it's not just the cops I'm worried about. I mean, in the list of worst case scenarios, they're actually preferable. At least let me go in there with you."

Alex let out a sigh of exasperation that put her hackles up. "We went over this. I'm just going to see if he's there and let him know we want to talk. After that, if the situation is safe, you guys can meet."

The plan sounded so simple. She hoped it could be that easy. "Okay, fine. We'll do it your way."

Liz tried to ignore the little smile of victory that crossed over Alex's face. He grabbed her hand and gave it a squeeze. "Don't worry. This will work." His expression got more serious. "Just promise me you'll stay here and out of sight until I get back, okay? Don't give me a heart attack like last time."

She rolled her eyes, but agreed.

Liz kept Alex in sight as he picked his way around the perimeter of the backyard. It took him ten minutes before she lost sight of him. Now the real waiting began.

She'd just settled into a more comfortable position, when a long, high-pitched wail filled the air. Her pulse hammered in her throat as she jumped to her feet. *Oh, no...*

From her vantage point, she could see the red and blue lights of multiple cop cars reflecting in the windows around her. They had been so careful! How had they not noticed the place was being watched?

Needing to see what happened, Liz crept through the trees in the opposite direction Alex had taken, hoping no one would see her passing.

What she saw had her heart dropping to her stomach.

Alex was bent over the hood of a police cruiser, his hands cuffed behind him. She wondered if he was experiencing flashbacks from a few nights before. A long-faced, lanky man who was taller than Alex walked up, wearing a slightly rumpled suit and a five o'clock shadow. He pulled Alex upright and exchanged a few words before helping him into the backseat.

That must be the agent she'd heard so much about, Matt Hagen. She hoped he was as interested in finding the truth as he was in climbing the ladder over at the MDEA. Otherwise, they were screwed.

Liz struggled to fight off the voice screaming for her to step out of the woods and turn herself in with Alex. All she wanted to do was stop this entire maddening situation.

But she couldn't do it. Liz had promised him that she'd follow through with their plan before going to the police. Not only that, but with Alex taken in for questioning, she knew their version of the story would be relayed. She hoped he'd have a chance to tell it before someone tried to stop him.

She had to stay out of the cop's reach, protecting their interests until this whole thing could be cleared up.

Finally, the three squad cars departed. Their sirens had been silenced but their lights continued to flash. Liz was surprised they hadn't knocked on Paul's door, or dragged him in for questioning. Then she knew, Paul wasn't even there. It had been an elaborate setup all along.

Liz debated going in to check right then, but decided it would be more prudent for her to wait until things had settled down. She doubted anybody else was watching the house, but it was better to be safe.

CHAPTER THIRTY-NINE

LIZ MUTTERED A silent curse as her pants snagged on the top of the fence. Why did these things always look so much easier in the movies? She grunted as she landed in a flower bed below.

She crouched in the shadow of the fence, waiting to see if anybody had heard her. It had been hours before she'd wound up the courage to approach the house. Surveillance must have gotten what they'd come for, because as far as she could tell, they hadn't come back. Her joints were too stiff to wait any longer. She had to move.

Her heart pounded as she approached the back door and dug the spare key out from under a rock. She slipped into the laundry room and promptly stumbled over a basket left in front of the dryer.

Oh yeah, you're real sneaky, Liz. Frozen in fear, she stood and counted her breaths, straining to hear any noise inside the house. All was quiet, so she made her way towards the hall.

"Paul? Jimmy?"

Nothing stirred. Would they have brought Paul back to the station? That seemed like an excessively long time to question somebody. Had he been arrested, after all?

Liz strode into the kitchen, feeling more confident now that she was in the house. Her new-found hope was dashed when she spotted the mess at the table. Warning bells rang in her mind. Whatever had happened didn't look voluntary.

Rushing down the hallway, she checked each room as she went. Other than a couple piles of laundry and some unmade beds, nothing seemed out of place.

Stymied by the lack of evidence, Liz made her way back to the dried puddle of milk at the kitchen table. A pad of paper sat near the overturned bowl. She picked up the pencil lying beside it and started to trace over the top page. Maybe those spy movies weren't complete fiction, after all.

She recognized the address as it slowly began to emerge. The problem was it was clear across town. It didn't seem like a very good idea to go back to the sedan they had parked a few blocks away, considering cops were probably searching for it from the moment Alex had been taken.

But Jimmy's car was sitting out in the driveway. Going back to his room, she searched the top of his dresser and bedside table with no luck. She was just about to give up when she spotted the set of keys hanging from a hook by the door.

Oh, thank goodness! The thought of stealing yet another car was unbearable, but so was walking clear across town. After a quick glance to make sure no one was visible, Liz let herself out of the house. The rattrap that Jimmy called a car had never looked so good.

It wasn't until she was a block away from the address that Liz began to doubt herself. Should she try to contact the police? After all, the people hunting her had already proven to be dangerous and willing to kill. She knew Josh certainly was, anyway.

Making her way along the sidewalk, she debated her next move. As she drew nearer, a figure stole out of the back door of the house. Not Jonesy. This guy was stocky and shorter. It was too dark to make out the person's features, but they were obviously eager to get away from the premises. Without thinking, Liz chased after him.

"Hey!" She ran across the yard in the direction the shadow was headed before finally coming to her senses. What on earth was she doing? Just this morning she'd learned Peter had been murdered. What exactly did she expect to have happen if she caught them?

She stood with her hands on her hips and gulped down large breaths of air and logic. Shaking her head, she turned back towards the house. There had to be a reason why the person was fleeing.

The back door was open and swinging, tapping the wall in the light breeze. She quashed the fear it raised in her throat. How could something so innocuous sound so sinister?

Other than the door, the house was still. The windows were dark and full of secrets. If she hadn't seen someone leaving, it would have been easy to see the place as deserted.

Liz poked her head in before stepping through the doorway. Light filtered in from the hall. She was lucky there was power, since the house itself appeared to be vacant. She found herself in the middle of an outdated kitchen with avocado green cabinets that would have been amusing if things had been different. Instead, she barely managed a wince before heading deeper into the house.

In the hallway she noticed large, brown rings that bore evidence of water damage on the plaster ceiling and walls. She entered the dim living room and instinctively searched for a switch. A ceiling fan illuminated the room. She stifled a scream as she crossed the threshold and took in the scene before her.

Paul sat tied to a chair in the middle of the room. There was blood and sweat caking the front of his shirt. His head lolled so far back that it looked like his neck was broken. Drool dripped down his chin.

She raced to his side and shook him, "Paul? Paul!" He didn't respond. His eyes were swollen shut and turning a dark purple.

He'd been beaten badly. Frantically, she lifted his eyelids, but his eyes had rolled to the back of his head.

She pressed her fingers to his neck, relieved when she found a faint, thready pulse. He coughed. Tears rushed down Liz's face as she helped to lift his head. "Paul? Paul, can you hear me?"

Liz watched as he forced his eyelids open, barely a slit, but she could see his urgency as he focused on her face. "They took Jimmy. Find him, Liz," he begged. "He doesn't have anybody else."

Paul struggled, his neck moving like a loose ball bearing. He rolled his head back towards her, trying to maintain focus. Wonder and self-loathing infused his voice. "Oh God, Liz. The rush! N-no wonder she's hooked." The last sentence trailed off into barely intelligible mumbling.

Liz leaned forward. "Hooked? Who? Who is hooked, Paul?"

Paul's eyes drifted off to a spot just beyond her shoulder. "My sister. She owed them so much money. I tried to help her. I did. They threatened to kill her if I didn't work for them." His face scrunched up with regret and guilt.

Her stomach dropped at the revelation. "You were hiding the heroin?" No, there had to be some misunderstanding.

"Secret compartments in s-s-specified vehicles." Paul began to sob. "I let them know when they could come in and stash the supply." A pained look crossed his face before the drug once again overwhelmed him.

Liz grabbed him by the shoulders and gave him a hard shake. "Come on, Paul. Don't pass out on me again. You gotta keep talking."

His eyelids fluttered, he began to mutter. "Be careful, Eliza. It's not who you'd expect. They're after you."

"What do you mean 'they'? Who did this to you?" Paul's whole body twitched violently and he began gagging. Liz realized with horror that he was choking on his own tongue.

"Paul!" She tried to lift his head, but the terrible sounds

continued. And then, just as suddenly, an ominous silence filled the room.

Reaching over his shoulder, she gave his back a hard pound. "Dammit, you are not dying on me!"

Registering what needed to be done, she blanched at the slimy process and tried not to hurt him any further. Liz gingerly pried his mouth open and pulled his tongue forward. "Ew, ew, ew…shit, Paul. This had better work!" With his air passage open, Liz moved behind him and tried to give him a modified version of the Heimlich maneuver, pressing on his chest instead of his sternum.

Nothing. The utter lack of response was infinitely worse than when he'd been choking. Somehow, she needed to get him breathing again! CPR was out of the question until she could get him untied from the chair.

Distraught, she tugged on the knots fastening him to the chair, but they were too tight. What to use? What to use? Liz made a mad dash to the kitchen, wrenching every drawer open. Seriously? Couldn't there be a knife? Scissors? Anything?

Stymied by her lack of resources, Liz rushed back into the living room. Paul's face was beginning to turn a distressing shade of blue, his stillness a dark omen. Desperate, she pushed him more forcefully than she intended. The chair fell backwards to the floor with a crash.

Liz winced as he landed on his arms, his hands trapped beneath the back of the chair. "I know that must have hurt, but you can complain to me about it later." She tilted his head back, pinched his nose, covered his mouth with hers, and blew two hard breaths in. Placing her hands in the center of his chest, she pressed down and pumped hard and fast.

"Come on, Paul, you gotta tell me who did this. Stay with me!" Each downward press pushed a puff of air from his lips. She couldn't remember if it was twenty pumps or thirty. What did it say about her that she could break out of handcuffs and steal cars, but wasn't sure about how to administer CPR? Liz counted out thirty presses and covered Paul's mouth again, all the while she kept up an unconscious litany of words.

Over and over she pressed on his chest, willing him to stay breathing. With each compression, she fought the rising tide of despair. Her surroundings, the drug ring, everything else faded into the background as she struggled to keep Paul's heart going.

He coughed. Gratitude filled Liz at the sound. The noise he emitted couldn't be construed as words, but it was obvious he was trying to say something. Liz leaned in, "I can't understand. Can you say it again?"

"I'm sorry..." He began to cry, silent tears tracking out of the corner of his eyes and into the hair at his temples. His voice took on a hazy quality. "I never meant to hurt you..."

A lump grew in Liz's chest. "Shh, whatever you did, it will be okay." Who was this withered old shell of a man that had replaced the strong, vital person she'd come to see as a second father? How had they gotten themselves in this terrible position? Emotion welled in Liz's chest. Her voice quivered as she asked, "Why didn't you tell me? I would have helped you."

He gasped as another shudder overtook him. Liz leaned forward. "Paul, no!"

CHAPTER FORTY

LIZ WASN'T SURE how long she attempted CPR. It could have been a few minutes or a few weeks, but she refused to admit defeat. His lips and fingers had turned a slight bluish color. She could feel his heartbeat slipping through her fingers. A sob bubbled up and out of her throat.

"Awww."

Liz whipped around at the sound. Dammit. It had been careless of her to forget where she was. Josh stood looking down at her from the kitchen doorway. He gave her a cruel grin. "Having a bad day?"

He stepped into the room and loomed over her. "I'm here to clean up the trash. Who knew I'd get such a bonus?" He nudged Paul's body with his toe. "You've been a hard person to track down, Liz. I gotta admit, I'm impressed."

She scrambled to her feet, wiping tears away with her sleeve. She would be damned if she'd let him see her vulnerable. "You son of a bitch!" All the hurt, anger, and grief rose up and crystallized into a solid, breathing beast within her. She lunged, satisfied to feel her nails scrape across his face and carve deep gashes across his cheek and chin.

He roared in surprise and pain, but Liz was animalistic. No longer willing or able to hold back her rage. She bucked against him, just avoiding being caught in his vise-like arms, and slammed her foot down against his instep.

Howling, he grabbed at her, this time managing to get his arms all the way around her. He lifted her off the ground, his arms squeezing hard enough to crack a rib. She thrashed from side to side, but her movements were limited with her arms pinned.

Liz screamed. She kicked her feet out, desperately hoping to find purchase in something soft and vulnerable. Her whole body twisted and jerked as she tried to free herself.

"Damn you!" Josh grunted with the effort to control her. "You fucking hellion!"

Liz tossed her head forward and caught him on the underside of his jaw, cutting off whatever else he may have said. He yelped as his jaw slammed shut on his tongue. "Bitch!"

Her forehead throbbed where it had connected with bone, but that didn't stop her struggles. The fist Josh slammed into her jaw did. Pain ripped through her cheekbone as her head snapped back on her neck. Liz slumped forward on legs no longer able to support her.

Josh flung her in a heap at his feet. He leaned down and grabbed her by the front of her shirt, twisting it at the collar so tightly that it nearly choked her. She could feel his spit as he pulled her face close to his. "I'm going to hurt you *so* bad. I'm going to take you someplace where they'll never find your body and I'm going to make you scream for days, weeks…maybe even months. You'll be begging for me to kill you by the time I'm done with you."

Liz stared into Josh's eyes and a cold spear of fear stabbed her through the heart. She was looking into the face of pure evil.

"Police! Freeze!"

Shocked, he whirled around to see two men standing in the doorway pointing their guns at him. Another officer came down the hall, his gun trained on Josh.

Liz was horrified as a mask of normalcy fell over Josh's face. He smiled and stood facing the cops, propping her up in front of him. "'Bout time you boys got here! I caught our most wanted suspect right after she murdered her partner."

"That's not true!" Liz protested. She tried to twist out of Josh's grasp, but he held on to her tightly. Instead she gestured toward Paul, still tied to the chair and lying on his back on the floor. "Please! You have to help him!"

Another man stepped in from the kitchen and walked towards them. It was the same person who had captured Alex. He seemed to be assembling something in his hands as he walked over to Paul and checked his pulse. Everybody in the room held their breath, wondering what he'd find.

"You," Hagen pointed a finger at one of the uniformed officers, "get an ambulance here now." His voice was calm and controlled, belying the tense situation. The officer immediately began calling dispatch and stepped out of the room.

Shoving the plastic applicator up Paul's nose, he pressed the plunger, and then proceeded to do the same with the other nostril. Within seconds Paul was gasping for breath. Liz couldn't help the hysterical tears streaming down her cheeks. Relief flooded her system, her own dire situation temporarily forgotten.

Another thought occurred to her. "Jimmy! They may have kidnapped Jimmy, too. Please, you have to believe me!" Liz was practically bent in half by the way Josh was holding her around her collar. She craned her neck up, trying desperately to make eye contact with the other man.

Josh clenched her shirt tighter in his fist.

Agent Hagen's voice was clear and firm, leaving no doubt about who was in charge. "Thank you, Officer Carver. You can release her. We'll take it from here."

Indignation and defeat filled Liz. Everything she and Alex had feared would happen was coming to pass. Of course they were going to believe an officer of the law, one of their own. In a he said / she said situation, Liz was never going to win against him.

Her frustrated gaze sought out this new man and was surprised to see a flicker of kindness and compassion cross his face. "You don't understand, he's evil! He's the one who is behind all of this! Please. If you lock me up, he'll kill me."

He took her firmly by the elbow and guided her to one of the officers. "Will you please escort Ms. Harper to the car?"

"Yes, sir, Agent Hagen."

Liz turned back towards Josh as she was led away from him. The smug little smile on Josh's face was infuriating.

Her hands fisted by her sides. Dammit, the bastard was going to get away with it. The young officer ushered her out the kitchen door.

CHAPTER FORTY-ONE

AGENT HAGEN STEPPED up to Josh and gave him a pat on the back as if to congratulate him, and then, in one fluid motion, disarmed him.

"Hey!"

"Josh Carver, you are under arrest. You have the right to remain silent. Anything you say can and will be used against you…"

"What the hell are you doing? Is this some kind of joke?"

Anger, raw determination, and something that looked like disgust crossed Hagen's face. "The only joke I see here is you wearing that uniform, asshole. You're a disgrace to this entire unit."

Cold ferocity infused his voice. "Our investigation has suspected for some time that there might be a link to the drug ring working within the department. I went back through the files of past drug activity for this department. You know what I discovered? You were the officer working nearly every single case."

"We also discovered a partial fingerprint – one of yours – at the murder scene over in Brunswick. A crime scene that was out of your jurisdiction, which means you had no official reason to be there."

"But it was interviewing Alex this morning that truly got us on the right track. He had a lot of interesting things to say about what happened that night. Accusations that had us checking the

GPS tracker on your patrol vehicle. Imagine our surprise when your log proved that you had been at the garage hours before the time you stated in your report."

"This is all circumstantial! I told you that I'd noticed some suspicious activity at that location. I was on patrol. It was my duty to keep an eye on the place."

"Perhaps," Agent Hagen grinned like a shark that smelled blood. "Then how do you explain the recording?"

Josh's face blanched. "Recording?"

"Yeah. Another thing Alex mentioned was that he'd tried to record what was happening in the garage." Agent Hagen smirked as confusion and outrage warred on Josh's face. "Ah, but you destroyed his phone, didn't you? He said as much."

Hagen's voice turned almost conversational. "You know, I lost my phone once. Left it in the back seat of a taxi. By the time I realized what had happened, somebody had stolen it." He moved closer, crowding the other man. "I was bummed. It had pictures of the Red Sox game I'd attended the weekend before." He stepped back and continued circling Josh. "But then a great thing happened."

Suspicious of where the conversation was going, Josh was hesitant to ask. Hagen waited, letting Josh sit in silence until he couldn't stand the suspense any longer. "What happened?"

"Ever heard of the cloud?"

"The c-cloud?"

"Yeah, the cloud. There's a way to back up the photos and video you take on your phone to the cloud, instantly and automatically. Lots of people use it, including our good friend Alex Weston."

The blood drained from Josh's face. He swallowed, thinking about what must have been recorded on the damning phone. Hagen leaned in, close enough to practically whisper in his ear. "Technology is such a wonderful thing, isn't it?"

Josh reared his head back and threw his hands up to shove

the other man aside, but Hagen was expecting it. Quickly countering the move, he caught his arms and wrenched them behind him. Josh soon realized it was no use. Every cop in the room had their gun trained on him. The click of the handcuffs sounded like a death knell.

"We have enough evidence without Ms. Harper's testimony to ensure you stay behind bars for many years. We'll have even more if Paul Rowland manages to live." Agent Hagen clucked his tongue. "An ex-cop, in prison? They're going to be long, long years.

CHAPTER FORTY-TWO

LIZ SLID ONTO the vinyl seat and fought to keep the panic from rising up the back of her throat as the young cop closed the door. The bars separating her from the front seat made the space feel even smaller. Liz gripped her seatbelt and struggled to keep her breathing even.

Getting into the backseat of the police cruiser had been difficult, especially given the last time she'd been in one. At least this time she wasn't handcuffed. She watched as an ambulance swung into the driveway. Two paramedics carrying a stretcher made their way into the house.

Willing Paul to be okay, Liz focused on the red and blue lights flashing in the driveway. She saw Paul on a stretcher and being put into the ambulance. They took off moments later with their sirens blaring.

It was nearly an hour before the officer who had placed her in the back seat came back. "Is Paul going to be okay?"

The officer rushed to reassure her. "The paramedics got him stabilized and he was conscious." He turned in his seat. "I'll get a report from the doctors for you when we get back to the station." Liz felt the knot in her chest ease. She smiled back at him, appreciating the officer's empathy.

Even after everything that had happened, she was thankful

Paul would live. Some part of her sensed that resolving her feelings about him would be a long process. He'd betrayed her trust, set her on this destructive path, and ruined her reputation. Yet, despite recent events, his death would have left a gaping hole in her heart.

Why hadn't he come to her?

Liz suspected this entire incident would have her questioning her judgment for a long time. She was so cautious about who she let into her inner circle. Until yesterday, Paul would have been included in that handful of people. But now?

How could she have worked with him every day and not noticed the stress he was under? Was she so wrapped up in her own head that she'd missed the clues? What kind of friend did that make her? It was time to admit that her emotional walls caused her to fail the very people she should have been relating to.

The officer started the car. "Where are you taking me?"

"To the police station so we can take your statement."

The little knot sitting in her chest loosened slightly as he turned in the direction of the station. Hoping conversation would help cut the tension further, she asked, "How did you guys find me, anyway?"

The cop glanced in the rearview mirror before returning his attention to the road. "I'm sorry, Agent Hagen will have to give you those details. This is still an active investigation. I'm not at liberty to discuss it."

Liz leaned her head back on the seat. "I understand. Things would have ended much differently if you weren't there. I owe you my life."

"Just promise me something."

Caution entered her voice. "What's that?"

"Next time, come to the police. We're not all bad apples, you know."

"I know." She sighed and turned her head to watch the

landscape go by. "Can I ask you a question? What's going to happen to me? Do you know?"

He made a left turn into the police station's lot and parked in a spot close to the front doors. Leaning back, he turned to face Liz. "Well, they could charge you for running and evading arrest, but given the extenuating circumstances…it's only my guess mind you, but I don't think they'll be charging you with much. Especially if this whole situation leads to the apprehension of the largest drug ring in the state."

Liz smiled at him, reminded again of the fact that most officers were good people that want to help their community. "Thank you for that."

He shrugged, as if embarrassed to by his kindness. "Let's get inside. I'll set you up in an interrogation room and then Hagen will fill you in on the rest of the details."

"Am I under arrest?" Liz asked.

"No. We just have some questions to go over with you."

As she walked into the station, Liz spotted Olivia, Fiona, and Mason standing in the lobby. The last ball of tension in her shoulders eased.

"Oh, thank goodness! Liz!" Her sisters ran across the room, both wrapping their arms around her in a giant hug. She winced, but the pain in her ribs was nothing compared to the comfort of being with her sisters again. Inhaling deeply, she let their love and concern wash over her.

"We were so worried!" Fiona said, giving her an extra squeeze.

Liz returned the embrace for another moment before stepping back. "I was worried myself for a while there."

The sound of a throat being cleared caused the whole group to look over at the officer who was escorting her. He glanced apologetically at Mason. "I'm sorry to break up this reunion, but we still need to interview Ms. Harper."

Olivia's face fell in disappointment. "Even now, with Josh in custody? I thought we might be able to skip all that."

Mason put an arm around her shoulder. "We're going to have to do everything by the book, especially because we're connected. It wouldn't do to have it look like she got special treatment because of her relationship with us."

He gave Liz a reassuring look. "Don't worry. Agent Hagen has a good idea of what's happened here. He'll still want to sit down and ask you some questions – just to get the details. You should go with the officer now."

"Don't worry. I'll be okay." Liz gave her sisters another big hug. "Where's Alex?" They'd been so inseparable over the last few days that it felt strange not having him with her. Olivia and Fiona exchanged an uncomfortable look. "What?"

"I'm sorry. We haven't had a chance to tell you. Alex's father has been admitted to the hospital and is in critical condition," Fiona said.

"What?!" Liz couldn't believe it. After everything they had been through, couldn't the universe have cut him a break? "When?"

"Last night." Olivia put her arm around Liz. "Last time we checked, he was still alive, but not doing very well. We haven't gotten an update for a few hours, though."

"That's terrible."

The officer stepped forward. "Look, I know the timing is bad, but we need to get you inside."

Knowing that cooperating would get her out faster, she smiled at him. "You're right. I'm sorry. Let's do this." She turned to Olivia. "If you hear from him, let him know I'm sorry."

"Don't worry, honey. I will."

CHAPTER FORTY-THREE

THE ROOM LIZ waited in was little larger than a walk-in closet and sparsely furnished with a table and two chairs. It wasn't long before the door creaked open.

"Hello, Liz. I'm Chief Hamilton."

"Oh." Liz shook the hand he proffered. "Hi."

He smiled, setting a cup of coffee down in front of her. "You look nervous." Liz leaned against the wall as he propped a hip on the table. It didn't seem like a natural position for him, almost like he was trying too hard to appear nonchalant.

It took her a moment to realize he was expecting a response from her. "I'm just surprised to find the chief looking in on me, that's all. I would have thought somebody else would be on baby-sitting duty. Thanks for the coffee."

He chuckled. "Well, that's true. But you happen to be a part of a bigger case, and it has already gotten a lot of attention in the local news. I figured it wouldn't hurt to see how you're holding up, especially given your relationship with Mason." He leaned forward. "Besides, it was one of my men who put you in this position, and that's not something I take lightly."

Liz shuddered at the memory of Josh holding her by the collar, his eyes gleaming with malice. "It's not something I'm likely to forget anytime soon, that's for sure."

"I understand you overheard him talking to somebody else on his phone while in the garage. Any idea who that might have been?"

She let her head lean back against the wall and looked up towards the ceiling. "No. I've been wracking my brains for any clues, but that's the one thing neither Alex nor I could figure out."

Chief Hamilton stood up and brushed his pants off. "Well, that's a shame. Maybe when things calm down you'll figure it out. Sometimes all it takes is remembering one small detail for everything to come to light."

Liz nodded. "I hope you're right."

He walked towards the door, but turned at the last minute. "By the way, where'd you stash the phone? Neither you or Alex had it, so I'm guessing you must have put it somewhere safe?"

"It's in the warehouse office. I stashed the parts separately. You'll find Josh's gun there, too. I'm sorry, I should have mentioned it earlier. I wasn't trying to withhold evidence."

"Don't worry about it. You've been under a lot of stress." With that, the chief let himself out. Liz went back to rehashing the events of the last few days. It was over an hour before Matt Hagen came in to see her. By that point, she'd paced every corner of the room and her nerves were frayed.

Hagen walked through the door looking as tired as she felt. He set a cup down on the table and took a long swallow from his own. "Please, take a seat, Ms. Harper. I wasn't sure how you took your coffee. Oh, it looks like someone has already taken care of you."

"The chief was nice enough to bring me a cup, but thanks. I can always use more." Liz fought not to wring her hands. "Have you found Jimmy?"

"Yes, we found him. He was bound and gagged in one of the bedroom closets in the house Paul was in, but was otherwise unharmed."

Liz sank into her chair. Instantly, her knee began to bounce. "What can you tell me about Paul?"

He sat in the chair across from her and leaned forward. "Well, quite a bit, actually. But before we get to that, I have some news."

She tensed, unsure if she could handle anything else bad happening.

Seeing her reaction, Hagen hurried to continue. "Paul was admitted to the hospital and is expected to make a full recovery. He has agreed to testify in exchange for a plea bargain. We've already heard his version of events and have a greater understanding of what happened and why."

Liz gulped and blinked back tears. She'd known Paul was involved. With his drugged confession in the living room, of course she'd known. But hearing it confirmed still felt like a twist to the heart. Looking down at her hands, she remembered how it had felt, pumping his chest and struggling to keep the life in his body. "I'm glad he's alive. Regardless of what happened, I'm thankful for that, at least."

Agent Hagen looked at her with sympathy, seeming to understand the emotional conflict. "I'm glad I could get there in time."

"Did he say who overdosed him?"

The question had Matt sighing. "Unfortunately, no. Whoever it was kept a mask on and wore gloves. Jimmy didn't get a good look at him. All he could say was that he wasn't very tall and had broad shoulders."

"That's not a lot to go on." Liz rubbed her forehead. "So that means there is at least one person out there unidentified."

"I'm afraid so, yes." She watched the agent take a bracing swallow of coffee and then wince. Whether it was from the bitter taste of the coffee or the case, she couldn't tell.

Liz nodded. "He…" Her voice cracked and she reached for the cup of coffee, taking a fortifying sip of her own before continuing. "It was hard to understand him, especially since I was panicking at the time, but I think he said his sister got him into this. That she was an addict."

"That's what he told me, as well. He mentioned that she'd racked up quite a debt and they'd started threatening his nephew. Paul was forced into an arrangement where he created secret compartments in vehicles to help transport drugs over state lines. In exchange, they agreed not to kill his sister or nephew."

"Oh, shit." She leaned forward across the table, desperate to convince the agent. "I swear to you I had no idea about any of this! All I knew was that his nephew came to stay with him a couple of months ago. Paul said it was because he'd just finished high school and didn't have any plans to go to college. I hired Jimmy to help out with some of the office work and to keep him busy. That's it. I wish Paul had told me. We could have come up with a better plan, gone to Mason for help."

"I believe you." He leaned back in his chair and gave her a candid look. "I might not have until I saw the video that Mr. Weston managed to record before being discovered. No one could fake the look of anger and confusion on your face. Not to mention, I think we can both surmise what would have happened to you if you hadn't managed to get away.

"We're still going to need your official statement, but as far as I'm concerned, you're completely exonerated. You simply had the misfortune of being in the wrong place at the wrong time." He chuckled. "As cliché as that sounds, it does happen once in a while."

The twin iron balls of stress and fear sitting in her stomach released. "Okay." Liz blew out a breath in relief and finally let herself relax back into her chair. "So, now what?"

"Now you'll need to record all the events that have happened to you these last few days. Be as specific and detailed as possible. Once we've reviewed and signed your statement, you'll be free to go home. There will be some additional proceedings, of course. But, in essence, you'll be able to pick up your life from where you left off."

Pick up where her life left off. As if it could be that simple. Everything had changed. "What proceedings?"

"We're going to need you to testify against Mr. Carver when he goes to trial." He shot her an apologetic look. "I'm afraid it's not quite over yet, but that will be something for the future. And there's still the matter of you stealing two cars, but I have a feeling the district attorney will be having you do community service for quite some time. For now, the important thing to know is you are no longer a suspect in either the drug case or the murder case."

At the mention of Peter's murder, Liz was reminded of how lucky she was to be sitting there talking to Agent Hagen. She wished things could have ended differently. "But what about whoever Josh was talking to that night? There's still someone out there who is pulling the strings of this whole operation. We're assuming it's the same person who kidnapped Jimmy and nearly killed Paul, but what if it's more than one person?"

Agent Hagen stood. "That's where I come in. This case is a part of a much larger one that I've been working on for a while. The good news is we've identified one of the key players and managed to expose corruption in the police department in the process. But the fight isn't over, and probably won't be any time soon."

He reached into his wallet and handed her a business card. "Obviously, if you think of anything going forward, you should contact me directly. It doesn't matter how small you think the detail is. I want you to let me know."

Liz got up and shook the agent's hand. "Thank you. I'm sorry for running the way I did. If I'd known you were this reasonable, it may have been different."

"It's always better to come to the police." His stern expression softened. "But, given the situation, I can see why you made the decision you did. I'll send someone in with pen and paper so you can get started on your statement. Take care, Liz."

CHAPTER FORTY-FOUR

LIZ STOOD IN the doorway and contemplated the man in front of her. The oversized bed made him seem smaller than she'd ever seen him. Or, maybe it was the recent events that were coloring her perception. Either way, Paul had always been larger than life in her eyes. Now he'd been reduced to the size of an old man hidden under covers.

His broken cough pulled her from her thoughts. She stepped into the room and hovered over the bed. His eyes welled at the sight of her and he quickly averted his gaze. "Liz."

She reached for his hand. "Paul."

"I don't know how to tell you how sorry I am." A sob broke through his self-control and he struggled to swallow it back.

"Oh, Paul. Why didn't you tell me? You know I would have helped you!"

"The last thing I wanted was for you to get caught up in this. Do you think I would have dragged you into this mess if I could help it? My greatest concern was keeping you and Jimmy out of it." He turned his head away from her. "I failed miserably. I won't blame you if you hate me."

"Paul," Liz squeezed his hand, "I don't hate you. I just wish you'd felt like you could come to me. Thank goodness it's finally over and you're okay."

The older man shuddered and Liz got a sinking feeling in the pit of her stomach. "It *is* over, right?"

"I…" Paul hesitated and wrinkled his brow.

"What?"

He shook head. "Nothing." He leaned further back into his pillows. "I'm sure it's over."

"Are you still concerned about the person who overdosed you? Do you think they'll be back?"

Doubt crossed his face before he could chase it away. "No, no. There'd be no reason for him to come after me. I've already given my report to the police."

"Have you remembered anything else since then? What happened at the house that day?"

"After I got the call that Jimmy had been taken, I went straight to the address they gave me. The front door was locked. When I went around the side of the house, I noticed the back door was propped slightly open."

Liz could see it in her mind's eye. She'd been in that same spot just hours before. "Go on."

"Well, I pushed the door in. The house was hot and dark. It was obvious that it had been sitting vacant for a while. As I made my way through to the living room, I thought I heard a sound in the back bedroom. Whoever it was knocked me out before I even knew they were there. Next thing I knew, I was tied to a chair and…" Paul gulped, remembering the high. He looked at Liz, but seemed to see right through her. "I've never felt anything like that before."

"I thought you were going to die."

Paul wiped his brow. "You know, it's funny. I was feeling so good with that drug running through my veins that the possibility didn't even cross my mind until I heard him on the phone. He called someone…"

"Josh." Now it was Liz's turn to shudder. She raised a hand to the bruises on her face.

He nodded. "Yes, Josh. He'd called and told him to 'handle the mattah,' and suddenly I realized *I* was the matter that needed to be handled. It was the last thought I can remember before blacking out."

"Holy shit, Paul." Liz clenched her fists. Everybody said Detective Matt Hagen excelled at what he did. She could only hope he'd get the bastard that had done this to her and her friends.

*

Alex slumped forward in the uncomfortable hospital chair, grateful that the corridor was empty. He had known this was going to happen sooner or later. In fact, he'd been trying to prepare himself for months. But now that the moment was upon him, he realized the folly of his own hubris.

No one could be ready for a parent dying.

He had thought it would be different this time. He'd lost his mother at such a young age that his memories of her were faded and well-worn, they were like old photographs. A comforting presence, but otherwise stored in a bin in the back of his mind.

He'd hoped that by being older, his father's passing wouldn't hurt him so much. Maybe he expected he'd be able to outgrow the anguish. Alex was discovering that wasn't so.

What made it worse was that he hadn't been here. He'd been a fugitive, running from the cops while his father laid in a hospital bed, dying alone. A sharp point of sorrow twisted deeper in his gut.

Preoccupied with his thoughts, the sound of rubber soles flopping on linoleum barely registered. It wasn't until a pair of orange flip-flops stopped in front of him that he looked up.

"Liz, what are you doing here?"

"I heard about your father. How is he doing?"

He couldn't speak past the lump in his throat as he shook

his head. Her expression filled with sympathy. "Oh, Alex. I'm so sorry."

Alex thought back over his rocky relationship with his father. He'd spent years resenting his father for sending him off to boarding school. Even after graduating, Alex had refused to come home for the holidays, not answering the phone when he called, not being here for him. They had wasted so much time, mired in pride and stubbornness, unable to communicate honestly with each other.

A few months ago, they'd started to make progress towards rebuilding their relationship. When he'd gotten the call, and learned his father was sick, he'd finally been able to set those old resentments aside. He'd worked hard to understand why his father had been so emotionally distant after the death of his mother. Now it was too late. When his father had needed him most, he'd been absent. Chasing after a woman who was just as emotionally walled off as his father had ever been.

Alex didn't think he could go through another experience like that. Grief quickly changed to a toxic mix of fury and frustration. In some ways, it was a relief. Better to be unreasonable than have to face the tragic fact his father had died alone.

He stood up, needing to get out of there. Not sensing the direction of his thoughts, Liz wrapped her arms around him. He set his hand on her shoulder and held her at arm's length. "Look, I appreciate that you came down here, but I need some space."

Alex tried to avoid seeing the way her face fell, telling himself it would be better to nip what they had in the bud before it could get any more complicated. They both had a chance to go back to normal now. Maybe one day they could even be friends.

"Alex...if this is about last night..." Liz looked down at her feet. "I know I didn't handle things well between us."

Had it only been last night? An image of Liz moving above him flashed through his mind. No. This was the last thing he needed. He stepped back. "Hey. I get it. We were both under a lot of stress, but I can't think about that right now. I need to focus on my father's funeral and getting your sister's restaurant finished. It's just…" He looked away, running his hands through his hair before turning back towards her. "I'm sorry, Liz. I gotta go."

The stunned look on her face punched him in the gut. Before he could change his mind, or say something to make it worse, he turned and walked away.

CHAPTER FORTY-FIVE

THE NEXT MORNING, Liz woke from a deep and dreamless sleep. The conversation with Alex played in her mind on a loop. It had been hard to reach out to him, but seeing him there alone, in the hospital corridor, had compelled her to set her usual reservations aside. All of which made his rejection cut even deeper. More than she wanted to admit.

She stared up at the ceiling and indulged in the warm comfort of her bed for another moment before forcing herself up to face the day. There was no way of knowing what to expect. Her face had been plastered all over the news and, as of a few hours ago, people still thought she was guilty of something.

Shaking the disturbing thought away, she got dressed. There was nothing that could be done about it. The police would be able to set the record straight as more of the story was revealed. Until then, she needed to focus on what she could have a hand in fixing.

And that started, first and foremost, with her business. Liz brewed herself a pot of coffee and stood at the counter eating a bowl of cereal for breakfast. She was half-tempted to turn the television on and see what the news was saying about her, but decided she'd find out soon enough.

As she unlocked the back door to the garage, the fear she'd felt the night she'd stumbled on the intruders came flooding back to her. She stood in the doorway and fought to catch her breath. "No! I will not let this place be ruined for me."

Memories of the afternoons she'd spent here with her father and Paul came surging to the forefront of her mind. The way her dad would sing loudly and off-key, or the hours Paul had spent teaching her the inner workings of an engine.

This was where she'd fixed her first car, helped her first customer, and discovered who she was. It was more than just a business; it was her home. She'd be damned if she'd let a few assholes take away something the three of them had spent so much time building.

Noise from the front office startled Liz. *Oh no, not again!* Moving stealthily, Liz grabbed a crowbar before cautiously making her way down the hallway. Somebody was moving behind the counter in the front room. Jimmy looked up to find her arm held up above her head, ready to swing. He raised his hands in alarm. "Whoa! Liz, it's just me!"

Feeling equal parts foolish and relieved, Liz lowered the crowbar. "Jimmy!" She quickly rounded the corner and caught him up in a giant bear hug, ignoring the pain in her ribs. "Thank goodness you're okay." Pulling away from him, she assessed his face and noticed the bruise blooming across his cheekbone. "*Are* you okay?"

Blushing a little, Jimmy nodded. "Yeah, Liz. I'm okay. I'm sorry about Uncle Paul. I had no idea."

Liz shook her head. "It's not your fault. I never suspected either." Tears swam in her eyes as she thought about the last time she'd seen him. "I'm just thankful he's alive."

"I could hear you in the living room. Thank you for saving him." He looked at the bruises on her forehead and around her neck, assessing the damage Josh had done in those final moments. "You put up quite a fight."

A look of discomfort stole across his face as he took a step back out of her arms. "I'm sorry you were dragged into my family's mess. I knew my mom had a drug problem, but she did her best to hide it from me. What she didn't keep from me, Uncle Paul did. I didn't realize he was so caught up in it."

"That must have been really hard for you, growing up."

He tried to shrug it off, but Liz could see the truth. "I thought things were going to get better once I moved in with Uncle Paul. I was out of school, I had a job, and I could help out with the bills and things. For the first time in – well, ever since I can remember – I was excited about the future." He looked around the office with a wistful grin. "But I guess I'm back at square one. I don't blame you if you want to let me go, Liz. I just came by to drop off your key and pick up a few things that I left here."

"Wait." Liz's heart ached for the young man in front of her. She knew he was smart and a hard worker. He couldn't be blamed for the hand life had dealt him. The night she'd lost her parents, Paul had stepped in and given her a foundation to cling to. Maybe this was her chance to repay the favor. "I never said I was firing you, Jimmy."

A spark of hope entered his eyes and reaffirmed her decision. "You aren't?"

"No! In fact, I'm going to need help around the shop now more than ever. Especially if I'm the only mechanic. I'll be too busy working on the cars to have to worry about the phones and stuff. Plus, you know how much I loved doing that before. Can you imagine how it's going to be now that my face was on every television in the state? It's going to be a fricken zoo!"

Relief, pure and bright, filled his face. "Oh, I didn't think about it. Sure, I can totally help out with that."

"Good." She gave a short nod, as if punctuating the conversation. "Then it's settled. You have a job here at the garage for as long as you want one, Jimmy. We'll take everything else as it comes.

"In the meantime, I could use some help cleaning the garage

up and getting this place back to normal. Think you can handle a broom?"

"I'm on it."

"Oh, and don't bother changing the sign on the door. I think we'll stay closed today."

"Okay. Hey, Liz?"

She turned back towards him. "Yeah?"

"Thank you." Jimmy's eyes welled up before he looked away. It was the exact same move his uncle had done the previous day in the hospital. Her heart ached. If only there was something else she could do for him. He swallowed, his eyes red-rimmed, but dry. "Did you see? There's a crowd of reporters out there."

"What?"

He pointed out the front door windows towards the parking lot beyond. Sure enough, there was a small crowd of news vans and reporters.

"Great, that's all we need." She sighed and handed him a broom. "Come on. Let's go tackle something we can control."

CHAPTER FORTY-SIX

THE MID-AUGUST DAY was heavy with humidity. A trickle of sweat left a trail down Liz's spine as the sun took full advantage of her all-black ensemble. Beneath their feet, the grass was dry and crunchy, more brown than green. She shifted the two bouquets she was holding into her other hand. How much longer was this service going to take?

Quite a few people had stared when she walked up to the gravesite with her sisters and Jimmy. It had only been a week since the ordeal, but Liz was looking forward to the day she wasn't recognized by total strangers on the street. She glanced over at the young man standing beside her. If she was feeling overwhelmed by the scrutiny, it had to be a hundred times worse for Jimmy. She sent him a small smile of encouragement, and was rewarded when he lifted his chin a little higher.

Liz took a moment to look around as a man pushed the button to lower the casket into the ground. Alex stood across the plot from her, his face set in a somber expression. It was the first time she'd seen him since their conversation in the hospital. He looked good, the sun just over his shoulder glinting in his hair and turning it to gold. There had been a few times she'd felt his eyes focus on her during the ceremony, but he never openly acknowledged her or gave any indication of what he was thinking.

The distance between them felt foreign after the time they'd shared. She wished she could comfort him or ask him how he was feeling. After the funeral, there were so many people who were waiting to talk to him that she decided to hang back.

Heck, she wasn't even sure if she was welcome. After all, the phone call with the funeral details had been made to Olivia. She'd briefly debated not coming, but after everything that had happened between them, it felt disrespectful. He had stuck by her through one of the most challenging situations she'd ever been through. The least she could do was attend his father's funeral.

A pang of jealousy shot through her when she'd recognized Cynthia, a permanent fixture by his side. She looked perfectly elegant in her black dress. Liz wondered how she didn't faint from heatstroke, with its black sleeves and long hem. It had to be hotter than what Liz was wearing, and she was in danger of spontaneously melting into a giant sweat puddle at any second.

After the services, she crossed the cemetery to another freshly dug grave. The headstone at this plot was simple and only contained two dates and a name, Peter Mullin. She stared down at the lonely mound of dirt and remembered the boy she shared her sandwiches with.

A moment later, Liz wiped the tears from her cheek and laid her last bouquet of flowers down. The group that gathered for Rod Weston's funeral had already begun to disperse. Liz made her way back to the car and watched as Jimmy and Mason talked on the hillside. She wondered if she needed to make an appearance at the reception, of if she could find a reason to get back to the shop.

Fiona walked across the grass to join her. "Are you doing okay?"

Liz snapped out of her gloom. She'd been so lost in thought that she hadn't realized she was no longer alone. After leaning into Fiona's hug, she stepped back and rested against the car. "Yeah, I'm okay. Why?"

"You've kind of had a scowl on your face all day. I can only imagine how uncomfortable it must be with all those people staring at you."

"Not as hard as it's been for Jimmy, I'm sure."

"It's not a contest, Liz. It can be difficult for you, too."

Liz instantly regretted her surly tone. She gave her sister another squeeze. "Shit. I'm sorry, Fiona. This whole month has sucked."

"I know. I'm sorry." She pulled back and gave Liz an assessing look. "Why do I get the feeling this also has something to do with a certain handsome contractor?"

Liz felt herself crack. She'd been trying so hard to keep her feelings in check. Leave it to her little sister to be able to see right through her walls. Knowing she'd hit a soft spot, Fiona continued. "Have you seen him since everything happened?"

"I saw him at the hospital the night his father passed away, right after I returned from the police station. Things didn't go very well."

"How so?"

Liz tried to tamp down the pang in her chest as she remembered their exchange. "He shut me out." She sighed. "We haven't seen each other since."

"That was five days ago!" Fiona paused. It was obvious she was debating whether to say more. "Liz, you know I love you…"

Liz grew wary. "Yeah."

"But you're not the easiest person to get to know. You have a tendency to hold people at arm's length. Have you ever considered that this is how people feel when you shut them out?"

Ouch. "Gee, thanks for pulling your punches, Fiona."

She watched as her sister blushed. "I wasn't saying it to hurt you! It's just, you know, maybe you could cut him some slack. It isn't like you haven't pulled back from someone before. Don't you think he deserves another chance?"

Liz hated to admit she had a point. How could she explain her fear of opening up and letting herself be vulnerable? Of allowing someone like Alex to get close? How could she relay the pain of him pulling away right as she was reaching out?

The problem was, she couldn't help but doubt whether she was good enough for him. Even despite everything that had happened – or maybe because of it. What they could have together seemed almost too good to be true.

Her inner turmoil must have shown on her face because Fiona bumped shoulders with her. "Do you love him?"

"Yes, and it scares the shit out of me." Liz rolled her eyes as her sister laughed. "I'm so glad I could amuse you," she groused.

"I'm sorry. I'm not laughing at you." She calmed down and got serious. "Eliza Harper, I have never known you to run from something that scared you. You've always been the badass that stood up and fought for what you wanted, or what you thought was right. Especially when it came to the people you cared about. You're stronger than this."

"Hey, what's going on over here?" Olivia walked over to where the two sisters were talking.

"Liz was just about to tell me what she plans to do about her feelings for Alex."

Olivia's eyebrows shot up. "I knew it! Something *did* happen while you were on the run."

Liz had kept most of the details about the night she'd spent with Alex to herself, but now realized she hadn't been as good at keeping things secret as she'd thought. So much for being discreet.

"Yes. Something amazing happened." At the look that passed between her two sisters, Liz felt obliged to add, "Amazing, that is, until I went ahead and sabotaged it directly afterward."

"Oh." Olivia's face turned to disappointment. "Was it really that bad?"

"Well, it wasn't good. Things were still uncomfortable between us the next day when I watched him get arrested. Then Paul overdosed, the cops came, his father died…"

Olivia grimaced. "It's hard to believe so much has happened these last few days. I'm thankful the worse is over."

"...and now we're all just supposed to go back to normal? I don't even know what that means anymore! How can a romance forged under those conditions possibly be real?"

The question had been asked rhetorically, but Olivia seemed to weigh her response carefully before answering. "Isn't that up to you?"

Liz opened her mouth to respond, then shut it again. Her brow furrowed. "What do you mean?"

"Regardless of whether Alex is 'the one' or not, you can't let fear be the reason you don't try and find out. Who knows? Maybe you both live happily ever after, or maybe three months from now you end the relationship because he doesn't squeeze the toothpaste tube from the bottom. You might both live together until you're ninety, or one of you might end up getting hit by lightning."

She continued, "Look at our parents. Do you think they expected to die in a car accident, leaving three young daughters behind? Of course not. But I still think, even knowing how it all would end up, that they would have chosen to be together."

"Me too." Fiona's voice cracked. "What they had was beautiful."

Olivia placed a hand on Liz's shoulder. "Nothing is guaranteed. You have to decide what's going to hurt more – opening up to Alex, or spending the rest of your life running away from all the potential good this world has to offer because you're too afraid."

"Geez. Between you and Fiona, I'm going to start getting a complex." The knot in Liz's stomach grew. "Talk about a bleak future."

Olivia sent her a commiserating look. "I'm sorry, but it's the truth. Any relationship, whether it's this one or a different one, requires a certain amount of vulnerability. You have to be willing to open up and communicate honestly. If you can't accept that, you're looking at a very lonely existence."

"But what if it's too late?" Liz couldn't help picturing Cynthia standing by Alex. Had she blown her shot at love before it even had a chance to start?

Fiona said, "If you want it, you'll find a way to make it happen. I have faith in you."

"Me too." Olivia got a sly smile. "In fact, I have the best idea! Alex and I were talking about the restaurant opening, and he assured me he'll be able to make up for the lost time. We're still on schedule to open next week."

"Oh! That's awesome! I can't believe you let me go on about my pathetic life while you're sitting on such great news."

"Thanks, but don't change the subject." Olivia rubbed her hands together. "Why don't you take the time between now and then to think about what you want? If you decide life is better with Alex than without him, you can use the restaurant opening as an opportunity to patch things up."

"That's a great idea!" Fiona beamed at her sister.

"But you have to make sure you're willing to do what it takes." Olivia warned. "That means laying it on the line with him. Can you make that kind of commitment?"

In her heart, Liz knew she already had.

CHAPTER FORTY-SEVEN

MATT HAGEN STUFFED his laptop into the bag and checked to make sure he hadn't left anything on the desk. Most people would count this case as a win. Jonesy had been picked up in Boston earlier that morning and would face drug charges for what happened at Liz's garage. Unfortunately, there was a credit card receipt that could prove he'd been in Massachusetts when Paul was being overdosed.

Josh already had his lawyer talking plea deal, but there was nothing Matt could do about that. It was disturbing to discover a fellow law enforcement officer was dirty, but gratifying to have caught him. He had secured enough evidence to build a solid case in court, and knew a conviction was likely.

That didn't mean he was the most popular guy in the Bath Police Department. For all of Josh Carver's faults, there were officers who were still willing to close ranks and stand by him. Matt knew the faster he could get out of there and move on to the next case, the better. All he had to do was say good-bye to the Chief and he'd be headed back to Portland.

He glanced around the conference room that had served as his temporary office for the last week. Matt knew he was missing something. He'd spent most of the previous night poring over his files, unable to identify the feeling of discontent that gnawed at him. Who had been on the phone with Josh the night Liz and Alex had gone on the run? Damn, he wished they had found the phone in the warehouse. By the time they had gone through Liz's statement and went to retrieve it, it was gone.

And who had overdosed Paul in the abandoned house? He knew it wasn't Josh. He'd been at the debriefing earlier that day, and the timing was off. Which led to the fact that this puppet master wasn't just calling the shots from behind the scenes. He had taken an active role in how events unfolded. Either that or there was another lackey. The questions plagued him. It felt wrong to leave that loose end hanging, it felt like the case was incomplete.

Recognizing that he wouldn't be able to solve it by staring into an empty room, Matt stepped out and made his way to the Chief's office. This wasn't the first time he'd worked with Chief Hamilton. He knew that final piece of the puzzle was bothering the other man just as much as it was him.

He knocked on the door and was waved in. "You taking off?"

"In a few minutes. It doesn't look like there's much else we can do with the case, at the moment. Certainly not from here."

"I appreciate you coming down here and helping us out."

"My pleasure. I'm sorry about your officer."

"Me too." Chief Hamilton sat down heavily. He looked tired. "We've had some disciplinary issues with Josh in the past, he's a bit of a hothead, but I never would have guessed he'd be a part of this. Although, when I look back on past cases, he was usually the first to respond on a lot of them. Almost as if he was on call to do damage control."

Hagen shifted the bag on his shoulder. "See? That's what I keep coming back to. We know there's someone else out there. Josh isn't smart enough to come up with an operation like this on his own, but he's not the kind of guy who would answer to just anyone. Either they have something on him, or they had access to some resource he didn't."

"You'd think that would narrow our search, but I can't come up with a viable suspect."

"Me neither."

Chief Hamilton looked down at his notes on the case. "I keep going back to the real estate. How did Josh know all these properties were sitting vacant?"

"I don't know. I agree, it's a decent lead, but I haven't found anything concrete. However, it's certainly a thread I'll be following up on." Hagen stepped forward. "At any rate, at least this part of the investigation has been resolved. Now the ball is in my court."

He reached across the desk to shake the Chief's hand. "We've both been in this business long enough to know these things usually shake loose sooner or later. My money says that once Josh gets a clear idea of how much time he's in for, he's gonna plead out. In fact, I've heard he's already working on it."

A funny expression raced across the other man's face before he nodded. "That, or Paul might remember more about who his attacker is."

Matt agreed. "It's a possibility, although I doubt it. Memory can get messed up when you're on heroin, especially considering it was his first time and he wasn't used to the drug's effects. Not to mention he was beaten before-hand. Either way, I wouldn't be surprised if we get another break in this case before it's over. You have my number. Give me a call if you come up with anything."

The Chief gripped his hand congenially. "Will do. You do the same. I'd like to know if you end up catching the guy."

After assuring him he'd return the favor, Matt took off. All he could do is hope his subconscious would nudge him in the right direction.

CHAPTER FORTY-EIGHT

LIZ TRUDGED UP the back steps to her apartment. After the funeral, she'd changed clothes and spent the rest of the afternoon down in the shop. Business was still slow, but she was happy there were a few cars she could work on. Nothing helped clear her mind better than working on a car.

Thinking about the future of her business, she was too preoccupied to notice the man waiting at the top of the landing until she nearly stepped on him. Yelping, she jumped back.

A firm hand held her shoulder, ensuring she wouldn't fall down the stairs. "Liz."

"Alex, you scared me! What are you doing waiting here in the dark?" Dammit, that's not what she'd meant to say. *Hi, I'm sorry about your father. How are you holding up? I miss you.* Why was it so hard to say what she was feeling with him?

"I saw you this afternoon. You didn't come to the reception after."

Liz stuffed her hands in her back pockets. "I just...you were busy and I didn't want to intrude." How could she explain how terrible she'd felt about the gulf between them? That she was so damn afraid it was a distance they couldn't bridge?

Then again, he was here, wasn't he? Lifting her chin, she gathered her courage. "Alex..." Liz saw his shoulders tense, as if he was expecting another rejection from her. She moved closer and gently put a hand on his chest. "Did you want to come in?"

Reaching up, he traced her bottom lip with his thumb. He leaned in, so close that their mouths were nearly touching. "I'm not interested in playing games with you. If we go in together, I plan on sticking around afterwards. None of the bullshit that happened last time." He pulled back and pinned her with a look that cut through the twilight. "Can you handle that?"

Her pulse raced as he stared down at her with such intensity. Liz reveled in the hard length of his body, but his hands were gentle as they came up to frame her face. He leaned down, his mouth hovering over hers. His eyes flicked to her lips as they opened to respond. His voice was rough with barely restrained desire. "Can you handle it, Liz?"

"Yes." The word leapt like a breath from her lips. She strained towards him, aching to feel the press of his mouth to hers.

And then she waited no longer.

His firm lips closed over hers, possessive. His tongue swept in, laying claim. She couldn't help the groan of satisfaction as he tightened his hold. She loved the feel of his strong fingers as they threaded through her hair, tilting her head up to meet his.

Long minutes passed with nothing but the sound of their breath intermingling. Finally, they pulled apart. "So, are you going to let us in, or are we going to stay out here on the landing?"

"Hmm?" It took another moment for his words to sink in. "Oh! Yeah." She turned and unlocked the door, barely managing to cross the threshold before he had her back in his arms and pressed against the door. In that moment, there was nobody else in the world but the two of them.

Sensations swirled through her system as he gradually lightened the kiss. She swayed towards him, as if his body had a stronger force of gravity than the world around them. "I'll be damned if we do this on the couch again." He took her hand and led her down the hall. "Where's your bedroom?"

They entered the room together. Liz was surprised to find herself a little nervous. He was the first man she'd ever allowed into her private space and some part of her was eager to see if he liked it.

Pausing in the doorway, he scanned the room. "Nice." He reached for her, wrapping his hands around her waist. "There are so many aspects of you to discover. Every time I uncover a new layer it feels like I've unwrapped a present."

She liked that he seemed intrigued, but wasn't quite sure how to handle it. "I'm not that complicated."

He brushed a finger down the side of her face, then back up to trace the sensitive shell of her ear. "You are, but your layers are subtle. It's an honor for you to share them with me."

His touch was sending shivers down her neck, and she could feel her nipples begin to respond. He smiled, knowing the effect he had on her. He followed the long line of her neck down to her collar, teasing the pulse he found there. "I think this afternoon was the first time I've ever seen you in a dress."

"I don't have a lot of reasons to wear one. My job can get dirty."

"I do love it when you're dirty, but you look good cleaned up, too." The comment seemed to ignite the air between them. Liz reached for him, stroking her hands along his broad shoulders and down his chest. Before she could reach his buckle, he captured her hands in his own.

He took a moment to kiss her palm, making his way to the fine bones of her wrist before sliding up her arm and kissing the inside of her elbow. His tongue darted out, licking the pulse point there. Alex gave a satisfied hum when he felt it jump. "I love the way you respond to me." He treated her other arm to the same care and attention before deliberately placing them down by her side. "This time it's my turn to set the pace."

Liz couldn't help feeling vulnerable. What if he saw too much of how she was feeling? There was a reason she took control of these situations.

Sensing her hesitancy, he continued. "So exquisite." His voice was deep and low, almost as if he'd spoken to himself. Alex reached up and traced her bottom lip with his thumb.

"So beautiful." He leaned forward and kissed the sensitive spot where her neck met her collar bone. Her head fell back, granting him better access.

"So hot." She gasped as his hands reached around and grabbed her ass. He hoisted her up around his waist and walked her backwards to set her on the edge of the bed. She squirmed as his thumbs teased the flesh just above the waistband of her jeans, sending flutters through her stomach and down between her legs.

Friction from his rough hands sent heat and need streaking throughout her system. His touch was patient as he slowly raised her t-shirt, revealing the silky skin of her torso. He pulled her shirt up and off, leaving her open to his perusal from the waist up. "Ahh, sweet Eliza. No bra?"

"They're uncomfortable." She fought the urge to cover herself, instead keeping her arms by her side. Her chin subconsciously went up a notch. "Besides, I'm small. It's not as if I really need one."

"Not small. Perfect." Liz gasped as he leaned in and suckled one sensitive tip, his fingers caressing the other mound. Her head dropped back as she was lost to the sensation of his mouth. Softly, he laved the perky nub, plucking it with his lips. "And, so responsive."

His hands shook slightly, revealing how much the moment moved him, too. She reveled in the effect she had on him. Satisfied that she wasn't the only one losing control.

He unbuttoned her jeans and slid them down her legs,

groaning at the scrap of black lace that was revealed. "If I had known what you had under your jeans..."

Alex settled his weight between her thighs and ground his pelvis into her. She gasped. The rough texture of his jeans sent flickers of heat up along the inside of her thighs until she was writhing beneath him. She curled her legs around his waist and thrust her hips up, letting him know exactly what she wanted.

"Shhh, there's no need to rush." He grabbed her arms and held them up above her head, stroking his hand languorously down their length from her wrist, to her shoulder, to her hip, and back up again. Bending down, Alex captured her mouth, drugging her with another kiss. Liz felt her desire stretch into something deeper and warmer. Still hot, but now purring like a fine-tuned engine under masterful hands.

Liz watched as he slid his way back down her body. He pressed his lips to the valley between her breasts, slowly making his way across the smooth expanse of her stomach before dipping his tongue into her navel.

There he teased her, sliding his fingertips along her thighs. He thumbed the damp evidence of her desire, the heat and pressure between her thighs building and begging for more.

"Alex, please..." She needed to feel him filling her. Liz never realized just how erotic the sound of a zipper could be until it filled the silence between them. Alex dragged his shirt over his head and then pulled his pants down off his hips. He stood before her, content to let her look at him.

Then he began to pull her panties down. It was the most vulnerable she'd ever felt, splayed out before him as he stood between her legs. He lifted her knees up and bent forward to kiss her thighs before wrapping her legs over his shoulders.

Her sex throbbed with anticipation as his hot breath fell on sensitive skin. He licked his tongue along the crease of her outer lips before dipping it between the folds. His hands came up to grip her hips and keep her positioned for his leisure.

Liz melted, her desire liquefying around his mouth. Her hands clutched the bedspread in a vise grip. Every part of her was focused on that one needy point.

She writhed. Pressure and need built to a fever pitch until she was out of control with want. Desire wound tighter and tighter in her core. And then everything burst in a shower of pleasure so keen she cried out with it.

Liz fell to the mattress panting, her body boneless. Alex looked up at her from between her legs. He shook his head and smiled, his eyes burning with desire. "I'm not finished with you yet."

She gasped as he grabbed her hips and pulled her off the bed to stand in front of him. His erection was a hard mast against her belly.

Alex turned her around to face the bed and leaned her over. She could feel his tip and spread her legs, silently begging him for more. All thought fled as he gripped her hips and slowly began to enter her.

Oh, yesss, she thought. He was so big. She could feel her most private inner walls stretching to accommodate him until every ounce of her being was filled with his flesh, until he'd fully buried himself in her silky heat. His reached around and lightly fluttered his finger over her sensitive bud.

Instantly, she catapulted to the precipice of another climax. Liz pressed herself back against Alex, silently begging for him to take her back over the edge. Something in him snapped because suddenly he was driving into her, giving her everything he had. He hit her so deeply that she couldn't tell where she ended and he began.

The pace grew frenzied. He grabbed her hands and held them behind her back, using them as reins as he rode her from behind.

Liz had given up all semblance of control, her face in the mattress, her ass in the air as he pumped into her.

He controlled every part of her body and filled it with pleasure. So much pleasure Liz was sure she'd burn up in flames. Then her whole world exploded. The orgasm ripped through her, milking him until he gave a shout of his own. Time stopped. Every part of them strained towards each other.

The air was filled with the sounds of them panting, trying to catch their breath from the freefall. Alex ran his hands up Liz's back, following the line of her spine. He loved the sight of her body beneath him. The long line of her back and waist and the way her hips flared out to such a lush ass.

He grimaced slightly when he saw her hips were red from where he'd held her. "I didn't hurt you, did I?"

Liz turned her head. She was a little embarrassed to admit how much she'd loved being manhandled. But seeing the concern on his face, she knew she needed to say something. "You didn't do anything I didn't want you to do."

Alex slid from her body, leaving a void behind him. She frowned until he laid down beside her and pulled the covers around them. He wrapped his arms around her and held her nestled against his chest. "Good."

They dropped off to sleep wrapped in each other's arms.

Chapter Forty-Nine

IT WAS CLOSE to three in the morning when Alex jerked awake. In his dream, there had been unseen eyes everywhere he went, and he could still feel their weight on the back of his neck.

His eyes roved around the shadowy room, his mind not quite ready to give up the last remnants of his dream. Technically, he knew it was a product of recent events, but it had left a dark omen looming in his mind. The fact that they had never caught the person behind Josh and Paul bothered him.

Alex shuddered and huddled deeper into the warmth of the covers, squeezing Liz's warm body a little closer to him. He'd never known a more passionate lover. It felt right, being there with her. Now that he'd gotten past her barriers, he was eager to see more of her warm, loving side.

His hands slid over her silky skin along the subtle curve of her hip before he wrapped his arms a little tighter around her waist. He let his fingers tease her nipples until they stood at attention, begging for more.

Liz stirred, but didn't wake. Alex felt his own body grow in response. He didn't think he could ever get tired of making love to her. He nibbled the back of her neck where he'd discovered she was most sensitive, and was rewarded with a sigh from her parted lips.

He drew her out of sleep, letting her mind slip from heated dreams into steamy reality.

She turned towards him and wrapped her arms around his neck, offering her mouth to him in a long, languorous kiss. Neither of them spoke, but he could see her eyes were open and focused on his as he slipped between her legs.

Love was a long, slow glide that gently swelled between them, lifting them up to a crest before letting them float back down. He could feel her body as it welcomed him, squeezing him from the inside until he had no choice but to give her everything he had.

Including his heart.

The realization struck Alex like a truth that had always been there, as natural as breathing and just as vital. He stroked her cheek as she lay beneath him and caught her breath. Finally, she broke the silence. "I think I like having you in my bed."

He smiled down at her. "It's a good thing, since I'm hoping to be here for a long time." Alex was gratified to see there wasn't any fear in her eyes at his declaration.

It was hours before either of them woke again. Liz stretched and turned to look at the clock. "Shit!" She bounded from the bed. "The shop was supposed to be open thirty minutes ago."

Alex admired her backside as she walked to the bathroom. "I think people would understand you taking a day off, considering the terrible ordeal you've been through."

He knew it was futile to suggest it even before she started to shake her head. "No, the sooner I get back to some semblance of normalcy, the better. People need to see that I'm not hiding and I'm not acting guilty."

"You aren't guilty." Alex pointed out.

"I know that. You know that. But the public may not be so sure of that. Think about it. They had over forty-eight hours of the news cycle proclaiming me as a 'person of interest.' Which, in the court of public opinion, means "guilty." The best way I can push back from that is to be the reliable business owner that I've always been."

Alex sighed, knowing she was right. "Okay." He thought about the events that had brought him to her apartment last night. The loss of his father would sting for a long time. He'd always regret the time squandered between them. "I need to meet with my lawyer about Dad's estate, anyway. And I have to give Cynthia a call and let her know to put any rental contracts and sales on hold for now.

Liz stopped in her hunt for a pair of jeans and turned to him. "Cynthia?"

"Yeah. Remember? She was my dad's property manager?"

He saw a look of relief wash over her face and wondered about it. "You didn't think we were still together, did you? Liz, that was back in high school." He gave an exaggerated shiver. "Besides, have you seen her? She's way too high-strung, always stressed and jittery. Makes me anxious just thinking about it."

She threw her head back and laughed. He loved how relaxed and confident she'd become around him. It was like watching her blossom before his very eyes.

Liz crossed the room and wrapped her arms around his neck. "Just do me a favor and meet her someplace public. I get the distinct impression she wants to be more than just your father's property manager."

He wound his arms around her waist and hugged her a little closer. "You know you can trust me, right? I don't want Cynthia. Or any other woman, for that matter. I just want you."

He watched as her cheeks flushed with pleasure before she rolled her eyes and tried to play it off. "Oh geez, we've reached the sappy stage." She kissed him, letting him know she was teasing, then pulled away. "Do what you gotta do, just know I have a very large wrench and I'm not afraid of cracking heads with it."

"Oh, I've seen what you can do with a wrench." They left the apartment together, taking another moment to share a kiss before saying good-bye. Alex drove away wondering how things had changed so quickly.

He felt on top of the world.

CHAPTER FIFTY

LATE SUMMER SUN slanted across the front of the restaurant, casting it in a golden glow. Liz stopped to admire the effect and wiped her hands down her dress. If she was this nervous, she could only imagine what Olivia was feeling right now.

The last couple of weeks had been a big push to get everything finished for the grand opening of Eclipse. She and Alex barely saw each other during the day, but they'd made a point of coming together each night.

Liz never expected to find someone she could be so easy with. He wasn't one to make grand gestures, but she quickly discovered he was full of little surprises. Sometimes that meant stopping by in the afternoon to drop off a latte, or taking her trash out when he left in the morning. Other times, it was the way he reached for her hand when they were walking down the sidewalk.

More surprising was how she was learning what he liked. She knew he preferred raw sugar for his coffee, that he put hot sauce on everything, and that he liked to double knot his shoelaces. She also knew that he had a funny three-note hum when he was feeling particularly content and that there was a sensitive spot just behind his ear that drove him wild.

And she knew she loved him. In fact, Liz was beginning to discover she had a huge capacity to love Alex.

Someone jostled her. "Oh, excuse me." With her thoughts interrupted, Liz realized she was blocking the entrance. A stream of people was walking towards the front door, dressed in their finery. Olivia must have invited the whole town to come celebrate her soft opening.

Crossing the threshold, the hostess at the front desk greeted her, then invited her into the dining room. Ordinarily, parties would be seated separately, but for this evening's celebration they'd left the tables open. Able to stand, walk around, and mingle, people were happily taking advantage of the freedom.

Liz felt Alex's eyes on her before she saw him. He was standing next to a massive stone fireplace, and her pulse jumped in response to his heated gaze.

Then she noticed who was standing next to him.

Who could mistake the polished gleam of blonde hair? Liz watched as Cynthia leaned closer to say something to him, placing a hand on his arm. She scowled right as the other woman turned to follow Alex's gaze towards her.

Cynthia's small smile morphed into a cruel twist and she shifted her body closer. Then Alex bent down and said something that wiped the expression off her face. He extricated himself from her grasp and began to walk towards Liz.

Trust and triumph surged in her chest as Liz watched him make his way across the room. "Hello, handsome."

Alex took her by the waist and gave her a kiss. "You look stunning." Liz had donned a racy little black dress that accented her lean curves to perfection. Hell, she had barely recognized herself in the mirror with her carefully applied makeup and her pixie haircut styled into a sleek side part, let alone the fact that she was wearing heels!

"Thank you." She smoothed his shirt with her hand. Not because he needed it – he looked impeccable – but because she savored being able to do so. "The place looks amazing."

"Why don't I give you a tour?"

Alex walked her around the room, pointing out the various bits of interest, including the original beams from the barn, the fireplace, and the antique wooden bar they had salvaged from another restaurant that went out of business. There were brass fixtures and Italian glass pendants hanging over the tables. They walked to the far wall that was filled with floor-to-ceiling windows overlooking the cliff.

Olivia had timed the event to perfectly coincide with the sunset, naturally showcasing the beauty of the location. Liz stood and looked out over the water, admiring the way the vivid oranges and hot pinks painted the horizon and were reflected in the water below. It was like watching two sunsets at once.

"Wow," she said. "I'd want to eat here every day."

Whatever Alex was going to say was interrupted by her sister. "Oh, thank goodness you're here! I need your help."

Liz turned. She recognized Olivia's stress, lurking under the surface. "Sure, Livvy. Whatever you need."

"Actually, I need to steal Alex away from you for a moment." She turned to him. "Can you head down to the basement and bring up a couple more cases of champagne for me?" Olivia looked down at her chef's coat, currently splattered with food. "There's been an incident in the kitchen, and I've just been informed that a food critic from the Portland Herald is here. I need to go change!"

"Of course." Alex dropped a kiss on Liz's cheek and handed her his glass. "Duty calls. I'll be right back."

Olivia rushed off to change, and Liz found herself standing alone in the middle of the room with a drink in each hand. She wove her way through the crowd, stopping to say hello to a few familiar faces on the way to the bar. She smiled at Mrs. Crowley and Mr. Hamilton, canoodling like a couple of young lovebirds in one of the corner booths. They might be in their eighties, but that hadn't stopped them from dating over the past winter. It had been the biggest topic in the local rumor mill up until Liz's ordeal.

As she was dropping her glasses off, a conversation near the bar caught her attention. The police chief was holding court with a couple of the local businessmen. Frank from the hardware store on Main Street patted him on the back.

"Don't worry about it, Mike. We know you were just doing your job and following the leads the case gave you. Although, if you'd asked me, I would have told you there was no way our Liz could have done it." Liz was relieved to see a number of heads bob in agreement around the police chief. Grateful that the group hadn't spotted her yet, she turned slightly away and strained to hear more of the conversation.

Frank continued. "Look, this drug stuff is an ugly business. We all know you've been doing your best with limited resources. I never thought we'd see the day when our small town had to deal with this kind of nonsense."

"Well, Frank, I appreciate it. It means a lot. But, I assure you, we're gonna handle the mattah. Whatever it takes."

Her head shot up. Cold dread and certainty speared through her heart. Just then, Mike Hamilton, the freaking *chief* of police, looked up. Their gazes locked before Liz could wipe the horror from her face. She quickly shifted her attention to across the room, hoping he hadn't seen the knowledge in her eyes.

Oh, shit. Oh, shit. The CHIEF?

It felt like her heart was going to jump out of her chest. She needed to get her pulse under control. Not bothering to wait for her drink, Liz made a beeline towards the bathroom. Diving through the door, she was grateful when the place appeared empty.

She couldn't catch her breath. She was going to hyperventilate. Liz faced her reflection in the mirror and tried to talk herself down. Was it possible she was jumping to conclusions? The phrase wasn't *that* uncommon, was it?

Liz turned the faucet on and quickly splashed cold water in her face. Maybe this was all just a product of her overactive imagination. Even as she debated with herself, she knew better. It was confirmed a moment later when he entered the bathroom.

She turned as the stocky man stepped further into the room,

making the spacious restroom suddenly feel cramped. He pushed the trashcan in front of the door, then glanced towards the stalls before focusing on Liz.

Liz was desperate to maintain an air of civility, despite the growing evidence that something was seriously wrong. "Chief Hamilton? What's going on? You're not planning on questioning me again here, are you?"

"No need, since I have all the answers. Although I imagine you're still harboring a few questions." He shoved his hands into his coat pockets and leaned against the wall. "You know, one of the things I've learned over the years is you can never leave loose ends. You'd be surprised. Half the bad guys I've caught were taken down by the smallest of details."

"L-l-loose ends?" Liz glanced around, but the counter was clear. There was nothing she could use as an impromptu weapon. Even the soap dispensers were attached to the wall.

He sighed and paused, as if she'd said something deeply meaningful. "Loose ends. They have a way of unraveling, like a thread on a sweater. If you pluck it long enough, the whole thing falls apart."

"And you're implying I'm a loose end how, exactly?"

He gave a dark chuckle and shook his head. "Liz. I appreciate you playing the clueless act, but I think we both know why you're a loose end in this scenario. I was hoping it wouldn't come down to this, but I think it's time you and I go for a walk." The gun he revealed from his coat pocket belied his conversational tone.

Liz gulped. Up until that point, there hadn't been anything overtly threatening about his behavior other than being in the wrong bathroom. She'd been desperately hoping he didn't know she had overheard his conversation, or that she had managed to connect the most dangerous dot to the overall puzzle.

"Come, we're going outside. If anybody asks, just tell them we'll be right back."

Liz stiffly walked towards the door and, at his urging, moved the trashcan aside. The hallway led to Olivia's office, the basement, and an emergency exit. The door led out to the backside of the restaurant and overlooked the lawn. A path meandered across the slope. Outside, the dusk air was warm and inviting, filled with the scent of phlox and sun-warmed grass. The restaurant windows glowed on the hillside. Every once in a while, a trill of laughter could be heard floating on the breeze.

"You were the person on the other end of the phone call that night, weren't you?" She gulped back her fear. "You were the one who overdosed Paul."

"Ah, see? There's the straightforward talk that I've come to expect from you. Playing dumb doesn't suit you, Liz."

"Look. I don't have any evidence. Hell, I barely even had a suspicion until you walked into the bathroom. Why don't I promise not to say anything and we can just sweep what's left of this situation under the rug?"

Even as she said it, Liz knew she wouldn't be able to do that. But, if she could somehow convince him that she would, it was worth a try. Liz attempted to look back at him, but was prodded by the barrel of his gun. "Keep walking."

Taking a deep breath to calm her nerves, she asked, "Where are we going?"

"Just keep following the path towards the cliffs."

That word – cliffs – struck a note of dread in Liz. She had to do everything she could to make sure they never made it there. "You mentioned loose ends, but I can't possibly be the one you're worried about. What's to stop Josh from entering a plea bargain and giving you up?"

"It's already being taken care of."

The statement stopped Liz in her tracks. It was only after the Chief bumped into her that she started moving again. "What do you mean 'being taken care of'?"

"Do you know how dangerous it is for a police officer to be

thrown in jail? They aren't exactly the most popular people in any prison. That's why they tend to be kept in isolation. But if there's a mix-up, perhaps an oversight in paperwork, they may find themselves in with the general population. At that point, anything could happen."

Holy shit, Liz thought. Did he just admit to having Josh set up to be murdered in prison? Before she could remark on the horror of that, he continued. "As far as your offer to stay quiet, I can't take the risk you wouldn't fold at some point. All it would take is for your integrity and sense of honor to creep up on you one night, and you'd be spurred into action. That's assuming you weren't planning on double-crossing me the minute I let you go." He shook his head. "I'm sorry, but that's not something I can afford to have hanging over my head."

The tone of regret in his voice disgusted her. She doubted he felt any true sense of remorse. Instead, Liz tried to appeal to his logical, pragmatic side. "Isn't this also a large risk you're taking? Especially here, with all these people around?"

"A bit, yes. But it's better to pick my own time and place than to wait for you to surprise me. Besides, if I do this right, nobody will suspect a thing other than you had a horrible accident."

"You can't possibly think it will be that easy," Liz said. "What about Paul? He's made a full recovery and has already filed a report with the police."

"True," Chief Hamilton paused, "but I took special precautions with him. He never knew who I was. Even when I was injecting him, I had my mask and gloves on. There's no way he'd be able to identify me. Plus, he was so messed up, it would be easy to question his memory. I doubt his testimony will be considered valid."

Liz couldn't believe the nerve of this guy. She wondered if his talking conversationally and pretending to be nice was just his way of mitigating guilt over her death.

The evening sky deepened as the cliffs drew nearer. Water lapping against the rocks below grew louder. Liz realized that she'd never make it if Mike forced her over the edge. If she was going to get away from him, she'd have to make her move soon.

Doing the first thing that came to mind, she tripped and fell to her knees. She didn't have to fake her moan of pain as she hit the rough gravel.

Mike growled. "Get up! NOW!" The menace in his voice caused her stomach to heave. "If you're not standing in two seconds, I'm shooting you in the head right here."

Liz rose from the ground slowly. In the deepening twilight, she hoped he didn't notice she was no longer wearing one of her shoes. Instead, her body tilted slightly away so her hand wasn't visible from his angle.

Liz held her body gingerly, sucking in a breath as if in great pain.

"Did you seriously just hurt yourself *walking*?" He gripped the gun more firmly and let out a sound of disgust.

"It's not like I'm used to walking around in heels, y'know. Especially out in the dark and on gravel." Liz was balanced mainly on her left foot, her shoe held in her right hand with the heel facing outwards. Her left hand held a fistful of pebbles and dirt. As far as weapons go, they were woefully inadequate, especially against a gun. Still, a shoe was better than nothing.

Liz sidled a half step closer to him and pretended to limp a little. "I've never understood why people wear these things." The hand holding the gun dipped lower. She was only going to get one chance at this.

With as much force as she could muster, she flung the rocks into his eyes and lunged to the left. Roaring in anger, he jerked his weapon up and brandished it towards her face.

Liz swung the shoe up and buried her heel in the police chief's shoulder.

CHAPTER FIFTY-ONE

CYNTHIA DUCKED INTO the stall and locked the door with trembling fingers. There was a slight sheen of sweat on her upper lip and she wiped it off with her sleeve before digging into her bag. The glasses case rattled in her hand as she opened it. Inside was a small vial of white powder, a syringe, a cotton ball, a small spoon, a lighter, and a straw.

She looked at the syringe longingly, but knew there were too many people around for her to be that incapacitated. Injections were best left for evenings at home. For now, she just needed a little bump to tide her over and even out the edges. Cynthia pulled the straw and vial out.

Next she pulled her credit card out of her wallet and knocked a bit of the off-white powder onto the back of the toilet. By that point, her jaw was beginning to ache from clenching her teeth so tight. She'd just begun to cut the powder with her card when the door to the bathroom slammed open.

Cynthia froze. *Dammit.*

She climbed onto the toilet as quietly as she could and pulled her feet up. Leaning slightly to one side, she peered through the crack in the door. Her heart dropped when she saw Liz splashing water on her face and muttering to her reflection in the mirror.

Of all the people.

Cynthia swallowed back a groan of frustration. Liz was becoming a constant source of irritation. In fact, it was being rebuffed by Alex earlier that had put her on such edge and in need of the bump to begin with. At that moment, it had become apparent that she was never going to get back together with him.

It was hard to believe that the gawky little tomboy had grown up to snatch the very person that Cynthia wanted most. She held her breath, praying the other woman wouldn't realize she was there. The last thing she needed was to have Liz discover her secret. She eyed the small mound of powder on the back of the toilet. With any luck, Liz wouldn't linger.

Her hopes were dashed the moment she heard a man's voice fill the bathroom. At first, she wondered if she'd caught Liz in the act of cheating. It soon became apparent that the situation was much, much worse. Discovering it was the chief of police sent a fresh wave of panic through her system. The drugs sitting on the toilet behind her practically screamed, but she didn't dare move. There was more than just discovery and a drug rap on the line here. Once he threatened Liz and escorted her out, Cynthia's shakes were stemming from more than withdrawals. Fear skated down her spine, raising the hair on her arms.

She looked down at the case of drug paraphernalia in her hand, and for one brief moment, she hesitated. It would be so easy to do nothing. Not only would she get to keep her drug supplier, but with Liz gone, she might stand a chance with Alex.

The thought filled her with disgust and self-loathing. Even though she'd been using heroin for years, she'd liked to think she had it under control. After all, wasn't she a highly successful property manager? And, even though she'd had to make a few concessions, such as allowing Josh temporary access to some of the vacant properties she represented, she prided herself on always being a consummate professional.

Accessory to murder didn't fit that profile, no matter how you sliced it.

Her mind made up, Cynthia wiped the small pile of powder onto the floor and threw the case into her bag, hurrying out of the room. She wove her way through the crowd, scanning faces for the one person who she knew would help. He was carrying a large box and headed towards the bar. "Alex!"

A part of her cringed when she saw the hesitation in his eyes. "I'm kind of busy right now, Cynthia."

"Please, this is important. I need to talk to you."

Alex set the box down behind the counter and nodded towards the bartender before turning back to her. Before she could relay to him what she'd heard in the bathroom, another voice called out from the crowd.

"Alex!"

A tall, lanky man strode through the dining room, leaving a wake of people scattering behind him. Two other men followed right on his heels.

"Agent Hagen, I wasn't expecting to see you again so soon."

"Have you seen Chief Hamilton here?"

"Um," Alex glanced around the room. Fiona was watching their interaction intently and began making her way across the dining room. "No, I haven't. Why?"

Cynthia stepped forward, craning her neck to make eye contact with the other man. "I have. He has Liz."

The way she said it caught Alex's attention. "Okay, someone needs to tell me what's going on right now. What do you mean 'has'?"

Agent Hagen ignored him. Cynthia shuddered a little at the way he'd completely focused on her, pinning her with his inscrutable stare. "Do you know where they went?"

She nodded, her tongue suddenly tangled in her mouth. "Cynthia!" Alex's sharp bark brought her back to her senses in an instant. "Yes. That's what I was coming to tell you, Alex. Chief Hamilton came into the ladies' bathroom to talk to Liz. I was," she hesitated, her glance skirted back up towards Matt, "in a stall. The conversation wasn't friendly. He mentioned something about going outside and escorted her out of the bathroom."

"Did they say where?"

At this, the true enormity of the situation hit Cynthia. "T-the cliffs." Realization had her turning towards Alex, her face full of fear, but he was already sprinting for the door. Matt Hagen and the other two agents were right behind him. The crowd's conversation grew hushed before ratcheting to an even higher volume as the men's movement's and Cynthia's fear-laden voice alerted them to something big happening. The room became charged with speculation.

"What on earth is going on?"

Cynthia wasn't as familiar with the youngest Harper sister, but she did know her name. She grasped the other woman's arm and headed towards the door. "Fiona, Liz is in trouble. Come with me."

They reached the door right as Mason and Olivia did. Behind them, a small crowd gathered as more and more people started to tune in to the developing drama. After giving Cynthia a cursory glance, Olivia asked Fiona, "Where's Liz?"

Tired of the interruptions, Cynthia cut to the chase. "She's in trouble. Alex and Agent Hagen are going to find her. Somehow the police chief is involved." With that, she strode through the door. Unsure of where to go, she was just about to head toward the bed and breakfast when a loud boom reverberated through the air.

Fiona gasped. "Holy shit."

"Was that a...?"

"Gunshot." Mason confirmed Olivia's unspoken question and began running towards the back of the restaurant. Even Cynthia could hardly catch her breath out of fear. She could only imagine what the two sisters were going through as they all ran down the dimly lit path.

CHAPTER FIFTY-TWO

LIZ DOVE JUST as the Chief pulled the trigger, but the shot went aimlessly up into the sky. An acrid smell of burnt gun powder filled the air. "You little bitch!" Rage had replaced all semblance of civility.

Recognizing that she was still in danger of being shot, Liz grabbed his wrist and wrestled for control of the gun. It barely budged, his forearm a solid branch of muscle.

Grabbing her hand, it seemed like he barely moved before her arm was twisted painfully behind her. The slightest pull up had her bent forward and screaming in agony. Her knees buckled in pain as he shoved her towards the ground, slamming her face into the damp grass. Soil smeared across her cheekbone and up her nose. Desperate, Liz dipped her other shoulder and rolled, trying to leverage his weight up and over her. He was pulled off balance, and the gun went tumbling away.

He recovered faster than she would have guessed, given his physique. He threw his body forward, and they rolled end over end until he loomed over her again.

Breathless and staring up into the face of the police chief, a new level of fear sliced through her. An undeniable truth became clear.

She was no match for him.

The knowledge didn't stop her from bucking and snarling like a wild beast, though. No way in hell was she going to die without a fight. Shouts began to filter down to them, echoing off the cliffs and over the water below.

It was too late, she thought. She was going to die.

"I wish I could say I'm sorry to have to do this. Ordinarily I would be, but you've been such a pain in my ass, frankly, it will be a relief."

Liz gritted her teeth. "Go to hell."

Chief Hamilton wrapped his hands around her neck. "You first." His grip tightened.

Oh, fuck. This was it. She dug her heels into the ground, desperately trying to dislodge him. Tears streamed from the corners of her eyes as Alex's face swam in the forefront of her mind.

Her ears pounded as her heart thundered in her chest. Liz struggled for air. Reaching up, she scraped deep grooves along his jawline. A warm gush of blood slid down her fingers and arms, but his hands barely loosened.

"Police! Freeze!" Three guns were aimed squarely at Mike's head.

Hagen's voice called out. "Come on, Chief. Don't make me do this."

"Liz!" Alex's voice echoed across the grass. Black spots filled her vision, and she could feel the edge of her consciousness dim. Suddenly, the weight on her chest shifted, but the iron bands around her neck persisted. A commotion grew around her, and she heard the hard thud of a fist connecting with flesh.

Cool, welcome air filled her lungs. It was all she could do just to breathe. Liz drew in a long gasp of air. Her throat throbbed in pain, but she was alive. Alex gathered her up and cradled her in his arms. His gentle hand framed her face. "Liz, baby. Talk to me."

She opened her mouth to respond, but couldn't make her voice work. Swallowing, she tried again without success. Nearby, a male voice was reading the Chief his rights. All the fight seemed to have left him the moment he was caught. Deep, wracking sobs filled the air.

"You came to the restaurant looking for him. How did you already know it was the Chief?" Mason asked.

Matt holstered his gun. "I was going over the case files and kept getting the feeling that I was missing something.

He crouched down, directing his explanation to Liz. "It always bothered me that we never found Josh's cell phone at the warehouse, especially since you said you'd separated the components and hid them separately. I couldn't figure it out. Then it dawned on me. That day you were in the interrogation room and I brought you coffee, there was already a cup sitting on the table for you. You mentioned that the chief had come in and spoken to you."

Liz nodded then raised her eyebrows in realization. Matt shared a look with her. "Did he ask you about the phone?"

Again, she nodded then glanced up at Alex. Taking her cue, he verbalized what she couldn't. "So, the only people who knew where to find that phone were Liz, me, and him – process of elimination."

"Exactly." Matt stood up. A chorus of sirens echoed in the distance. "I'm going to escort Chief Hamilton up the hill and let the cavalry know what's going on. The ambulance should be here soon."

"Thank you." Alex reached up and shook the other man's hand. "Really, I can't thank you enough. You're a hell of an agent."

"Well, usually I wouldn't advise running from the cops, but considering the extent of the corruption, I think it's what saved your lives. I'm just glad it's all going to work out in the end. Here's my card. Let me know if there's anything else I can do."

Liz gave him a warm smile, wishing she could express her gratitude better. She doubted it would be possible even if her voice was working. Matt gave her a nod, showing that he understood. "You two take care."

Olivia dropped to the ground beside them and brushed a stray tendril of hair back from her face. Looking up, Liz was surprised to find a circle of people crouched around her. Mason turned away and began talking to one of the other agents. Even Cynthia, hovering on the outer edges of the circle, was a welcome sight.

She smiled wearily at her sister, then burrowed further into Alex's arms. Liz looked up into the face she loved. Caught by the intensity of his gaze, she lost her breath for an entirely different reason.

A deep sense of contentment and joy overcame her, despite how bruised and battered her body felt. Fiona was crying as she took her hand. "It's over, Liz. Everything is finally over."

Alex shifted her more comfortably in his lap, tightening his hold on her.

Well, maybe not everything.

Some things were just beginning.

IF YOU ENJOYED SECRET NEED, PLEASE
LEAVE A REVIEW.

Consider recommending it to a friend, talk it up with your barista
while waiting in line, or even tell the lady sitting next to you on
the bus! Every bit of word of mouth helps.
I love hearing from my readers! Like my Facebook Page, follow
me on Twitter, or visit my author blog.
Subscribe to my newsletter to hear about giveaways and
new releases.

OTHER BOOKS BY SATIN RUSSELL

<u>The Harper Sister Series</u>
Secret Hunger
Secret Need
Secret Dream – Coming soon!

ACKNOWLEDGEMENTS

Thank you to Lynne Favreau for her friendship, strength and encouragement. Your insights and honesty have made this a better book. I couldn't have done it without you.

I'm lucky to have found a wonderful, active community of writers and authors. I want to give a big shout out to my WriNo-Shores writing group, especially Kelsey, Julia, Rochelle, and Paul, and to my Newburyport Writers group for all their knowledge and support. Thank you for all the inspiration, write-ins, commiseration, and writing advice. Thank you to my editor, Debbie, and to my beta readers for your invaluable input.

Lastly, to all the people out there who read local, encourage new authors, and support indie writing.
"Thank you!"

ABOUT THE AUTHOR

Satin Russell was a financial advisor for many years up until she decided to pursue her dream of becoming a writer back in April 2013.

It took her a full year of saving and planning before she was able to commit to her goal full-time. Secret Hunger is her debut novel and was published in April 2015.

Satin lives in Massachusetts with her husband. Other than writing, she loves reading, supporting fellow authors (especially self-published ones,) traveling, and photography. She's also partial to a good whiskey now and then.

Satin loves to hear from her readers. You can visit her website at www.satinrussell.com or email her at satinrussell@hotmail.com.

If you liked this book, please consider leaving a review and supporting Satin as a new author.

Thank you!

Made in the USA
Columbia, SC
08 February 2020